ANGEL FOOD

Brittany Tuttle

ISBN: 978-0615987453
ISBN-10: 0615987451

Vesuvius House Publishing
This is a work of fiction. All of the characters, events , busi-
nesses and establishments portrayed in this novel are inventions of
the author's imagination or are used fictitiously.

Cover design by Trey Tatum
Wing art by Katie Litchfield

Tuttle, Brittany
Angel Food / Brittany Tuttle 1st ed
Vesuvius House Books are available for special promotions.
For details, contact the author.

Printed in the United States of America
10 9 8 7 6 5 4 3 2

Angel Food

For Noah,
for everything.

Angel Food

ACKNOWLEDGMENTS

I would like to thank my earliest readers for their valuable insight and encouragement. Mercy Tatum, Marie Wreath, Suzanne Stauss, Margi Finch, I am grateful for all of you. Thank you to the Kiwi Gelato Book Club, especially Terri Trimble, Heather Layton, and Leslie Logemann. To Elizabeth Aquino, Mary Moon, and Rosemarie Robotham for your support. Your kind words shored me up when all else failed. To Amy Brown, my darling friend. My deepest gratitude to Sara Baker, whose sharp eye refined the story and improved it immensely. I owe you a whiskey. (All mistakes are mine). Thank you Trey Tatum for the kickass cover and for being so patient in the process.To my mom, who always believed in me, and my dad, for instilling in me a great love of books. Thank you both for loving the book even though you are Lutheran. To my sister, Heather. To Ayla and Indy, the lights of my life. Most of all, I am indebted to my husband. I could never have done it without you. I love you most of all.

WEST OF MEMPHIS

AN ANGEL HAS BEEN on their tail since Tusca-
loosa. They picked it up taking a wrong turn through sacred
ground. To the angels a Methodist cemetery counts as sacred
ground; Anson wouldn't have expected it either. Why any angel
would hang around in a graveyard is a mystery to him, but it's
not like any of this has ever made sense, and by now he's quit
trying. They'd been in South Carolina but had fled quickly
when a tsunami hit Myrtle Beach, figuring there'd be tons of
angels in the area soon. Last night they pulled over at a rest
stop, the shady kind with a dumpster and concrete commodes.
While River whined about the machines being out of peanut
butter cups, Isidore left to hunt the angel, out in the bushes
where all manner of unwholesome act occurred. She'd returned
embarrassed, apologizing to her brothers with her eyes for an
unsuccessful mission. Anson had tried to trick it, then, by pulling a fast U-turn on a two-lane country road. They were easy
enough to trick, sometimes, but this one had proved wily.
Now, as if being in Arkansas weren't bad enough, they still
have the thing on them and it's making Anson edgy. But the
worst of it is that Anson can hear River eating his onion rings,
and they stink.

   "Maybe they've always trailed us," River says from his
lazy position in the Airstream's navigator seat. At least he

doesn't put his bare feet on the dash like Is, but his mouth is full and even though Anson keeps his eyes on the road, he can see, or maybe feel, the food in there. "And we just haven't noticed—"

"Chew with your mouth closed," Anson tells his brother. For an answer, River throws one at him. It hits Anson on the nose and Anson doesn't flinch, but he makes his Anson gestures—flexing his grip, rolling his shoulders, like a boxer pumping for a fight or a fitful toddler. This alerts Isidore that it's probably time for a rest stop.

"They've never followed us before," she says, leaning forward from her perch on the sofa just behind the navigator seat and the storage closet. Then she slurps up the last of her milkshake in one long suck, a rattle like an old man dying and trying not to.

"Well," River says, shrugging. "She would know."

"You're telling me you're not freaked out about this?" Anson says to Isidore. She moves from the sofa to sit on the dusty floor between them. Anson waits for an answer, but she slurps the shake again. He reaches back and snatches it out of her hand. He slides open the window, the screen purposely removed for combat situations, and tosses the paper cup out. The highway wind snatches it away. Isidore whines lamely. River laughs.

"You're driving me crazy," says Anson. "Would you chew with your mouth closed? It's disgusting. I can see food spraying out." They are driving into the final dregs of sun, day-old orange and merlot seeping like life out of dark blue clouds. There is no telling when Anson will be able to sleep.

"Maybe they're coming more," River says.

"They always come more," says Isidore.

Despite his sister's inability to put together a grammatically coherent sentence, Anson knows what she means. They come more often all the time. When she was an infant, after the horror show in the delivery room, they'd drop down only once a year, like well-meaning but detached aunts. Then once turned to twice, and twice to every few months, until eventually she turned eighteen and the angels were gatecrashing dinner every Sunday. Eighteen must have been official slaying age, or maybe God just got tired of playing around. Now they show every few days. Anson doesn't wonder when they're going to quit playing nice and wage an all-out attack, because it's a messy thought. What can he do about it? How do you prepare for an angel battle royale? You don't. Or maybe you do, by having lots of sex and beer and porterhouse steaks, but Anson can't do that. So you see his point.

"I can't believe you threw out my shake. And littered. Stole and littered."

"There was nothing left in it. That's why it was slurping like that."

"No. It was slurping because some shake was still coming up. If it was empty, it wouldn't make any sound at all."

"She's right," says River.

"She's not—" Anson begins, and then catches himself. He's not going to do this, he is not. "We still got angel tail?" Somebody has to maintain order here. Someone must be in charge, and as the oldest, it's always been him. He realizes he's driving too fast and slows down. He didn't even want to stop for dinner, but they overruled him. Now that they've had their milkshakes and fried onions you'd think they might be satisfied, but no. Now they show signs of mutiny.

From the corner of his eye, he sees Isidore shrug. Thin shoulders rise up and down fast, her gestures childlike. Drives River crazy, he thinks it's an affectation. Anson's generally too tired to care.

"You could get up and—"

"Fine," she sighs. Plenty of elbows in Anson's face are required to help her stand. The blinds flutter violently at the back of the Airstream, over their one bed. Anson can count on one hand the number of times he's had the privilege of sleeping in it. "I don't see anything. Which means nothing, as usual. I think you oughta pull over, Annie."

"Could you not jerk the blinds like that? I don't need to pull over." Those blinds would be expensive to replace.

3

"I think you should."

"Isidore." Anson uses his tone. River is laughing. Anson wishes for a button. He would push it and it would eject his brother out of his smug little seat. The highway wind would snatch him, too.

"Fine then. I'll be in the bedroom," Isidore says, which is fine with Anson. Isidore doesn't like to be alone herself, but at least she gets that Anson does. Once River senses he's not going to be any fun to dick around with, he'll leave for the Xbox over the couch. Then Anson will be alone with the road, which is all he needs. On a good day, all he needs is a strong cup of coffee, good music on the iPod, and the open road sprawling ahead of him, the back roads and lonely highways, the obscene swells of sky. On a good day there are no angels, and this is all he asks.

SOMEWHERE ARKANSAS

ANSON DOESN'T WANT to stop but they need gas and he can't risk running out on a lonely highway in Arkansas. Though he knows most of the country's highways like other people know their way to the grocery store, Anson is not familiar with Arkansas. When he is in the south, because Isidore gets a wild craving for sweet tea or southern gentlemen, Arkansas is what lies between him and Martha in Tulsa, and nothing more.

He exits the highway at a truck stop oasis, hoping to avoid being caught alone in a rural area at night. Rows of banked semis watch from the far side of the lot like horror movies waiting to happen. No one else is in the parking lot, but Anson is comforted by the lights of a Waffle House across the road where there appear to be a handful of teenagers and at least one friendly drunk. Isidore is sleeping on the couch. At least, he thinks she is. He is seventy-five percent sure she sleeps. Maybe sixty. She has to sleep. He goes to her and slaps her on the thigh. "Rise and shine, bitch whore," he says.

Isidore sits up and does a good impression of an awoken human. Rubbing her eyes, she looks out the window to the black fields beyond the fluorescent light and outdated pop music blazing from the filling station platform. "We're not in Tulsa?"

"I can't go to Tulsa, Isidore," he says. He's trying to be patient but even he can tell he's failing. Of course he'd like to see Martha. He just doesn't believe showing up at her house and calling down angel Armageddon would make a great impression. Man of doom is not really the persona he has cultivated with her. "We've got a tail, remember?"

"Right," says Isidore. "Where are we, then?"

"Nowhere, Arkansas," Anson says. "Need gas. Food."

"We have food," Isidore says. Anson waits for her memory to catch up. They had food. Then Isidore got bored and snacked her way through the white cheddar popcorn, beef jerky, and the salty remains of a tub of trail mix. "Oh," she says. She does her attempt at a winning smile. Anson winces.

"Yeah. Hope you enjoyed it."

"It was The Hungry Hunky's fault," she says, referring, Anson thinks, to the cooking channel. He hopes it is not some new nickname for River. Isidore and River sometimes watch Food TV for nine or ten hours straight. Anson chooses to view it as bonding and doesn't worry about the endless hours they both spend slack-jawed in front of the screen, not bothering to ask where Anson's driving them to next because they don't care and it doesn't matter. He pulls back a fist, winding his arm in the air so Isidore can see it coming before he lands it hard into her thigh. Catching her by surprise is a mistake and could result in death. Isidore grunts lazily and gets up. Anson pushes her down.

She gets up again. While River snores in the back, Isidore hurries ahead and leaves Anson to gas up. Of course it would never occur to her that anyone else is capable of putting gas in the Airstream. It's possible she doesn't know what gas is. Leaving the hose pumping into the trailer, Anson heads into the station, jittery and anxious to get back on the road to Vegas, where surely God will abandon them. They've never had heat in Vegas, and he trusts that once they hit Gomorrah's city

6

limits the angel will panic at the den of iniquity and fly back to where it came from.

The moment he enters the station, Anson senses something is wrong. The clerk behind the register has his back turned, watching motocross on a silent television. The store is cavernous. Full not only of stock service station sustenance but also of fancy novelty candies in pretty bags—chocolate covered cinnamon bears, garlic flavored pistachios—and all manner of depressing tchotchke. He doesn't see Isidore. His hand goes to the gun at his waist and Anson waits, ready for the angel to make its appearance.

From the back of the station, down a dim hallway where the bathrooms are, Anson hears a noise. A cry and a scuffle. He moves quickly, ignoring the lone clerk as thoroughly as the clerk ignores him, and rounds the corner with his weapon drawn. There in the scummy gray hallway with ghastly flickering lights is not an angel, but a man. His back is to Anson. He has a sad bald patch at his crown and he is pressing Isidore up against the wall. The mop and bucket beside them have been overturned. The guy has one arm pinning Isidore's chest to the wall and another covering her mouth. His knee grinds into her groin, which is gross. Isidore glances up and makes eye contact with Anson.

Anson drops his weapon. He turns back to the rack of jerky, which is what he came in here for. His favorite kind is hot chili, but if they don't have that he'll take peppered. He had elk jerky once, from a roadside stand up in Wyoming. It was fine, but what Anson prefers is the cheap gas station brand, tough as leather. It takes time and effort to chew, and will help pass the long hours he's about to spend on the road in the dark, aiming for Vegas and hoping not to die. He hears Isidore whimper and moves farther down the aisle, away from her and toward the door. It turns out to be lucky, because here is where the peppered jerky is, next to a new variety. Hot Chili with Soy, it says in green neon lettering. Anson grabs himself a pack of each. River will want some. But if River wants some, dammit, he can get his ass up and come in for it himself. From the hallway there is a moan that walks a disturbing line between arousal and terror. Anson closes his ears to it. He gets halfway to the register, then turns back and grabs two extra pouches of jerky for River. He really doesn't want to share his jerky.

Anson pays and gets out quickly. In the lot, he scans the skies for angels but there is only light pollution and weak star shine. He takes the gas hose out of the Airstream and replaces it in the slot. Inside the cabin, River is awake. He is rotating in the navigator seat like a kid in daddy's office chair, messing with the iPod. No doubt planning to put on some whiny emo shit Anson can't stand. Or dumb-step, Anson calls it, always laughing at his joke. River yawns, sleepy and content.

"Would it have killed you to finish up with the gas?" Anson says. "We're kind of in a hurry here." He can hear the heat meter whining through the layers of clothes they've stuffed it under.

"Gross, Anson. Those things are full of germs."

Anson throws the beef jerky pouches at River like a punch. He opens up the glove box and fishes for the hand sanitizer. The only one left is the one scented like an Oompa Loompa, Isidore's scent. It remains because Isidore never uses it. He squirts it on his hands and a sickly sweet scent fills the Airstream.

"Chili Soy?" River says, wrinkling his nose.

"Go get your own, if you don't like it," he says, glancing at the station for Is. It's taking too long.

"Can we stop somewhere—"

"How are you possibly hungry?" Anson says. "You ate three hours ago and you've been sleeping ever since. How could you possibly have an appetite now?"

"Like you've been working so hard," River says. Anson snaps fast, leaning out of his seat and punching his brother's arm. He looks less like an assassin and more like a perturbed schoolboy. River throws the Chili Soy jerky at him and it hits him in the face.

"Goddammit—"

"Let's move," Isidore says, coming up the steps with a

massive coffee clutched in each hand. She gets on River for always eating food she refers to as Cancer Yum and then she goes and drinks these sugar and plastic concoctions almost constantly.

"You're seriously going to drink both of those?" Anson says.

Isidore looks wounded. "One's for you," she says, holding it forward.

Anson's mouth goes tight with the effort to hold in a pretty stream of curses. He honestly doesn't know if she does this intentionally. She knows he doesn't like this stuff, doesn't she? How could she not, by now? But she seems so earnest. He can't tell if, by drinking it, he's sparing her feelings or giving her something to laugh at behind his back. He takes the coffee.

"What took you so long?" River says.

Isidore makes a lewd tugging gesture at her crotch. "Mr. Happy Hands," she says, pleased with her theatricality.

"And he wanted you?" River says, looking away from her groin.

"Shut up," Isidore says. She's waiting to see if they'll ask her how she dealt with the problem—or disposed of it—but Anson does not want to know. He turns the key in the ignition and starts the trailer fast, before the door is closed behind Isidore. The sudden motion sends Is and River sprawling. "Jesus," Isidore says, clinging onto River's chair to avoid falling out the door. Anson grins as River leans over and slams the door shut, nearly falling out of his seat, and Isidore spills coffee into his hair.

FLAGSTAFF
ARIZONA

THE AIR CONDITIONING cycles off and renders the sucking and slapping noises suddenly juicy and visceral. Isidore tilts back her head and laughs. She's panting blissfully above him, no soreness or even irritation from his knobby knees poking into her thighs. Her boobs bounce rigorously like she's leading a hell of a work out. It's like she was made for this. Isidore could do it for hours. A couple of times she has, picking up Tantric sex therapists down around Sedona and working a little brain magic on the brothers so they won't get antsy to leave.

At the sound of her laugh, he opens his eyes and grins. He's baby-faced and blonde, which is not her usual, but the full lips really did something for her at the bar and she'd felt like she'd explode if she didn't kiss them. He's thrown her around like a trapeze artist or ice dancer; it was nothing less than a delight. She likes working men, cowboys and carpenters, and she hasn't asked this one what he does because she's pretty sure the answer would be "work out." He squints again, screwing up his face and Isidore knows it's almost over. She feels bad about this part. They always have such a great time until they come,

10

and then, in a tragic twist, the happy times are decidedly over. She doesn't do it on purpose and she can't stop it. Wouldn't even know how to try. She hopes the time she shows them before the finish makes up for it.

As soon as it's over he goes limp and closes his eyes, panting. Isidore disengages quickly, it feels rude to linger. She rolls off to the side, stretching her muscles luxuriously. Next to her, on the bed, he's doing what they always do. Isidore pretends not to notice. It embarrasses them. Men screw her and then they cry, it isn't ideal, but that's the way it is. It would be kinder to tell each one that he's not alone, that she does this to everybody. But she doesn't want them getting ideas. You never know what fantasies they'll cook up in their heads. The last thing she needs is some lovelorn Lothario realizing he'll never feel this way again and tracking her and the brothers across the country, swearing he'll make her happy if she'll let him.

This one is different though. Usually they seek immediate privacy to tend their shaken egos. Usually that's when she puts on her clothes and sneaks out the door. But baby face stays put. Stretched naked across the plasticky spread, Isidore admires her soft belly and begins to search for the remote. He reaches his hand out and slaps it down against her bare thigh. Companionably, like they've done this before and will again. Isidore's afraid she's been made. Made is her favorite term from Alias. She's been calling Anson "Boy scout" lately, and it's freaking him out. "Call me 'Mountaineer'," she tells him, just to see him make that face where he wonders if someday she's going to kill them in their sleep. She and Anson are life partners by default, like an arranged marriage or conjoined twins. She supposes normal women must sometimes turn to their husbands, sleeping next to them in the dark of night, and wonder who it is they've really married, who lurks beneath the black socks and pleated khakis. If they don't, they should. Isidore likes to keep Anson guessing. It is her way of spicing things up a bit, even though they both know they're not going to get old together.

Having lost their tail in Vegas, she and the brothers

11

are lingering in Flagstaff, blaming their procrastination on Isidore's insatiable sex drive. They blame it for a lot of things, actually. The tire went flat because Isidore needed sex. The Broncos lost because Isidore needed sex. They got pulled over because Isidore was in heat. They'd like to blame it for the angels, but the math doesn't come out right. The angels wanted her dead the moment she drew her first breath, for some original sin passed to her through the birth canal or blood, and unless infants are capable of harboring unsavory desires, it doesn't add up. Isidore thinks it's the other way around. That being hunted has kicked her loins irretrievably into overdrive. "Think about it," she says. "If you knew you were gonna die—and you couldn't go to Greenland—what would you wanna do?" Isidore doesn't dream of spa weekends or shoes. Like a Hindu goddess, she was made for battle and banging.

"That was strange," baby face says.

"Yeah?" she says hesitantly. This is better than the usual sobbing. She's relieved not to have to pat him on the back a few times before taking a sneaky leave.

"Yeah." He runs his hand through his wavy hair. Isidore isn't sure she likes it. "You must have felt it. It was like—something else was here. Like a presence. You must have felt that."

Isidore doesn't answer. She reaches down and fiddles with the turquoise around her ankle. She bought it from an Indian woman at a rest stop in Utah. There'd been a bunch of families out there with their daughters standing over silver and turquoise charms and Isidore had felt guilty and lifted sixty bucks from Anson's wallet to buy something from them all. Later, at a Shakey's Pizza, Anson asked where all his money went. Isidore whipped a bracelet at him and ran out the door.

"Beth," he says. He's not going to let her go.

"Yeah," she says. "You were amazing." She tells them all this. It seems a kindness, after they have pleasured her and been reduced to tears.

He laughs. He's flush and generous, sprawled inside the sheets with his legs sticking out at angles. Isidore studies him with a contentedness in her selection that slowly prickles and shifts toward alarm. His blond, wavy hair, his Ken-doll limbs. He's golden, she realizes. Of hair and skin and heart. She is forced to admit she picked him because he looks like a Gabriel. God, she is sick. Honestly, can she blame God for wanting to kill her? She curses under her breath. The boy doesn't hear.

"Don't flatter me," he says. "It wasn't me. It was like you became something else. Something more. Does it happen every time, with you?"

Isidore wonders if Jesus is playing tricks on her. She's always seen him as a prankster, having the gall to fake his own funeral and bust in late with the good wine. First she takes this Gabriel lookalike to bed with her, and then he zeroes in on her little problem like no other guy ever has. It's an energy, she knows that much. Something soft and old and glowing descends over the room. They always, always cry. Except for the one in Reno two or three years back, the really bad choice. He didn't cry, his dark goal was to elicit hers and five minutes later she'd opened his throat.

"Yes," she admits. She folds her legs up tight to her breasts. She's starting to feel naked.

"I had that feeling once before," he says.

"Yeah?" Isidore is curious. She'd like to know more about her super sex power, she's just never imagined there was anyone who could enlighten her.

"I was in church."

Isidore flinches. She wonders if angels planted him here, to lure her away from the brothers and kill her. She unfolds her legs and goes to get her underwear, dropped on the floor at the foot of the bed. Pulls it back on. It's cold in the hotel room. She's naked. It's sticky between her legs. Isidore has never felt guilty about her thriving sex life until this moment. Sex with her is different from sex with other women. She knows this, and yet she has never felt ashamed of it until this moment.

He asks her what's wrong. He sounds sweet. He must

not be an angel after all.

Isidore is regretful. Usually she's smart enough to get out before it gets messy. They're so vulnerable after the sex. "Look," she says. "Whatever you felt, it wasn't holy. It wasn't even good. It's some kind of taint, some bad energy. You know. Tainted lo-ove," she sings. This is the best way she's found to describe it. She knows it's inadequate.

He frowns. "Beth—"

"My name's not Beth," she says, tugging her shirt over her head. "It's—" she freezes. Anson has warned her about this. "—Roxanne."

The boy is deteriorating from blissful to baffled. "I don't get it. Are you telling me you're a hooker?"

This is hilarious to Isidore. Just because she likes to have sex doesn't mean she wants to do it for a living. Despite her rush to leave, she giggles. "Yeah, that. And I'm on the run from my primp. So I gotta go."

"You mean your pimp."

"Really?" she says, shrugging on her jacket. Primp makes so much sense. Such dapper dressers.

He's not buying the pimp story. He's beautiful in his concern, emoting even with the tips of his hair. For a moment Isidore considers pulling one over on them all and lingering another day. "Did I do something wrong?"

"No sweetheart," she says, remembering the throwing. "You were pretty fucking good. Like an ice clowner." She thrusts her foot into her jeans, stumbling sideways.

He shakes his head, like trying to dispel an enchantment. "Well. You don't have to go. We could order a pizza, or. Breakfast."

"Thanks for the offer, Braxton," she says, and means it. Just because she doesn't want a pizza doesn't mean she doesn't want one offered. "But you don't want me to stay. Trust me." She thinks she's just being honest, but it upsets him. She's desperate to get back to the brothers, their shallow interactions, their lack of emotional demands. She doesn't want to snuggle, doesn't want a phone call or pancakes or even, really, tender words, because what's the point? She wants to have an orgasm with a man, plain and simple, and is shocked at just how difficult a goal that is to achieve.

"Whatever," he says. He frowns as Isidore shakes her feet into her boots. Sits forward. "It's Brandon. Let me at least give you a ride—"

She's on her way to the door. His kindness stops her. "Look. Whatever you felt—it isn't good. Good things don't like me. Good things—" she almost says want me dead, but Anson's voice kicks into her head. You never know who you might be drinking with or fucking. Don't tell strangers you're heaven's most wanted, Isidore. It might not go over well. "Run away from me," she says, which is near enough the truth. "You shouldn't feel bad about it. You were a really fun lover. Seriously a cut above. I mean, this thing?" she says, holding up two fingers and wiggling them. She only means to show her appreciation but he stares at her, uncomprehending. She sighs. "It's a compliment."

Brandon is naked and limp, puzzled like a tricked child when she leaves him at the door.

FLAGSTAFF ARIZONA

ANSON AND RIVER are enjoying themselves, if you must know. It's embarrassing to have a life in which the high points are comprised of a motel bed and your brother, but so it is. Anson's bought the nice beer, the kind in bottles, and they've kicked off their boots because their assassin-bait kid sister is safe, for the moment. The new Tina Fey movie is on cable and Anson, in particular, is enjoying himself immensely. He finds himself attracted to Tina Fey, an attraction that worries and disturbs him because he doesn't know if it is socially acceptable to think Tina Fey is hot. He has no male friends to test it out on, he only has River. He said something once along the lines of "Man. Tina Fey," shaking his head, waiting to see if River would bite. He did not.

He has splurged on another motel because it's a luxury not to have to sleep sitting up in the dinette, giving River the sofa like he always does. The remnants of a good sandwich lay on the bed, corned beef with cheese, pickles, mustard, and a hot pepper spread. His belly is full, his sister is safe, and Anson is satisfied. If pressed, Anson would be forced to admit it doesn't rival the distinct charms of Charleston, South Carolina, but still. Few places do.

Then, of course, the door opens. He sees Isidore from the corner of his eye and doesn't look at her. Tina Fey is shirtless and screaming on the screen and he's enjoying this, dammit. He is enjoying this.

"You guys," Isidore says. She marches over to the TV and snaps it off. "You guys. Listen." She's panting, her skin and eyes shimmering like treasure from the sea. "Shut up. No, shut up. I have to tell you this. It's important." Anson sits up. He reaches for his boots because he doesn't know what this is about, he's only certain it will require fleeing and possibly fighting for their lives followed by dishonorable death. Isidore pauses, gathers herself. Touches her fingers to her clavicle. "Some dude and I. Just had the most amazing sex—"

"Goddammit!" River shouts, sputtering on his beer. "Goddammit, Isidore!"

"It took me an entire box of tissue to clean up my—"

"No!" River shouts. "No no no."

"Shut up," Anson says, less hysterical about Isidore's sex life, and Isidore in general, than River is. He throws the first thing he can find at her, which happens to be the remote. She catches it. "Turn the TV back on," he says, immediately regretful.

"I just thought you'd want to know. Your little sister was in good, good hands tonight. Good hands." She accompanies this with a particularly evocative motion of the fingers.

"You're sick," Anson says, but Isidore snaps the TV back on and then, mercifully, heads to the bathroom to take a shower.

It's two a.m. The motel air is mushroomy, like a dank forest trapped under glass. The air conditioning rattles and annoys her. Isidore is lying on the fake-Navajo print couch, staring at the ceiling. She insisted on taking the couch, told Anson she'd wake him if she got uncomfortable. It's sweet, she supposes. The way he clings to ideals of her, like Isidore is nearly a normal girl and on top of that, one that sleeps. She has read for a few hours by the fluorescent parking lot lights, but eventually she always gets antsy. Isidore has spent countless hours lying in beds pretending to sleep, reading or entertaining sexual fantasies in the dark. She can't sit still for long, her inner fire burns too hot. She decides to get up and go to the machines for a Coke and maybe a Hershey bar. Rising from the couch, she pulls on her jeans and fishes for change in the pocket of Anson's jeans, in a heap beside his bed. She's careful not to be too quiet; accidentally waking one of the brothers wouldn't be a bad thing. She's bored and could use a little company. But neither one of them stirs in their sleep, even when she slams the dead bolt open and rattles the knob closing it. Good thing I'm not an angel, Isidore thinks. Or we'd all be dead.

The machines are in the dead center of the boxy U of the motel. There are only two other cars in the lot, the Airstream parked around back. Isidore scans the area furtively, thinking maybe a rapist will accost her. It would give her a few moments' entertainment, but no luck. Tonight, the motel sleeps safely.

The machine does not stock Coke and Isidore takes it personally, cursing and giving it a kick. Feeding in the quarters, she settles for water. The stuff from the tap tastes like sulfur. She doesn't hear it coming. There is an intense heat at the back of her neck and instinct guides her. Her body knows, somehow, that the only way to save her head is to duck forward and down. She can move with a speed so intimidating the brothers pretend not to notice it. Even this isn't enough to spare her from the Gabriel's sword, which kisses her neck and razors away a fat chunk of her beautiful blonde hair.

Head saved, she can turn. There are three of them. Three of God's self-righteous, brainless minions. They look just like the old paintings, the Gabriels. Fair-skinned and golden-haired, the lips of a woman and the muscles of Sparta. Isidore's darkest desires are of having sex with one of them. This is something so twisted she knows not to share it, even with Anson. But really, is it Isidore's fault that they're so beautiful and intoxicatingly focused, even if the object of that focus is her own demise? She doesn't take it too personally anymore; after all, they're just obeying orders. The way they wield a sword is a definite turn-on, Isidore doesn't think there's anything aberrant in her liking that.

Usually she can stay in a place about twenty-four hours before getting heat, but it's only been eight hours since they pulled into Flagstaff, and she realizes this is their tail, finally showing with his bigger buddies. Isidore doesn't know what methods of communication the angels use, she only knows it isn't cell phones. News spreads surprisingly slowly among the agents of heaven and as long as Isidore doesn't spend more than a night in one place, she's usually fine. There are exceptions, of course, but nothing the brothers need to know about.

Isidore spins on a round kick and then they are neatly engaged in a battle so precise that to an outsider, it would appear rehearsed. It's like they were made for each other, she and the angels. Like sex and tequila. When sparring blow for blow with three angels—not two, not four, but three—Isidore experiences a deep warm rush that is only comparable to that moment just before an orgasm breaks, when there's no doubt she's going to come, she is absolutely going to come, but she hasn't yet. Two are too easy. Four might kill her. Three is the g-spot. The first of her three levels: g-spot, Hulk, and Armageddon. Yellow, orange and red. The trick is to try and stay in the sweet spot, and most of the time she can. Hulk isn't usually necessary. She doesn't tire like a real human. There is hot energy in her, her own molten core, which never needs to be replenished. Anson calls it the pit. "How's the pit, Is?" he'll say, if she's been battling for a while and he wants to make sure she doesn't need a hamburger helper. The pit is always good.

They trade thrusts for a while, Isidore allowing it to draw out because it slakes some thirst in her, for a little while at least. The angels move like they've been choreographed and are aiming for the Tony. They are generally predictable, using the same combinations of moves over and over again. Isidore is pretty sure they don't have brains, and they definitely don't have personalities. They are obedience combined with intent. They never question their orders.

They're having some fun together and managing to keep things surprisingly quiet when Isidore takes a good gash to her shoulder and the blood starts to flow. At first it's only ticklish on her back, but as it courses down her arm and hits her palm it becomes a danger. It makes her hands slick. Isidore likes to imagine she is starring in her own TV show. She imagines this scene. The camera would show her bloodied hands and then cut to her face: "Trying to grab an angel with bloody hands is like trying to catch an oiled pig," she would say to Anson, the sidekick. "And I never really cared for rodeos."

Isidore allows one angel to thrust too close, grabs his head, snaps his neck. Then she pulls her knife out of her jeans and takes the next two down quickly.

She doesn't bother entering the room quietly. They won't be staying. Anson is up almost immediately, brandishing his weapon. Now he snaps to it, where was he ten minutes ago when she felt like a chat? He's got the gun trained on her face, but Isidore doesn't take that personally. It's not as if she believes the thought has never crossed his mind, but she doesn't have a feeling it's going to be tonight.

"Three." She realizes she's smiling. Anson's used to it, she doesn't have to hide.

"You're okay," he says, before he sees the back of her shirt, blood soaked, and swears.

He thumps River twice and then he's behind her with a washcloth, pressing.

"Is," he says quietly. It's so tender, this voice. Startling from a man. It makes Isidore feel soft and wobbly. Like her potbelly.

"Dammit." She is certain she could face down anything as long as Anson doesn't get all tender about it. "I was fine."

"They almost took your head off."

"Not almost," she insists. "He would have had to get deeper for almost."

Anson ties a tourniquet around her bicep while River throws their things into the big navy and tan duffle their mother ordered for them from Land's End. Embarrassingly she had their initials stitched into the sides so that it reads A.C. R.C I.C like an unsolvable riddle.

Isidore doesn't want to leave. She wants to stay in this moment. They are on a journey to hell, yes, but sometimes more literally than others and this next leg of their trip promises a particularly tragic ending: a family gathering lies at the end of it. Her eyes meet Anson's in the mirror. In spite of himself, he smiles. He loves this too.

"Why didn't you call us?" River says, bitchy.

"They don't exactly phone ahead," Isidore says.

"Actually, they're supposed to," River says frowning. "Shit."

Anson is scooping a pile of shoes and jeans from the floor to the bag. He pauses and stares at River. Possibly the only good thing his little brother has done his entire wasted life is rig up a device that detects when angels are approaching by the extreme amounts of heat they give off, and, to River's ridiculous delight, plays "When The Saints Go Marching In" for alarm. "Where's the heat meter?" Anson says quietly.

"I must have left it in the Airstream," River shrugs. "Sorry." He knows this nonchalance will enrage Anson.

Isidore pipes up before they attempt to reenact Cain and Abel. "More will come and I'd rather run than fight. Come on."

They're back out the door in seconds. The angel's bodies are gone. This is convenient for all parties involved, the fact that heaven cleans up after itself. It wouldn't benefit anyone to leave angel carcasses lying all over creation, definitely not great P.R. for heaven. Anson takes the wheel. Isidore sits next to him, still buzzing. Her skin tingles, her muscles beg for more fighting. When she was little this urge was impossible to ignore. She bloodied the brothers all the time with an overwhelming instinct for combat. She knows Anson can feel it on her now because he is alert. Sometimes she still strikes out, like those people who shout swear words in public. She's busted a nose or jaw more than once.

They are barely out of the parking lot when the heat meter starts to sing.

"Is," Anson says, but it isn't necessary. Before he can complete the thought she's popped the hatch. Using the dinette as a stepping-stool, she pulls herself up on top of the Airstream and releases the Minigun. The heat meter begins to scream.

"Back her up," Anson orders. River is already moving, Anson sees him in the rearview, hoisting himself out the hatch. There's room for two, to defend themselves from front and back, but only one Minigun. Anson reaches down and grabs his Heckler & Koch semi-automatic out of the duffle. He shifts his eyes back to the road, which is a stretch of wet black one moment, and flurry of moonlit wings the next.

"Shit." He slams on the brakes and is raising his weapon when a multitude of angels rush his windshield.

The next thing Anson sees is a hazy River bent over him, scrutinizing his face. He's repeating Anson's name, alarmed in a way he usually reserves for when the Xbox flashes red. He says it again and Anson can't answer him, he is underwater, or stuck in the mud. The way they once were after a sudden thunderstorm in Nebraska when the heat meter had sung and Anson thought for sure he would have a heart attack trying to disengage the trailer from the mud before they all died there. Then River calls Is over and he finds his voice.

"Yeah," he manages. Speaking hurts like hell. Anson hears himself moan, he doesn't mean to, but he's sore like a giant used him as a billy club in a brawl with a rock.

"Are you—"

"I'm fine," River says. "Here." He holds water to Anson's lips. Anson drinks it. He thinks he's going to hurl violently. "Is?" The day will come when Isidore does not survive. Anson tells himself he's prepared for this. Then he hears a squelching sound, like someone shoving a fist into a tub full of Jell-O, and he has his answer.

"Right. We gotta move." After a battle, they change locations first, clean up later. It confuses the angels. River and Is good and well know this, would it kill them to follow protocol? For once? He doesn't understand why they're not moving. Everything is hazy, Anson feels as if he is watching life through a veil. River brushes at him, swats his hand around his face and shoulders like Anson isn't dying but is merely dirty. He jerks his head like a toddler getting his face cleaned. "Why aren't we . . ." Blackness swims around his eyes. It surrounds him, warm and quiet, a tempting lure.

"Keep your eyes open." River slaps Anson's face. Anson wants to push him away, but can't summon the energy to raise his arm.

"Keep his eyes open," Isidore scolds from somewhere inside Pacey. "Jesus, River."

"I'm fine," Anson growls. "Just give me a minute. Get us outta here, man. We gotta move. Our tail."

"That was our tail." The Airstream cabin is dark, but in the shadows Anson can see his little sister drag a still-twitching angel across the navigator's chair and dump it onto the road. She dusts her hands like a housewife over pies. From the depths of the trailer, Anson hears moans. The last pleas of dying angels. It's a surprisingly human sound; it could just as well be people dying in there. Anson can't remember ever feeling sorry for killing an angel, though he knows from the movies that taking a life is supposed to be emotional, the first time anyway. Anson killed his first Gabriel when he was eleven. The only emotion he recalls experiencing was the fierce need to keep Isidore alive and a raging blood lust for anything coming between him and that goal. Isidore returns to the cabin. There is a thick and woody snap. An angel moan ends abruptly.

"Riv," Anson repeats.

"Ok, except, I can't. You're still in the driver's seat."

Anson looks down and is surprised to see that River's right. He still has his seatbelt on.

"Well unbuckle me and—"

River says, "Don't move!" just as blinding pain tears down the right side of Anson's body, from his ribs to his ankle.

"Shit." He's afraid to look. "River. Am I gonna die?"

"If you move again you might."

"What is it?"

River gives him the truth because he knows Anson wants it. "You got a spear through your side pinning you to the seat." He pauses to let this information sink in. It doesn't come as a shock. It's almost a relief. A firm diagnosis.

"You wanna call Martha?"

Anson snorts. "And tell her what, exactly? I made the mistake of pitching Bibles to cannibals in Flagstaff, Arizona?" Martha thinks Anson peddles Bibles to poor pagans. Which maybe could explain the spear, he thinks. "Do you think she'd believe it?"

"We don't have to tell her about the spear," River says, exasperated. Like he'd prefer it if Anson would just hurry up and die. "What about Mom?"

"I don't know. Give me a minute. I've got a few minutes, I think."

"Mom'll be pissed if I let you die without calling her." This is a true concern for River. He hates being the target of his mother's displeasure. It will nag at him for weeks. He sees himself at Anson's funeral, his mom glaring shards at him across the grave. He shudders. "I think you should—"

"He's not gonna die," Isidore calls. "Jesus. Anson is not going to die." Anson can't tell if she's cursing Jesus or giving him orders.

"I really think you should call—"

"Just give me a second," Anson says. If he's dying, he needs time to think. Last words should be said, and all that. He feels he should tell Isidore something. He can't think what.

They wait. River tries to get Anson to drink but Anson asks for a trash bag. He would hate to be sick on the captain's chair.

"They're all dead," Isidore says, and then she's squatting next to Anson. "Or whatever they do. Shit, Annie." She looks like a nightmare. Her skin, normally egg-pale, is now flushed sunset with the heat of battle and draped in blood like war paint. Her hair is matted like a dreamtime warrior's.

"What happened?" he says.

"They swarmed when Pacey stopped. Busted in the door and we went hand to hand."

This makes Anson grin, which seems to trouble his siblings. "Did you stand over my lifeless body and defend me?"

"Yes," Isidore says, frowning. Anson can tell by the way she's looking at him: he's definitely going to die.

"We're gonna have to call an ambulance," says River. "We can't drive with him like this." His tone leaves it open as to which is the bigger inconvenience: Anson dying, or Anson dying pinned to the driver's seat and delaying their departure.

"You wanna explain that?" Isidore points to the spear in his side. Angel fashion moves slowly, Anson supposes, because their weapons look like something Spartacus would have inherited from his grandfather. And sting, by the way, like they piss on them first.

"Not really. But seeing as how we have no other options—"

"Shut up a second."

Neither River nor Anson likes what is about to happen. It forces them to look truth down the snout and pony up that Isidore isn't an actual human. That at best, their sister is merely human-ish. Like one of those Japanese fetish-bots. In the end, Anson's desire to live and River's desire to stay on his mom's good side trump any squeamishness. They decide not to stop her.

"Well hurry, then. He's gonna-"

"He's not going to die you idiot," Isidore says. "It's a flesh wound. Look, it went right through your side fat. Would it have killed you to get some towels?"

They think they're hiding it, but Isidore knows that every time she performs this particular parlor trick both her brothers wonder if it might be time to kill her mercifully and possibly save the world by doing so. If they got themselves beheaded, she's pretty sure she couldn't fix that. She might be able to stuff their entrails back in, should a Gabriel spill them, but why would she want to? She doesn't think that after handling her brother's innards she could ever be the same.

Isidore puts her hand on the wound, right up against the spear. Anson sucks air hard through his teeth. The thought of his pain makes Isidore nervous. She considers knocking him out first so she won't have to hear the noises. Since they are in a hurry, she tells him to shut up and begins to draw the spear slowly from his body.

Anson is trying not to scream when a feeling like warm honey washes through him and erases all the pain. He looks down and watches as Isidore extracts the spear, point intact, out of his flesh and tendon. The warm feeling glows hot and then it's gone. Isidore holds up a spear that has his own blood and fat clinging to it, like he is a cupcake and slightly underdone. He touches a hand to the spot. It comes away bloody, but the gash is gone.

"You'll be fine."

Anson glances up at Isidore. He swears, there is something off in those eyes. He wonders if this is it, that if he doesn't kill her now she'll go on to destroy the earth and he'll always regret not doing it when he had the chance. Isidore blinks at him innocently. She can't possibly know what he's thinking.

"Thanks."

"Weenie," she says.

"Is that—Anson?" River says, touching the gore clinging to the tip of the spear.

"Yep."

"Sick!" says River. "I've got your fat on my fingers, dude. This is like, tendon here."

"Get your hands off me," Anson says. "It's weird."

"Let's go. I'll drive," says Isidore.

Anson is tired like he hasn't slept in years. A fight always wears out him and River. Unlike Isidore, who is only invigorated by battle--in every possible way. They'll have to find her a bar. He wonders if she can find her own way. She always relies on him to do it.

"The blood," Anson says weakly. It's the last thing he wants to worry about, but he also knows from experience that a bloodstain is a bitch to get out of upholstery once it's set.

"We'll deal with it tomorrow," Isidore says. "Move your ass."

With River's help, Anson gets out of the chair. "Here you go, man," River says, spreading a blanket across the couch so that Anson won't have to sleep on the bloody upholstery. It doesn't occur to River to offer Anson the bed, even though Anson's injuries are—or were—much worse than his own. But Anson is used to this. He lowers himself onto the couch, talking the pillow River offers, and falls asleep almost immediately. Isidore drives them into the night.

KAYENTA
ARIZONA

DAYLIGHT WAKES ANSON. Isidore is still at the wheel, which worries him. He's earned a bloody death, and he's going to have it, dammit. He will go down swinging. Not trapped in a trailer inferno after Isidore gets distracted at the wheel and drives them off some ravine.

He gets up and pees, lifting his torn and bloodied shirt to examine his wound from the night before. It is gone, surely as if it had all been a dream. His skin is smooth. He wets some toilet paper to wipe the blood away and remembers he needs to dump the tanks soon. He has long ago given up hope of anyone remembering the tanks besides him.

In the bedroom, River is snoring, naked legs smothered in blue sheets, his hand down his boxers. Anson digs through the piles on the floor for a cleaner shirt, then shuts the door. He doesn't need to see that. The galley floor is swathed in blood, like it's been mopped with someone's insides. Anson eyes the couch, the upholstery, and then looks away, unable to deal with such mess so early in the morning.

His tongue is stuck to the roof of his mouth. His head aches at the temples. He needs water and caffeine. The sea of water bottles on the floor are all empty. The steel sink is full of dishes all rimmed with old coffee or syrupy soda. Anson grabs the next nearest thing, which is the coffee carafe. He fills it with tap water and drinks deeply. Then he opens the cupboard above the sink and reaches for the tin of coffee. It's too light in his hands. He pries off the lid and finds it empty. They always put back the empty cartons, River and Is, and Anson wants to throw them at their heads. He slams the carton into the trashcan, but the bin hasn't been emptied and that muffles the effect. Resigned, he sinks into the passenger seat. Isidore glances at him. She's got the music off to let him sleep.

"How you doing?" he asks, rubbing his face. The desert is an endless stretch of pink around him, the clouds wispy violet feathers. A few rock formations thrust skyward in the distance, otherwise this place is post-apocalyptically barren. It's the kind of landscape Anson loves, the world vast and lonely, making no pretense.

"Fine. I mean, I need sleep. I guess. You?"

Anson cracks the window. He wants to catch whatever lingers of the scent of desert night. It's an earthy scent, dust and a sweetness Anson can't name, so rich it makes him dizzy. "Fine. I'm not bleeding out painlessly, am I?"

"Don't think so."

They're passing through Kayenta. Anson knows the roads. Sometimes he thinks that if he needed to, he could steer by the stars. Kayenta means he's slept about three hours and Isidore has avoided temptation to go off course, to take any turn other than the ones she's supposed to, drawing them nearer to the thing they're all dreading.

"You wanna trade?"

"Don't you need coffee?"

"We're out. I'll stop at the McDonalds."

"It wasn't me. It was River," Isidore says immediately. "I've been drinking the gas station stuff lately—"

Anson rubs his face. "I don't care, Isidore. Come on. One. Two—"

On three, they both stand. Isidore drops back. Anson

moves across and takes the wheel. The Airstream drifts slightly. Anson gets a boyish thrill every time they pull this off, like popping a wheelie or finding a nudie mag. They made the mistake of doing it in front of their mom once. She'd panicked, yanked Isidore's hair so hard her neck jerked, and tried to ground Anson, who was twenty-six at the time.

"Good one," Isidore says.

"Get some sleep."

"Yeah," Isidore says slowly. "Mind if I leave the TV on? I, uh. Sleep better that way."

"Sure," Anson says. He does not question further. He does not want to know.

THE ROAD

THEY ALL KNOW where they are headed, though no one will say it aloud. The weight of their destination is like an anchor behind them, bumping reluctantly along the asphalt. Stalling, Anson stops in Cortez, buys Isidore pancakes and River corned beef hash, takes his own breakfast in a box to a laundromat across the street. He attempts to wash one whole outfit for each of them. He is pleased to find a dump station at the edge of town, but then River and Is abandon him to see to the sewage alone, as they always have and always will. Once, Anson had shown River his clever addition of a clear elbow pipe between the tank and the hose so he could monitor the fluids and River plugged his nose and backed away, staring at Anson like he was disgusting just for doing the job. Anson takes pleasure in knowing that, if he dies, it's only a matter of time before River and Isidore are swimming in their own shit. When Anson is finished with the dump, Isidore and River return to the Airstream bickering. River is clutching a bag of circus peanuts in one hand and red-dyed pistachios in the other. "You make me sick," Isidore says. River throws an orange peanut at her with an excessive degree of vigor. Before Anson can intervene, Isidore tells him his blood must be nothing but corn syrup and red dye, and River tells her to shut her fucking mouth, you stupid fucking whore. River and Isidore are always quick to flare. It is hard to tell if this is due to the persistently dire nature of their situation, or merely a deep, hereditary hate. By the time Anson has used two twenties and a six-pack to convince a teenager at the detailers that a stag had been shot and poorly, drunkenly butchered in the Airstream, it seems like every happiness in the world hangs on a hamburger and a beer and a moment of silence. River shuts himself in the back room and Anson drives them toward Durango.

DURANGO
COLORADO

"HEY, IS," RIVER SAYS, kicking her foot under the table. "Hey. Is."

Isidore is supposed to say Is not, but instead she kicks him back, hard. Silverware jangles and heads turn their direction. "Knock it off. I'm pissed at you."

"Oh yeah? Well fuck off."

"You shouldn't eat like that," Isidore says. "You'll get cancer." Anson tries to block them out. They are waiting for food at a joint off the main drag that is full of tourists. Behind River is a television screen where news outlets are covering over sixty tornadoes that blew through Iowa last night. Cedar Rapids is gone. Everyone is dead in Dubuque. They'd passed through Dubuque last summer, or maybe the one before, after Isidore had asked Anson to show her the Mississippi. He'd pounded on the steering wheel. "Goddammit, Isidore. Goddammit! Every single time." Fifteen, twenty times at least, Anson has driven Isidore across the Mississippi at her request. He doesn't understand why she never remembers. "Remember Dubuque? Right on the Mississippi?" he asks her now, testing. Isidore frowns and shakes her head. "We should really see it sometime," she says. "The mighty Mississippi."

Anson can't believe it. He rubs his eyes and shoves back from the table to go get another beer from the bar.

"It doesn't matter if I get cancer—" River says.

"Shut up." Anson smacks him on the head as he passes. He can hear River's continued ribbing as he makes his way to the bar and flags down a barman. He is regretting the fact that he can't get nice and wasted and live through the next couple days in a warm liquored haze, when he feels it. The unmistakable atmospheric charge of Isidore beginning to do the worst thing Isidore can do. They have sensed this power lurking in her since she was very small, and have spent their lives walking delicately around it. Living with Isidore is sometimes like eating breakfast and watching TV with an armed bomb that might go off if you insulted its outfit or laughed when it wasn't joking. Anson looks at the table, where River is slowly leaning back, away from Isidore, and Isidore is staring downward, gripping the edge, trying to hold back her own tide. Anson doesn't get the details, couldn't possibly, seeing as how he is fully human, but Isidore says keeping this explosion at bay is like trying not to sneeze. He ignores the ethical implications of the fact that their whole family has allowed a girl who might be able to end the world as easily as other people sneeze to live. He mentally pleads with the barkeep to hurry up with the beers while telling himself he can put a bullet through her brain to save the world, if he has to. When Isidore was seven she had grown angry and leveled all the trees in a fifty-yard radius. Their dad had taken Anson aside and told him that one day, Anson might need to kill his sister to save the rest of the world. "You'll be a hero," his dad had said. "I'll be a killer," Anson said numbly, staring at the weapon his father had placed in his hand. "The exact word is sororicide," Dad had said cheerily, setting up the target.

The energy in the restaurant has shifted. Only the brothers know what they are feeling. Everyone else experiences it as a ripple of apprehension. People who felt fine a moment before begin to worry about the children, the oven, the decline of the mountain trout. The second the beers are set on the bar Anson picks them up and walks toward Isidore calmly, making a wide arc so she can see him coming. He doesn't waste a dirty look on River, who won't meet his eye anyway. He sets the beer in front of Is. "Here."

She puts her hand around it and inhales. "I'm not going to end the world," she says quietly.

"You sure?"

"Mostly sure," she says, which is enough for now.

They sit in tense silence until the waitress arrives with the food. They've ordered identically, the blue cheese, bacon, and avocado burgers, but Isidore has added a root beer float. They're quiet for a few minutes as Isidore pulls the onions and tomato from her burger and River drowns his in ketchup. Anson just slaps his together and eats it, secretly proud of this workingman's austerity. As a child he was unduly influenced by his grandfather's collection of John Wayne movies.

"I've got a guess," River says at last. Food in his mouth, again, but Anson prefers it to the strained silence.

"Let's hear it," Is says, following the script. "What am I?" Her voice is her own and not the netherworld croak that Anson heard once and has been haunted by ever since. Something that was tight in him unclenches.

River pauses for dramatic effect. "Rougarou."

"Rougarou. Hmmm. Some sort of devastatingly beautiful fairy—"

"Hah."

"Who blesses her family and everyone around her with her gentle grace and wisdom."

"Close. More like a really ugly werewolf who eats Catholics if they don't follow Lent."

"Oh," says Is. "Sorry, I didn't realize we were guessing for you." She pops a french fry into her mouth, pleased with herself.

"There's seriously a monster that eats people for breaking Lent?" Anson says. "Hell isn't punishment enough?" The blue cheese bacon avocado burger might be the best he's ever had. He takes a bite, follows it with a long drink of the brown ale. Food brings out a sense of well being for Anson, and he thinks they can go on like this, maybe forever.

"It might also be a type of Native American bigfoot," River shrugs. "Hulking. Hairy."

"I do have a thing for Catholics," Isidore grins wolf-ishly.

"Goddammit," River mutters.

"I'm still going with demon queen." Anson's said this before. Guessing what, exactly, Isidore is and why, exactly, God wants her dead is a favorite family pastime. "God would definitely want to kill a demon."

"Dad used to say I was born of a virgin," Is says, spooning vanilla ice cream into her mouth with a fry.

"What?" Anson freezes, his burger halfway to his mouth. River jerks his head up. Her eyes meet theirs over her float. She looks like a kid caught in a lie. She was always a terrible liar.

"Mom wasn't a virgin," River says. This is obvious, as Isidore is the youngest.

"He didn't mean it like that. He meant like he wasn't really my father, like Mom just woke up pregnant one day or something." She shoves a huge spoon of ice cream between her lips, like if her mouth is full enough they won't ask her questions. River winces in anticipation of brain freeze. He's forgotten Isidore doesn't get it.

Anson can't keep up with this. "Dad always said you were born of a man and a woman." He repeated it, like a prayer. One that, if intoned often enough, would make Isidore human.

She shrugs. They wait for her to swallow. "He used to get drunk and do things."

"Things?" Oh god, Anson thinks. The therapy bills are going to be astronomical. He thinks, he cannot have this conversation. How did they used to put it? Bad touching. The thought sends a terrible itch down the length of his body. He puts down his burger and begins to scratch at his chest.

"You know," Isidore licks the back of her spoon. She has completely missed the lurid suggestion of her own words. River is pale and rigid, paralyzed by the weight of the moment. "You know. Like that time he painted the naked lady on the neighbor's door. Or he'd tell me I was no man's daughter. That I was born of woman and woman only. Stop scratching your chest, Annie."

River and Anson look at each other. There is no point asking Is if she's serious. It's possible she misunderstood dad completely, but she doesn't make things up.

"So you're not saying—he never—bad touching?" River manages.

Isidore freezes with the spoon in her mouth, dangling from her tongue. "Jesus, River. No. What the hell? Pervert."

"Is," Anson says before River can get offended. "What are the words that dad used, exactly?"

"Why?" She puts down the spoon and gazes at him solemnly.

"Welcome to the conversation," River says.

"You think it wasn't just. You know. Dad drunk talk?" she asks.

"I don't know. What did he say?"

Isidore looks at them. Her brothers have stopped eating and are staring at her, slightly pale, with all their worry lines showing. Isidore thinks that, in their life on the lam from heaven, whatever drunken ramblings their dad used to spout rate pretty low, but what does she know? She's not the real human here.

"He'd say, 'You, little Isidore. You are no man's daughter'." She does it in her deep dad voice, the one that makes him sound like an idiot inheritor holding forth over oysters. Which is, in fact, how dad used to sound. "Or, 'I don't know who made you, Issy, but it wasn't me and your mother doesn't cheat'." She even slams down her glass on the last word for maximum dad effect.

"Jesus Christ," River shoves his plate away, nearly spilling his drink, and thumps back against the bench.

"Jesus Christ," Is agrees solemnly.

"No—no, I mean like—shit, Isidore."

"I don't understand," she says, frustrated now with her inability to catch the subtext—or even, sometimes, the text. She looks to Anson.

He has to give her something. "It's just—we always thought you were Mom's and Dad's. Their natural child. Just different."

Now she looks like she feels sorry for him. "Anson," she says. "Are you stupid?"

PUEBLO
COLORADO

AFTER ANSON TURNED sixteen, while the adults sat on the back patio on sultry nights, smoking and drinking Coors, the siblings would sneak out and drive around looking for a restaurant where rumor said midgets walked around in sombreros filled with chips and salsa. Isidore thought she had never heard of such a wonderful thing. According to legend, one could sit at her table and reach out to dine off the midget's Mexican hats as the midgets roamed about the restaurant like dazed cattle. Even at sixteen, Anson doubted the veracity of the claim and was uncomfortable with its prejudice, but was content to drive Isidore around nonetheless. It made her happy, and attack was unlikely to occur on the streets of downtown Pueblo. The restaurant was said to be named Nacho Mama's. It wasn't in the phone book and this was before the internet, so they'd spent plenty of evenings in their dad's old Chevy Citation, driving the streets with the windows down, listening to whatever River insisted on hearing, searching for an El Dorado that may never have existed. Anson remembers River in the backseat, thirteen, puffing on a stolen cigarette and saying the midgets should walk around wearing ashtrays. Earlier that year he'd killed his first angel.

They never found Nacho Mama's. They did get caught once sneaking back into Grandma Ruth's, where the old woman had pulled out a wooden spoon and gone swinging at Is, shouting about dairy cows, and Anson had swung back at her. Grandma was younger then, not yet frail. She was lucky it was Anson who went after her, and not Isidore. Grandma called him a denigrate lowlife, went to bed, and rose the next morning to spend a day penning letters to his entire family outlining his faults in detail, including his "unseemly love for his own sister" and his "sub-par color-coordination skills". It wasn't long after the angels had killed their dad. Mom just rolled her eyes and burned the letters in the sink, cigarette in her hand and too much distance in her gaze, her bathrobe and hair both faded and bleak. Anson had muttered something about a ruined old bitch and his mother had slapped him, then looked stunned. She'd never hit him before and now, when he was eighteen and feeling pressure to give the kids what they should have had from a father, seemed a strange time to start. Is says there's more between Mom and Grandma Ruth than they can understand and Anson just takes her at her word.

Isidore's feet are on the dash, her leg is jiggling nervously. She is taking deep breaths and then sighing, over and over again, an unending cycle of determination and defeat. Anson exits the highway, drives past strip malls and Applebee's and Red Lobsters, past trailer parks where he momentarily envies the families there, who look so happy on their tiny lawns with their raucous children, and enters the outskirt area that was once primed to be upscale and is now inhabited by people who put bathtubs and painted tires and even one rusting iron bed frame into their lawns. It's here Grandma Ruth lives in her glass house.

Gripping the steering wheel hard, then catching himself and stopping so as not to upset Is, Anson turns down the gravel drive. There is the red pickup his mom bought to replace the Citation, extolling its potential for weapon storage and overlooking the fact that her four growing children could not all fit inside. Next to it is Grandma and Grandpa Campers' massive white Chevy Silverado, suggesting they're ranchers or horse people and not old folks who fight contentiously and besmirch one another over fried shrimp and coleslaw. Missing is the beloved white '77 Camaro that Anson threw up in when he was seven and has not been allowed to ride in since. It is their particular cross to bear that all their grandparents, save their mom's father who they never knew, are still alive.

"Don't make me," Isidore says, and Anson feels heavy with guilt. Isidore doesn't complain unless she is truly beyond her ability to withstand.

"Be a good girl and I'll drive you to that vaquero bar later." It's probably somewhat wrong to be plying his sister with the promise of vaquero sex, but they are not a normal family. Surviving this is going to be no Sunday picnic, and if Anson can't keep Isidore level, it could be everybody's last hurrah. Ever.

Isidore sighs. "The last one kept weeping and calling me mamacita. It was creepy. I don't care if they mean it as a compliment."

"Goddammit, Is," says River. "It's bad enough I have to be here without having to hear about your sex life."

"They almost always weep," Is says, and River clambers out of the trailer, slamming the door behind him. Isidore and Anson giggle helplessly at his tantrum, delighted that he is so easily and openly annoyed. Anson goes to the cupboard, bare except for a box of Cap'n Crunch and a bottle of Rye. He takes a swig, passes the bottle to Isidore, and snatches it back before one shot becomes four. Thus fortified, they throw themselves into the fray.

Grandma Ruth's glass-walled living room is full of their frustratingly extensive family and a small cluster of Grandma's friends who are gathered around her, peering down at her digital camera. Grandma has a penchant for green and everything is decorated in shades of snot and avocado, from the dampish shag carpet to the heavy drapes to the stiff, uncomfortable furniture. She smokes in the house and the scent hits them the moment they walk in, stale smoke and Febreze and mildew.

River has already disappeared in the crowd. When Isidore and Anson enter red-faced and giddy, Grandma Ruth's eyes fall on them like a hawk's. She scowls. Anson can already see her wheels turning. He puts himself in front of Isidore, like it's possible to shield her from matriarchal wrath.

Luckily, before Grandma can come after him with the claw, their mom comes out of the kitchen. She spots them immediately and beams. Isidore flies at her. They hold each other a long time and when their mom pulls back her eyes are teary.

"It's so good to see you," she says, touching Isidore's snowy hair. "You look thin, Isidore. You making sure she eats?" she says to Anson before kissing his cheek, pulling him in.

"Hi Mom." It feels good to hold her, to be hugged by his mom, in spite of everything.

"Annie," she says, patting his face. She's blond-haired and blue-eyed, like Isidore, but more angular in the face. Isidore inherited her pouty lips and apple cheeks from their father. His mother looks so happy to see him that it hurts; her love a weight he'd rather not carry. It makes him feel guilty for being gone, but he was here four weeks ago, dammit. Maybe six, but there's no need to act like it's some post-war reunion.

It wasn't always like this. Mom, when they were younger, was like a heroine from a 90's action movie, before heroines had to dress slutty and fall down all the time. She is maternal now in a way she never was when he was young and wanted it. She's been out of the game since Anson and Isidore, who was eighteen at the time, picked River up from jail, threw him in the Airstream they'd bought with bonds of Isidore's that had just matured, and hit the road together, just the three of them. That's seven years she hasn't had to worry about keeping Isidore alive, keeping out of the middle of nowhere in the middle of the night, making sure they're stocked on ammo and Isidore takes her pill, because Anson's been doing it. She sold the house in Colorado Springs, pointless by then as the angels were attacking too often for Isidore to live in it, and moved to an old hacienda in San Miguel de Allende. River had spent a few years terrified she'd become a lesbian. "Mom had an experimental phase before Isidore was born," he would whine. Then Raoul had shown up one Thanksgiving, wearing a shirt of pink paisley, sporting a thin mustache and sambaing loose-hipped in the kitchen while quartering limes for caipirinhas and making Anson wonder if he'd been raised by an impostor, some mother-faced proxy for the real woman.

"No Raoul?" says Anson.

"Oh honey. Family isn't something you inflict upon your lover. Where's your brother?"

"He came in already. Here, somewhere."

"Mom," Isidore says. She's eager, Anson knows, to get her away from the crowd, but it's too late. Across the room, Grandma Ruth rises from her chair like Cthulhu from the depths. She's shaking, claws gripping the armrests for support. Her old, soft body sways in its Hawaiian flower muumuu, her boobs unbridled in there and knocking each other like Bobo dolls desperate to take each other down. She swoops in for the kill. Is sidesteps her. Anson sees it coming, but it's too late. Her bony hand, fingers old and worn slick like a puckered orange peel, descends and talons close aroundal his forearm. She leans all her weight on him as if she might collapse, gripping him to a degree he's convinced she knows is painful.

"Hi Grandma Ruth," says Is.

"Hi Grandma," Anson says, his skin rippling its disdain of the claw.

"Did you get my letter, Linda? MY LETTER," she shouts. She ignores Isidore and Anson completely.

"The one with the pictures? THE PICTURES?" asks their mother. She is forced to raise her voice in response to Grandma's expression of bewilderment. Mom is more patient with Grandma Ruth than she used to be, because soon Grandma Ruth will die. They are counting on this.

Grandma Ruth looks at Anson, pretending she can't

hear his mom and waiting for translation.

"With pictures?" Anson booms loudly in spite of himself. Grandma wobbles, throwing all her weight onto his arm and squeezing the claw, as if the volume of his voice has nearly leveled her. "Pictures, she says? You want pictures? Well here."

Isidore laughs at his fate. Grandma releases her claw hold, but relief is short. She holds out the camera, squinting at it from a distance like it is an inscrutable artifact, when Anson knows damn well she's proficient at it. She was emailing him pictures of her hair up in rollers until he finally blocked her address.

"How do I turn it on, Anson? Is it the button? The BUTTON ANSON WHERE IS THE BUTTON?" Anson turns the camera on, which prompts Grandma Ruth to say what a treasure he is in a tone that falls just short of blatantly sarcastic. Then she holds the camera out to him and proceeds to scroll through pictures of her church choir, who stare down the camera like prisoners at a Gulag. Their mom says something to Isidore while Anson is forced to watch the slideshow.

A pink-haired woman with a fierce little mouth pops up on the display. She appears to be inflicting some nasty gypsy curse on Grandma Ruth. "There's Fizzy," Grandma says rancorously. Fizzy and Grandma Ruth are famous enemies. "You wouldn't believe it if I told you. The look that woman gives me! Turns around and just—" she glares to show him. "At me!" She glares again, and Anson knows she's only imitating Fizzy, but it's hard not to take it personally.

"Those are nice, Grandma," Is says, trying to come to his aid.

"Isidore, when you're not dressing like a man, you're dressing like a floozy," Grandma snaps. Isidore flinches and looks down at her own outfit. Anson's eyes follow hers, then jump up to Grandma Ruth. Her fake-lashed eyes gaze at him with reproach. As if she's just discovered naked pictures of Is on his laptop.

"Won't you think of your poor mother, Isidore? If not me, at least your mother. Think of how it must hurt her, to see you like this. Wearing those—cross-dresser short pants. What did they call them in our day?"

"Daisy Dukes," Mom says, at the same time Grandma Ruth says, "Shorts for whores."

This strikes Anson as funny and he starts to laugh. But he catches Isidore's face, and she's not amused. Little things that wouldn't get to him get to Isidore. He supposes she's still afraid that if she crosses some line she can't see, they'll toss her out. Their dad used to threaten it all the time, after all. "We'll toss you out to save ourselves, Issy, don't think we won't," he'd say when she spilled Kool-Aid or smarted off; somehow Isidore never got that it was his way of joking.

"They're not even that short," Isidore mutters.

"With that bosom hanging out," Grandma says. "I didn't know better, I'd think you were trying to attract—" She looks pointedly at Anson.

"Mom," their mom says.

"All right," Anson says. His voice is too loud. From over by the window, his cousins turn to look. Anson has a reputation among the cousins as being some kind of arsonist or schizophrenic. Stupidly, this has always bothered him. He can feel them now, watching him with their moon eyes. Arnie with his polo shirt and bald patch, Kara in her conservative cardigan and black skirt. Even Kelly, in his hipster plaid and black skinny jeans, tapping his American Spirits against his tattooed wrist, avoids Anson. In his own family, Anson is the good son. The black sheep is Isidore's role and not one he can tolerate. "That's—come on, Grandma, can't we—" he's at a loss for words. He knows it would be frowned on for a grown man to get mouthy with his nana. Losing it would feed the cousins' gossip for weeks. He doesn't' understand why they're supposed to pretend she's not a raging bitch, just because she's old.

"That's because I am trying to attract," Isidore says, and loops her arm around Anson's neck. "Is it working?"

"Oh my god," Anson says. "Too far, Isidore." He glances at Kara, who puts a hand to her mouth. Kelly pretends he didn't see.

"Hi Grandma Ruth. Happy Birthday," River says from behind Anson. Anson uses it as an excuse to shove Isidore away, make room for their brother.

"How nice of you to decide to come," Grandma Ruth says. "I know you've been so busy looking for work. Haven't you?"

Anson takes a swelling breath, and it is only Isidore's hand on his arm that halts his response. He wants to throw her off and pull his Glock on Grandma Ruth. Why shouldn't he pull his Glock? River risks death every day so that Isidore isn't abandoned, alone—never mind that River would certainly have overdosed by now without Anson's watchful eye, never mind that—and Grandma suggests he ought to be steaming lattes or bagging groceries.

"Really busy," River says easily. Always better than Anson at detaching himself emotionally. Grandma Ruth senses her remarks haven't hit their target and tries again.

"We've hidden all the drugs," she says. "Even though it's just enabling, if you ask me. Which is not to say you could-n't find them, if you looked hard enough. You'll have to ask yourself to show a little restraint."

This wounds River, which Anson finds tragic. She should be glad River was able to get off the meth at all, never mind that he drinks the equivalent of ten cups of coffee a day to make up for it. Some guy with a thing for little boys and a basement full of arcade games got him hooked at sixteen, not long after their dad died, and Isidore may or may not have killed that man. They don't talk about it.

Isidore edges away, toward the banquet table where there's a huge crystal punch bowl that inevitably will be full of Hawaiian Punch and melting rainbow sherbet. Anson lets her go, manning up and staying with River instead of abandoning him to Mumm-Ra in the muumuu.

Mom hugs River and tells him he's looking better. Like everything with River happened last week, instead of nine years ago. This is why Anson doesn't bring them to more family gatherings. On the road, it's possible to forget all the way they've screwed everything up. Their family is determined to keep the tender parts right at the surface. Grandma Ruth glares and Anson bids her a happy birthday.

"Thanks for humoring an old lady," she says. "I'm sure you're anxious to leave. I'm sure there are places you'd rather be than celebrating the birthday of a poor old woman. But I'm glad you're here, anyway. This is going to be my last one, Anson. My last birthday. I don't know, I can just feel it."

"We know, Grandma," Isidore calls from the buffet. She has abandoned hope of being loved and is going straight for the jugular. It suits her better, anyway.

"Stop, Mom," Mom says, covering for Is. Grandma Ruth touches her eye, like she's going to cry. Like that's something she's capable of doing.

Anson looks over to the banquet table. Isidore has stuck a black olive on each of her fingers. She waves them at him, smiling.

"Want a drink, Grandma? River and I will get you a drink." He abandons his mom to her own mother, tugging River away with him. He would rather face an angel than Grandma Ruth in her moods.

At the banquet table, Isidore fakes a pitiful cough. "Help an old woman, Annie," she mimics, forming her own claw and clinging onto his arm.

"There beer over here?" Anson says. He needs a beer badly. He knows exactly how this celebration is going to end, and he's determined to stay out of it this year. He absolutely cannot do that without a couple beers in him.

Before sustenance can be found, two hands grab Anson firmly by the shoulders and shake. His hand goes to his gun before he remembers where he is. A battleground surely, but not one that requires firearms. He pulls himself free of the grasp, and then turns to face his Aunt Jackie and her newest husband, Fletcher Mound, whom he refuses to call Uncle Fletch.

"It's good to see you kids," Aunt Jackie says. She's Dad's older sister and has no kids of her own. Which is a really good thing, considering her taste in men.

"Good to see you too, Aunt Jackie," Isidore says. She goes in for the hug, which brings her into dangerous proximity to Fletch Mound but Is doesn't mind. Anson thinks she's hoping one of these days he'll finally make a move on her so she can kill him.

Fletch stares at Isidore. Stares at her all over. The fact that Isidore is aware of it doesn't leave Anson any less disturbed. Then Fletch looks at him and River and waggles his eyebrows. Lustily. Over Isidore.

"Oh my god," River says flatly.

"Fletchy," Aunt Jackie scolds fondly. She looks at them smiling, like Fletcher has strapped on his suspenders and offered to dance a jig. "Isn't he just something else?"

"He sure is," Anson says.

"Been down at the crick all morning," Fletch says. As a result of the tacit approval he received in marrying their Aunt Jackie, Fletch makes no effort to hide who he is. Anson wants to kill him, but can't go through with it. Slaying angels is one thing; Anson has never killed a human. That's best left to Is. "Got three squirrels. Got two ducks. Got nine rabbits. Found a mama in her den. Had good luck, today."

"Got?" Isidore says, missing his meaning. Anson thinks he's going to throw up.

"With my pellet gun," he says. "Some of 'em ain't dead yet. Got 'em strung up in the basement now. Wanna have a look?" In his sweater vest and khakis, Fletch Mound does look like a pervert, but a dapper one.

"You shouldn't say these things out loud," says River. "You know that, right?"

"Aunt Jackie," Anson says, ignoring Fletcher. "Your husband has spent the morning torturing small animals. That seem normal to you?"

"Oh Annie," she says, swatting at Anson's arm. "You kids! Your father would have gotten such a kick out of you."

"Yeah," Anson says. "I'm not joking, Jackie."

"How was Vegas?" she says, abruptly, stirring a cocktail straw around in her concoction so that it looks like she's dissolving Rainbow Brite's pus into a cup of blood. Aunt Jackie doesn't look much like their dad, who had the bone structure of a cartoon hero and disturbing bee-stung lips. Jackie is drawn down, like Olive Oil without the figure. Her face is long and unfortunately horsey, her hair the color of a Barbie doll's and curly like a poodle. She's tied a big bow in it, like this is Halloween and she's going as Daisy Duck. She's wearing some kind of high-heeled sandal, her toes such a bloody red that it looks as if someone cut off their tips. Fletch Mound draws back his palm and slaps her hard on the rump. She startles, her eyes shooting wide like ripe blue cervixes. She smiles but Anson can tell she's embarrassed. He smiles back at her softly.

"Great," Anson says. "You should go to Vegas sometime, Aunt Jackie. You'd have fun."

"How 'bout it, baby? We could hop in the truck now, get us some ham salad and wine coolers," says Fletch Mound, twirling a lock of her hair.

"Not with you," Anson says. "I didn't mean with him. You could go with some girlfriends, Aunt Jackie."

"Oh! I suppose!" She smiles too brightly and Anson realizes she doesn't have any girlfriends. It makes him sad. He may have been dealt the bloody death card, but he's never had to face anything alone.

"Probably not a good idea for me to cross state lines, anyway," Fletch Mound says thoughtfully. River nods at him, raising his eyebrows at Aunt Jackie. Anson can't discern the greater cruelty: to make her see, or to let it go on.

"Fletchy is always one for caution," Aunt Jackie says by way of explanation. "He doesn't like to take unnecessary risks."

"Doesn't he?" says Anson.

"Did you get a gift for Grandma Ruth?" Isidore says.

"Sure, honey, you want me to sign your name to the card?" Aunt Jackie always had their backs when they were little. She bought Is forbidden, inappropriate clothing and let the boys watch banned horror flicks. At Aunt Jackie's house, Is would prance around like a tiny hooker and the boys would wake crying in the dark from nightmares of being devoured by clown-sharks. It was wonderful. She doesn't know about the angels. Mom would rush them to Jackie's house immediately after every angel appearance, desperate, Anson supposes, for a break and counting on the fact that the attacks were usually spaced a few days apart.

"Oh, I don't know. That's okay. That would be great," Isidore says.

"And the boys—"

"Just mine."

What the hell, Anson thinks, looking at Is. But then a voice pipes up from behind them and Anson comes to the detached realization that he was wrong. This could get worse.

"Well, there you all are. Hiding from me."

Aunt Jackie smiles at him. Fletch Mound eyes him up and down like sizing up prey, which, to Fletch Mound, he probably is. Uncle Mark presses himself, enormous belly first, into their circle. "How are you Jackie? Aren't you looking fine today? I swear, but you haven't found the perfect man for yourself, have you?"

This is exactly the kind of mind-fuck Uncle Mark has been working on Jackie and anyone else unlucky enough to share space with him all their lives. His tone implies he means the opposite of what his words have actually said. Aunt Jackie's smile freezes on her face and Anson can see her trying to work out whether offense has been given or not.

"Uncle Mark," River says. "You're here. That's not weird." Uncle Mark is Aunt Jackie's first husband, the man she was married to when they were little and who has earned the title Uncle by default. Anson watches him rub his enormous belly. He looks like he's expecting triplets and is happy about it.

"Aren't you pleased," Uncle Mark says, like he knows they aren't. "Had to take a couch in Ruth's basement. Asked if I could share a hotel room with these two but that one wasn't having it." He jerks a thumb at Jackie and Fletch Mound, respectively. He isn't joking. Uncle Mark is like this. He sees absolutely no reason why a man shouldn't share a hotel room with his ex-wife and her new lover. "Kara's damn kids all running amok down there. I'll tell you what, those boys have some real nasty porn. Their type always does."

In spite of it all, Anson finds his announcement promising. Uncle Mark in close quarters with a serial killer. "The basement?" he says. "Fletch Mound's claimed that territory for himself. Maybe this will work out after all."

Isidore snorts punch up her nose. Aunt Jackie frowns. "You can just call him Fletch, dear," she says quietly.

"I could take you down there," Fletch Mound says. "Show you what I got. Bunch of helpless things." His eyes shine lustily. Bless him, but he's trying to be nice.

"What do you think of this on the news here," Uncle Mark says, waving his Coors can at the TV. Anson wonders where the hell he found the beer. It hits him that Grandma Ruth may have hidden it to pretend like River's an alcoholic, too. "Anson? Eh?" Mark prods.

"Hmm?" Anson says. He's distracted by hunger, but the food all looks like June Cleaver took opiates and decided to experiment with pimento and Jell-O. "What is it now?"

"This volcano. What is it—Rubble?"

"Rabble," says Aunt Jackie. "In Papa's New Guinea."

"Papua New—never mind," says River.

"She blew," says Uncle Mark, shaking his head and making jazz fingers at the ceiling. "Took out a whole island. Everything that wasn't destroyed by the lava was taken down by the ash. That's what they get for living near a large body of water," he says. "I'm sorry, but what the hell do they think is going to happen?"

"Shame," Anson agrees. Suddenly Isidore is next to him, handing him a Coors Light.

"All they have," she says quietly.

"God bless you, Isidore," Anson says, pulling the tab.

"What's wrong with Coors?" booms Uncle Mark. Isidore has not been quiet enough. "You kids drove up to the Springs, got yourselves some fancy ideas, is that it? Coors is brewed with Rocky Mountain water, son. Coors is the life blood of your ancestors—"

"We're related to Adolph Coors, now?" River says. "That it?" Anson knows he should give River his beer to avoid ending up on the evening news, but he just can't bring himself to part with it. It is as if he has wandered into hell, and this sole, cool can is his Virgil.

"Prefer strawberry wine coolers, myself," says Fletch Mound. He licks his lips. "Love that pink color. Love that smell."

"You and your smart mouth, boy," Uncle Mark starts. He's always had it out for River, no one's sure why. "Maybe we are related to Adolph Coors—"

"Both of us? By coincidence?"

Uncle Mark makes a frustrated farting sound with his lips, all the bluster just puttering out of him. Anson takes deep breaths. Just about anything Uncle Mark says is capable of pissing him off.

"Gonna go find me a wine cooler," Fletch Mound says. "Toast. To the volcano."

"I just don't know about him, sometimes," Aunt Jackie whispers as he walks away. Her lipstick is bleeding into the wrinkles around her mouth, like she is leaking. Anson wishes some nice man would take her home and make her tea. "He's a real different sort. Late at night I find him looking at porn. You know, the serious kind."

"The serious . . .?" Anson blinks away an image of a solemn, sexy librarian in tortoise shell glasses. He wants to hear it as much as he doesn't.

"With the dead people," Jackie says in a stage whisper. "He leaves for days at a time and comes back with blood in his clothes. Isn't that something!" Anson realizes that the nasty porn Uncle Mark found did not belong to Kara's third-graders. Probably.

"Yeah," River says. "That's because he's a serial killer, Aunt Jackie."

Aunt Jackie makes a strange face, a strangled almost-smile and for a moment Anson thinks, they've finally made her see. He isn't worried about Fletch freaking and taking hostages, it's nothing Isidore can't handle and anyway, she's hungry for the excuse. But then the constipated look is rewritten into a cheery grin. "Oh," Aunt Jackie says, wagging a finger. "You kids and your sense of humor."

"No, seriously," River says, but it's too late. Aunt Jackie has hurried herself away, suddenly very interested to hear Uncle Mark's opinions on the exploding volcano and unrepentant heathens.

River rounds on Isidore. "Couldn't you have got me one?" he says, gazing at the beer.

"Annie got the last," Isidore says. She's angry. They're all on edge now, and River has apparently stopped caring that nothing is more likely to make Isidore go apocalypse than family. Anson hands River his beer. He wishes, for once, that he could be the person everyone else had to worry about. River says, "No man, I couldn't." Then he takes the can and drinks deeply.

"Come on," Anson says. "Don't make eye-contact."

As they sneak out the back door, Isidore disobeys orders and makes sexy-mouth at hipster Kelly. River punches her in the back. Anson knows better, but for some reason he doesn't heed his own advice and glances up at the last second. Grandma Ruth catches his eye. He smiles and waves. Her hateful glare lands like a poisoned-tip dart and protrudes from his skin as he hurries them out the door.

PUEBLO
COLORADO

ANSON WAKES UP on chemical-scented shag carpet with a crick in his neck and an almost sexual longing for the open road. He groans sitting up, hand to neck, and resents River, who sleeps open-mouthed on the twin bed between crisp cotton sheets. Anson has made do with an electric blanket that has the texture of leg hair and smells like old woman. He remembers the way their dad used to wake them with a foghorn, saying it was for their training but clearly enjoying himself. Anson wishes he could do that to River now but, lacking the resolve and the foghorn, settles for shutting the door behind him in a way that is not exactly quiet.

They have a few hours until the threat of death requires them to leave. He wanders downstairs in pajama pants and finds his mother browning breakfast sausages in a cast iron pan. "It's not Jimmy Dean," she says apologetically. The sight of her silk peach robe is mildly disturbing. She hasn't gone thick all over like most people's mothers. Mom could still wield a Gurkha knife in one hand and a semi-automatic in the other, if it was required. "Your Grandma Ruth bought these hippie sausages that don't have nitrous, or something. Because of the cancer. Can you believe it?"

Anson sits at the table. "I thought Grandma Ruth still believed cancer was caused by saying it three times fast." She used to swat them every time they said it.

"Apparently it's a combination of that and Jimmy Dean." She turns the sausages. They smell pretty savory and delicious for something cancer-free. While his mother makes coffee, Anson thinks of Martha. Now that they have lost their tail and made the required visit to family, he is planning to visit his girlfriend. He knows Isidore and River are counting on the Pacific Northwest for the cooler weather, where they'll eat fish and River will visit--again--the top of the Space Needle while Anson waits at the bottom with Isidore because heights are too risky. And he'll take them there. But he has a craving for Martha. He doesn't know if it's love. He figures it must be, since it sure as hell isn't lust--Martha is a twenty-six-year-old virgin, a hymenal one anyway. If it isn't lust, it must be love. He can't think of any other option.

There had been a strange desire to show up at her ranch outside Tulsa, trailing the angel, and letting her see the truth of his life, once and for all. It was a sick desire, evidence that he was fundamentally ruined in some shadowy way. Pursuing a relationship with her had required a silent promise to tuck the truth away, only a real bastard would whip it out now. All of Martha's friends are married and most of them have houses and babies. A few are even divorced. They've been seeing each other for two years. Anson understands that, in her circles, this is the point at which a ring is expected. He just can't bring himself to produce one.

The peace doesn't last long. The scent of meat summons River, he comes in scratching his belly and yawning. He passes behind Anson and Anson fists him in the thigh. River puts his dukes up lazily, but this jockeying is reflexive, not provoked. Isidore trails behind him trying to look casual, like she hasn't calculated the moment it would be safe to come down. But maybe, Anson thinks, he isn't giving her enough credit. She must have slept.

"Morning Mom," Isidore says, hedging away from her oddly. She squeezes herself between the chairs and the wall to avoid passing behind their mother. Their mom is turned to the stove, her back to them, and Anson raises his hands to ask Isidore what's up. She's not exactly subtle, not now or ever. She widens her eyes; it appears to be a plea for help.

"Sit down, Mom," River says.

"No no," she says. She swats at him with a spatula and Isidore startles. "Let me make you breakfast. I hated it all those years when you were young, frying eggs and flipping pancakes when all I wanted was a cup of coffee and the paper. Now, of course, I'd give anything to have those years back."

"Hated it enough to—" Isidore begins. Anson kicks her hard under the table. He thinks, he'd better get her an e-reader or something. Being up all night alone with her thoughts isn't doing her any good.

"What honey?"

"Enough to have all these kids after me," Anson says.

It's possible she isn't aware, as the rest of them are, that Isidore has always suspected Mom of making several attempts on her life. All failed. So far. He thinks he's covered but she rounds on them. Isidore dives beneath the table, mistaking the quick movement for an all-out attack. Their mom holds out a platter of pancakes and sausage and frowns. She looks to Anson for explanation. He rolls his eyes playfully. Crazy Isidore. He doesn't know what has happened between yesterday and this morning to put her on high alert, and he doesn't care. He wants to kick her, but in a lazy sort of way.

"Isidore, honey?" Mom says. "You all right?"

"She's fine," Anson says. "You're fine, Isidore."

"Just dropped my . . . thing," Isidore says, rising hesitantly.

Mom sits at the table, finally, and goes to pour herself a cup of coffee, but the carafe is empty. "I'll make more—" Anson says, and stands, but she tells him to wait. There's a tone, so Anson sits back down.

She looks at each of them, drawing out the suspense

as she likes to do. River is immersed in his pancakes and doesn't notice. Isidore taps her fork nervously against her plate, agitating Anson until he finally does kick her. She ignores him and cries, "What, Mom?" This act of their mother's drives her crazy.

Mom looks at each of them in turn. Isidore looks like she's trying to climb out of her skin. Anson keeps his eye on the pancakes, unable to bear either of them.

"Well. I guess I'll just say it, then."

"Say what?" Isidore says, sipping her coffee nervously. Anson wishes she would get ahold of herself. Mom has always done this to provoke Is, and Is always plays right into it. For someone who can do what Isidore can do, she can be absurdly insecure. Then Anson feels guilty, for thinking it, and growls out, "What is it?"

"It's Minxy," Mom says.

"Goddammit," cries Isidore. Anson agrees with her. All this suspense, for Minxy?

"What's wrong with Minxy?" River asks.

"She's dying. Minxy is dying, and I need you to go find your father."

Minxy is a caramel colored Cockapoo, and when Anson was in San Miguel de Allende last month, he'd been surprised to find her still alive. She was a puppy when Dad died. But that was sixteen years ago. Which is where they arrive to the major problem with what Mom's just said: Dad is dead, and Minxy already should be. It isn't natural, for that dog to still be kicking. She's what, seventeen years old now? Is that even possible, for a dog?

"She should have died a long time ago," says Isidore. Anson's thoughts exactly.

"Well she's dying now, and I need you kids to go get your father," Mom snaps.

"Dad's dead," Anson says. He's bored with it already, whatever stupid joke his mom is playing. "Haha. Seriously, how the hell is Minxy even still alive? Are you sacrificing babies for her, or something?"

"He isn't dead," Mom says. Anson's fingers squeeze too tightly around his fork. He realizes he is holding his knife like a weapon.

"Mom. Dad died in an angel attack. He died defending Isidore." This family lore is sacred. Their father died a hero's death and therefore Anson cannot resent the man for leaving and forcing him to take charge. He died defending his freak daughter. A death beyond reproach.

"No honey. That's just what we told you."

"What?" says Isidore. She's watching Mom distrustfully, like she expects at any moment the woman will rip off her face and reveal herself as God, or the Penguin, or Oprah.

"Your father didn't die, he just couldn't handle it anymore. He was tired of all the work, and the running. It's so hard, being a parent, guys, and your dad was never really cut out for it."

Anson thinks, this cannot be happening.

"Mom," Isidore says. "What are you saying?" Anson can't tell if she's about to spiral south. She sounds upset, but she's inhaling her pancakes with disgusting vigor.

"He didn't want to leave you, honey. He was just really tired." Anson catches her eyes darting toward the Sunday paper, like she's longing to take a look.

"Tired? Dad's not dead, he's tired?" Anson says.

"You know he really wanted to get into art therapy. He just couldn't focus with the angels always flying in, and you kids running around."

"Dad left us because of art therapy?" Isidore says. She looks at Anson with a terrible smile frozen on her face and tears just below the surface of her eyes.

"The important thing is for you kids not to take this personally—"

"Dad abandoned us because Isidore's little problem interfered with his art, and you want us not to take it personally?" Anson says.

"It wasn't just that," Isidore says defensively. "It was because of all of us. Right, Mom? What's your problem?" she snaps at River, who has made the mistake of looking at her with sympathy.

"The constant intrusions really disturbed his inner space. He wasn't like me. It was fun for me, you know. Like being in a movie. But your dad just couldn't work from the right place, what with having to kill the angels all the time."

"And the kids," Isidore says. "It was hard on him with all of us."

"Yes, Isidore," their mom says, placating. "It was hard because of all of you." Anson wonders if she's actually trying to sound insincere.

"How is this even possible?" River says. "An angel attacked that day. I remember it. Dad was lying on the ground. There was blood."

"You passed out," Isidore says. "You and Annie, both."

"I didn't pass out," River says. "I was knocked unconscious. You make it sound like I fainted."

"That's because you did faint. You panicked, and you fainted like a great limp dick." She makes a floppy motion with her wrist.

"At least I have a dick, Isidore."

Isidore asks him if that's what gets him out of bed every morning and then they are both saying shut up again and again, shut up shut up shut up.

"He's right," Anson says, ignoring them. "I remember Dad on the ground, and all that blood." Then he had come to, and the body was gone. Mom hadn't wanted them to see it. The result, of course, was that Anson had imagined his father eviscerated and in shreds. Like pork through the grinder. Worse than any horror movie.

"You remember what your father was doing, when the angel attacked?" their mom says gently. She tugs the Arts and Lifestyle section toward her.

"He was barbecuing," Isidore said. "I've always wondered if that's what drew the angels. Cooking meat. Like a sacrifice. You know, Moses." She raises her hands in an inscrutable manner. Like a football referee signaling touchdown.

"You drew the angels," River says. "That was you." Isidore flips the double bird, her hands still raised shoulder-width apart. River stabs his fork into his sausages and crams them in his mouth, smiling at her. "Nobody understands your gestures, freak." Anson feels that he could pull out his gun and shoot them both and only regret it over whiskeys on Christmas Eve.

"She's doing Moses," Anson translates. He raises his hands like Isidore's. "The Red Sea."

"It was an opportune time," Mom says to her pancakes. "He took it."

"But the blood—" Anson says. "Dammit Isidore, would you stop doing Moses?"

"Probably doing Peter, Paul, and Mary too," Grandma Ruth calls from the other room.

"What's wrong with that?" Isidore says. "Can somebody please explain to me—"

"The blood," Anson presses. "There was so much blood." In high school Anson had a recurring nightmare about punching a hole in a wall and watching the wall begin to course heavy seas of blood, gushing tides of it filling the house and drowning them all.

"It was ketchup, Annie," Isidore says. Finally she stops doing Moses. "Dad faked his death with a squeeze bottle of Heinz." She is being overly dramatic, like it's cute, and River actually starts to laugh. Again with the food in the mouth.

"He was just so tired," River says. "He couldn't catsup." Mom smiles at them indulgently.

"Was the angel real?" Anson says. "Or did you and Dad string something up with wires and fake feathers? What the hell is the matter with you two?" Their mother is telling them their father, who appeared to be dead, actually just wanted more time to do his art, and they're laughing about it. Like psychopaths. Anson bangs his fist on the table. It feels satisfying for a second, his display of ape-like superiority. But he should have known better. Isidore and River stare at him silently. Then, in unison, they raise their fists and bang them against the table.

"Are you monkeys or are you men!" Isidore shouts. Bang bang.

"Enough is enough is enough is enough," says River. Bang bang bang bang. They are both imitating Dad, which is, to Anson's great shame, exactly who he sounds like.

"The angel was real," Mom says. "And Isidore killed it. The effort knocked her out for a bit, too—"

"Or maybe you hit me on the back of the head with a baseball bat," Isidore says darkly. She is not entirely joking.

"Isidore!" says their mother. "How could you even think something like that?"

"And now we're supposed to go find him," Anson says. "He left us for all this time, and we're supposed to just go and pretend like everything's okay?"

"Everything's not okay," Isidore says. "Minxy is dying." She's glaring at her coffee. The reminder of Mom trying to kill her has turned her morose. Anson is too annoyed to care. If she triggers the apocalypse, at least he can say I told you so.

"They say she has a month, maybe two. I need you to go find your father. He wouldn't want Minxy to die before he got to say goodbye. "

There is no way Anson's agreeing to do this. "Mom. Dad faked his death to avoid his own children for the last fifteen years. And now you think he's going to come back—for a Cockapoo?"

"He enjoyed taking her for walks," she says. Like this explains it all. "They used to go every morning. Down at that—that strip, you know. What was it called?'

"The trail," says River.

"The green belt," says Isidore.

"The green belt? Are you stupid? What kind of name is that?"

"I thought it had something to do with—path. Walk? Wash?"

"What the hell does it matter what the trail was called?" Anson says, banging the table again. He wonders if his slow downhill metamorphosis into his father is inevitable.

"There's no reason to be so confrontational, Anson, please. Look, honey, if Minxy dies before your father gets to see her, I'll feel guilty forever. We don't want that. It's not like you have anything better to do. Plus, I need help. Moving this couch. Your Grandma wants it under the window."

"Anson'll do it," Isidore says.

"Anson never could. He drops everything." Anson wonders what the hell she is talking about.

"I can do it, Mom," says River.

"Don't be ridiculous."

"Because I dropped the pizza? That time we went for a picnic?" Anson says.

"It was all we had for dinner. We were so poor then, Annie. We couldn't afford another pizza."

"Mom, I was like—nine."

She shakes her head and waves at him dismissively. "There was all that gravel in the cheese. That's not the point. The point is, I need to see your father. He wanted Minxy, and I wouldn't let him take her. I felt better with her around. She'd bark, you know. At prowlers and rapists. Stupid dog. Now, you know what this means," Mom says. Anson feels his mother's desires like carbonite, pressing him on all sides. She takes a deep breath, seems like she's going to draw it out again, but Isidore gives her a look like she's going to explode, and since Isidore might, Mom's forced to come out with it.

"You're going to have to get Lulu."

Anson thinks his mom has lost her touch. If she really wants to get his goat, she's going to have to say something more believable than this. Get Lulu. Like he'd ever fall for that nonsense.

"Well, didn't you all take that well!" she says after the silence.

"We're waiting for the punch line," says River.

"Oh." She frowns. "No honey. You really are going to

have to get Lulu."

It's like she's speaking a foreign language. As if, by entering into this house, Anson has passed through a portal into a secret wonderland where nothing makes sense and everyone is ridiculous and insane.

"No," Anson says. "No way."

"I don't get it," River says. He looks at Anson, waiting for him to explain the joke.

"I'm sorry, Annie," Mom says, but she's not actually sorry. "That's just the way it has to be." Isidore is perking up. Not only is she lacking the appropriate dread Lulu's name should inspire, she looks downright excited about it. Anson can't fathom why.

"Why's it gotta be Lulu?"

"Use your head, Anson. He's been living alone all these years, building a life, perfectly happy without us. You think he's just going to give that up for any of you? It has to be Lulu. She's the baby. Your father always did anything she asked."

"I'm the baby," says Isidore, who is indeed two years younger than Lulu.

"You're probably the devil," River says.

Though Anson often feels like a robot programmed without consent to please Isidore, he can't imagine that taking Lulu with them on the road would be anything less than disastrous. Anson is aware of just how delicate their entire existence is, and Lulu has a way of exposing things best left unseen. She makes no attempt to hide her disdain for them all. She resents Isidore for being Isidore, Anson for "enabling" her, as Lulu put it, and River for sticking around, never striking out on his own. Their mutual belief that this is the right thing to do—sticking together, seeing it through to the end—is their religion. It's the only thing keeping them together, keeping River off the streets, keeping Isidore from a life of sex and tequila and Anson from abandoning her to it.

"It might be fun," Isidore says with a brightness in her eyes that Anson wants to both destroy and protect.

"No," says River.

"All of us, together again—"

"No," says River.

"Oh come on," says their mom. "What else are you going to do?"

"The Space Needle—"

"Would you stop talking about the Space Needle, River? It's creepy." River wilts under his mother's disapproval. Anson searches for the truth. There has to be a thread of it somewhere. He knows there is a ruse. Mom is telling him he needs both Minxy and Lulu to lure Daddy home, which is over the top in the way their family tends to be. One or the other should suffice. Thinking it's a done deal, his mom has finally absorbed herself in the newspaper. River is sulking over his pancakes, probably writing some emo ballad about syrupy dredges in his head. He looks at Isidore. She is giving him pleading eyes over her Tweety Bird coffee mug. She wants this reunion, Anson just doesn't understand why. He knows she feels guilty for breaking up the family, despite all the times he's sincerely thanked her for it. Did she watch some movie about a family reunion that made it look all Earl Greys and afghans? It doesn't matter. A person who is going to die young cannot be denied. Anson resigned himself to this a long time ago. He shakes his head at her.

"I'll check the oil."

ONTARIO
CALIFORNIA

ON THE DRIVE from the armpit of Colorado to the plastic climax of California, Isidore's trepidation is in direct proportion to Anson's. She knows Anson is doing this for her, and while the initial win of manipulating his will with her own felt good, she's beginning to worry about the fall out. River is drinking in the commode and Anson's wearing his tense shoulders. She puts on the Radiohead and hopes Anson will sing. Sometimes when he thinks they're all sleeping he does emotional renditions of Fake Plastic Trees. She feels calm when he sings, it is a comfort she knows to be quiet about. But Anson doesn't.

Normally they avoid California because of Lulu. Also because Isidore feels strongly that any day now God is going to sink Orange County into the Pacific and she doesn't want to give him the bonus points of being there when he does it. She assumes she could die by drowning, although she realizes now she doesn't actually know.

They drive through the miles of desert, through Vegas and Victorville, past canyons and ravines they can't see in the dark before dawn. At a gas station in Barstow the eastern sky glows orange and the hot wind makes Isidore edgy. The world seems restless for something. Around six a.m. they stop for coffee at a Starbucks in Ontario. While Anson waits with Isidore for her Frappuccino, River crosses the lot and buys a pack of cigarettes, a fix he resorts to under extreme duress. They all smoke one, leaning against Pacey in the abandoned end of the parking lot. They don't even bother to give River a hard time about it. The sun is rising like it would in California, slowly as if it doesn't really care, and the hurried masses are bright with hope and shrouded in smog. The concrete is black and sticky with tossed out Cokes from the Walgreens across the street. The highway roars above them, palm trees insisting vacation against a dirty, yellowish sky. A couple business guys driving black sedans with tinted windows look at them funny as they get into their cars with their iced coffees. They look wrong, Isidore knows. People who travel by Airstream are usually wealthy families with kids, old retired couples, or hipsters. Isidore's not sure what they look like, but it's not tourists or hipsters.

River looks at Isidore and squints, a James Dean expression he's been trying out. He's the only one who got their father's root beer eyes, hers and Anson's an unremarkable blue, and he's vain about it.

"You look like blue steel," she says. Most of the time she doesn't understand why River, or anyone else, does the things he does, but she knows this brooding leer is an attempt to look cool and she's pretty sure blue steel is what the cool guys do.

"You look like a crack whore."

"Takes one to know one," Isidore says without thinking, and politely looks away when it seems River might cry. She knows better than to tease him about the drugs, but sometimes it just slips out.

"Fuck," Anson sighs, and Isidore and River's eyes both jerk to him, like he's their dad and about to start swinging. But he's not swearing at them. He flicks the cigarette to the ground. "Too hot for coffee. Let's go."

Isidore tries to think of something she might say to brighten the mood or apologize to Anson for making him do this thing he's dreading. She thinks about how Anson always takes her to a bar and leaves her free to prowl after a fight or Grandma's house. "Do you need sex?" she asks him. River stumbles forward, squeezing his coffee cup so hard that it pops, sloshing hot liquid all over him. He coughs and chokes. Anson swats the back of his head. "She's not propositioning me. Shut up, Isidore."

As Anson winds through the sunny streets, Isidore clutches her melted coffee for comfort and pulls her wrap tight around her. Something about the dirty sunshine makes her want to hide. She doesn't have any makeup on but her skin feels scummy; the pollution, she guesses, and the sticky sea air, now that they've snaked through Los Angeles and are somewhere close to the beach. Isidore can smell the salty sea. Just because this was her idea doesn't stop an oily ball with teeth and hair from forming in her belly. Isidore's feelings about her sister are too complicated for her to dissect, especially considering she has never even been certain how to secure a parent's approval, something the brothers do without even trying. When they'd left Pueblo, Mom had clung to River and cupped Anson's face before kissing him. Then she'd waved at Isidore and told her to get herself a new bra.

They've never been here before, and Anson refuses to use GPS, but somehow he knows where to go and Isidore doesn't ask. He slows to a stop. Directly below them, one block downhill, is the great blue ocean. If Isidore wanted to, she could hear the waves. She leaves the windows up to spare her senses the assault of Lulu's large living.

"This is it?" she says, hoping there has been a mistake.

"Yep," Anson kills the engine and thuds back against his seat.

"Goddammit," Isidore says. The cheery yellow bungalow represents everything Isidore hates about Lulu. It is tasteful, slightly snug, and perfect. It has white trim, like Lulu's innocence, but it's old, like Lulu's wisdom. It is even a little condescending, staring down at them from its small hill, beyond the white fence, through the tulips. "It's a fortress of Lulu." Suddenly her beautiful Pacey, with his brushed steel sink and his blonde wood cupboards, feels cramped and dark and pathetic.

"What are you pouting about? This was your idea," Anson says. Nonetheless, he sounds sympathetic. Isidore doesn't know how to explain that she needs to see Lulu because she is her sister, even though she does hate her. There is no way to tell her brother that everything has begun to feel more urgent. That she finds herself aching for spicy foods and hot burning liquor, that the desert in the sun rise made her weep, that she is troubled all night with a longing between her legs so fierce it makes her writhe. She especially knows she shouldn't say that last part. She doesn't know what it means, that the earth is suddenly so vibrant that things like hot showers and brewing coffee are orgasmic with pleasure.

"Maybe we'll get heat," Isidore says, and for a moment they sit and enjoy this wicked desire, imagining Lulu, hair aflame and screaming, all her old instincts gone. Finally Anson takes a deep breath, bracing himself, and then gets out of the door and slams it decisively. Because it would be poor form not to, Isidore scrambles after him. River can do whatever he pleases.

Anson pounds on the door and Isidore hides behind him, cowed by Lulu in a way she never feels in battle. The doorknob turns and her belly flutters. She's not ready for this. She just knows Lulu is going to insult her yoga pants or her entire way of life.

The woman who answers the door and looks at them with pretty dismay is, in fact, their sister. They can tell, even though she's not doing a bong hit or mutilating China dolls, because she looks just like Isidore, only better. Lulu in her natural state has huge July-grass eyes, fat marshmallow lips, and a sweeter jaw, these three small changes lending Lulu the movie star looks and leaving Isidore just a normal blonde chick who isn't frigid, but who gets mistaken for it thanks to her Nordic palette and her icy eyes.

Isidore's one triumph over Lulu is Lulu's deep resentment of their physical similarities. Lulu spent the years be-
tween her twelfth and sixteenth birthdays chopping her hair
short and dyeing it a rainbow of colors, but mostly black, desperate to distance herself from Isidore. Whatever Isidore did,
Lulu did the opposite. Isidore tried to please her parents so
Lulu took up drugs and made art out of tortured baby dolls.
Isidore started having sex at fifteen, so Lulu dabbled in True
Love Waits pledges and purity rings, which were faddish at the
Lutheran high school their mother had sent them to figuring
God would be less likely to scourge the Lutheran kids than
those in the publics. Then Lulu turned nineteen, got into the
vintage Camaro that Grandpa left to her because she was eve-
ryone's favorite, and drove away to sunny California, leaving
Isidore to finish out school an abomination and alone.

"Hey sis," Anson says grimly,

Lulu's eyes are so shiny and wide they look like you
could buy things with them. She takes a long moment, looking
from Anson to River to Isidore to Pacey behind them. Then
she takes in Anson's boots, and the knife Isidore has strapped
to her thigh, and the bulge in River's pocket where he's got the
heat-meter. She brushes her snow-blonde hair from her face,
and she says,

"Jesus. Still?"

Just like that, Isidore is ignited. She kicks the door-
frame and the brothers jump, fearing an eruption. Lulu isn't
fooled.

"Still what, Lulu? Kicking? Sorry to disappoint." Anson's doing his James Dean, which, unlike River's, is convinc-
ing.

"I can't believe you guys," Lulu says, and then flinches
like she's sorry.

"It's okay. We feel sorry for you too."

Lulu gives the Lulu look, which really is impressively
derisive, if you can view it impartially. She's wearing Isidore's
outfit, only better. Black pants that hug her thighs and aren't

baggy in the ass with the fabric pilling like Isidore's. Her white t-shirt swoops in at her hips and shows what in L.A. passes for a tasteful amount of cleavage, though Isidore would like to hear what Grandma Ruth would have to say. She's even got a flowy top on, but hers is clean and beautifully cut, a green, thin fabric that matches her eyes and swims around her like sea foam.

"You look like a goddamn mermaid," Isidore says, and is ignored except for River's confused frown.

"You gonna invite us in?" Anson says. "Introduce us to the fam?"

Isidore knows her sister too well for Lulu to hide what she thinks she's hiding—pity charged with panic. Some actress, Isidore thinks. She says, "We don't want to be here either, you know."

Lulu appears genuinely hurt, which is confusing. "Well, thank you, Isidore. Thanks for that." Then she stands back, opening the door wide.

"Come in," she says.

SANTA MONICA
CALIFORNIA

ISIDORE IS DETERMINED not to look around like she cares, but Anson and River stand in the entryway and gawk. Lulu's interior is even tidier and more coiffed than her exterior, everything white and robotically neat. Just standing next to the white couch, flanked by white end tables, makes Isidore feel grubby. She worries that she clashes with the décor.

"You guys want coffee?" Lulu calls. Isidore follow her to the immaculate kitchen, leaving the boys to gape like monkeys at the opera.

"No," Is says. "We had a Frappuccino." Lulu nods politely. She does an actress trick where she looks like she's trying to hide her disapproval without actually hiding it at all. Isidore can't believe she's fucked up already and admitted to Frappuccinos. She scratches her palms. Anson saunters in and surveys his surroundings defensively, like he's got reason to believe Lulu is harboring an angel in her pantry.

"Doing pretty well for yourself here, aren't you Lu?" he says.

"I worked hard for this," says Lulu.

"That what you call it?" Anson says, feigning distraction. He's leaning down, inspecting the cabinetry like he knows

71

anything about it and would recognize a flaw. "You got something to drink?" he says. He thumps the countertop once, bestowing reluctant approval of the workmanship.

"There's orange juice. Fresh squeezed. Or I've got—acai," Lulu falters, realizing her mistake. She has given the brothers easy fodder.

"What are you, speaking Chinese now?" says River.

"It's not Chinese, it's a—never mind."

"Jesus, Lulu. Stop dicking me around," Anson says.

Lulu's mouth forms a pretty pink line. Was she always such a steel magnolia? Isidore can't remember. The last time she saw her was at a family Christmas party a few years back. Lulu had been hiding behind bug-eyed sunglasses, balancing an ugly leather purse in one hand and a fizzy pink cocktail in the other. She had managed to get drunk and stumbled on her heels into the tinseled tree. Anson had caught it before it fell on her. For one brief moment, Isidore had wished he hadn't.

"You want alcohol? Seriously? It's eight in the morning."

"Save it for Mom," Anson says. "You can play at country club all you want, Lulu, but we all know you can drink like a sailor with chlamydia." Isidore wishes she could disarm the anger like she can an angel, but she can't find a way in. It doesn't help that she agrees with everything Anson has said.

"Not anymore," Lulu says.

"You on a diet or something? Or wait—don't tell me you went straight edge again."

Isidore can see the moment when Lulu decides to tell them something she would rather hide. Her head dances up like a pony's, her eyes glitter with the certainty of her own righteousness.

"I don't drink on Mondays anymore, Anson. Because I'm a Mormon now." She delivers her line. A dainty Scarlett O'Hara resolve.

Isidore doesn't understand Lulu's angle. She knows that every choice Lulu makes is calculated, every action cultivated to convey not Lulu herself, but the Lulu she is willing to let others see. Isidore decides to meet her where she's at. "What's your motivation?" she asks.

"Oh my god, Isidore. Would you stop trying to appear normal? It just makes everything worse."

"So what, you gonna serve us mocktails now?" Anson asks. "You? Chug-a-Lulu?"

"Anson please," Lulu says. If hearing her old nickname has wounded, she doesn't show it. "Being a Mormon isn't about not drinking. It's about doing something of value with my life."

The trick with Lulu has always been to get her to stop performing. Anson never did understand this. He always tries to beat each persona as it arises, an impossible task. Like whack-a-mole with personalities; knock one down, another pops up. "You have to drink, Lulu? What else would you do at all the strip clubs?" Isidore knows what life in L.A. is like. She watched an awards show once.

"Just clubs, Isidore. Not every club is a strip club. Where have you guys been taking her?"

"To strip clubs," says River.

"I'm working at one now. I'm good. Make tons of money. My stage name is Demon Lady."

Lulu starts to laugh, and it isn't her stage giggle. The real Lulu laugh is rich and just as satisfying to evoke as her glares.

"I can just see you, Is," she chokes. "Two dollah, sir." It's an old joke of theirs, and for once, Isidore knows her line. Together they blurt, "Fiddy cent!"

It feels good to laugh with Lulu, even though the brothers roll their eyes, annoyed and possibly intimidated by the depth of the intimacy between the sisters. They carry on until Anson pushes behind Lulu, going to the glistening glass cabinets with their neat white bowls and plates stacked inside like museum displays. He opens a pantry, then bends low, finds only more virginal baking dishes.

Lulu sighs, wiping her eyes. "What are you looking for?"

"Liquor, sweetheart. I wasn't joking."

This ruins Lulu's laughing mood. "There's no whiskey, Anson. Lulu can't drink," says Isidore.

"Unless it's the weekend," says Lulu. "That's Utah Mormonism. I'm an L.A. Mormon."

"Aren't you gonna ask what we're doing here, Lu? Can we hurry this up? Jesus, Anson, I'm starving. I need a sandwich. Anson." River says. Anson shuts his eyes and touches his forehead.

"Is that what I'm supposed to do? Coffee? I've got the French Press or the pods." Lu doesn't look at them. She is diverting and Isidore doesn't care. Isidore shakes her head with her eyes wide and bright. It's her look.

"What? Isidore," Lulu sighs, understanding. Sometimes Isidore isn't sure if she truly is socially awkward, or if the brothers are just surpassingly awful at picking up cues. Lulu reads Isidore just fine.

"I assume I'm still the only one of us who can cook?" Lulu says doing peevish. Isidore knows she is secretly pleased.

"We've been kinda busy," says Anson.

"Right," says Lulu. "Chasing angels. Would you sit down, Anson? You're making me nervous." Isidore feels tender toward him. He looks like a cowboy at a country club, asking do they have Bud Light on tap. On the island in front of him sits a bowl of bright yellow lemons flanked by two glass vases of white tulips, their stems arranged to symmetrical perfection. Isidore's glad they're not lilies. Lilies remind her of Easter. It was a tough holiday, growing up.

"Not chasing angels," Anson corrects. "Running from them."

"Whatever. Sit down," she says.

"Where?" Like the white bar stools are so nice and pristine, Anson is somehow above them. He is making Isidore simultaneously guilty and angry.

"On your mama's lap. I'll make Isidore her pancakes."

"Yum yum," Isidore says, doing perky and pleased, as is required when Lulu does one a favor. She doesn't care too

74

much about explaining Minxy, Anson will see to that. Her main problems right now are a powerful hunger and Anson looks ready to shoot the knick knacks.

"So. Who's paying for all this?" River says.

Bent to retrieve one of her white baking bowls, Lulu pauses. Briefly, but they all register it. She slams the bowl down on the counter, jerks open the huge steel refrigerator. Inside Isidore sees expensive bubbly water in green glass, arranged in neat rows. Little glass containers of strawberries, raspberries, kiwi, carrots. Like Oprah and Dr. Oz are about to drop by and rate her for form and content. Back in Pacey, they have Spam and Pizza Combos and Trix, and Isidore wonders if a month or two on the road with them might actually kill Lulu. Or better yet, make her fat. Lulu takes out a brown carton of eggs, slams the fridge shut.

"I've been working, you know. You could see for yourself if you ever bothered to check my imdb page."

"You're you are what page?" says River.

"Sounds inappropriate," says Anson, finally lowering himself awkwardly onto the barstool next to Isidore. He doesn't know where to put his knees. Isidore bumps him companionably with hers. She'd been worried about her own survival, but Anson appears to be the one having a breakdown.

"It's a webpage. It shows you everything I've done."

"You're bragging about that now?"

"Shut up Anson. Do you want coffee or no?"

"No," they all three snap at once.

Lulu chooses not to notice, or maybe genuinely doesn't. She has always been out of sync with them, never learned the family dance. When the parents fought, Lulu would cover her mouth and laugh. Later, they'd be taken for ice cream and Lulu would cry into her mint chip. "I shot a pilot. It didn't get picked up. But one of the producers is big in sci-fi— you know, geek stuff—and he's working on something for me specifically. The female lead. I mean, nothing's for sure yet. There are studios and contracts . . ." she waves her hand. "But he's got a website devoted to him, I guess, and he goes to cons—conventions—and stuff. And he wants me for his new project. A re-imagining of the life of Jesus, or Tim Tebow, or something. The Steam-Punk Messiah, and he battles demons or. . . narwhals." Lulu shakes her hair from her face nervously, feeling her performance slipping, the true Lulu coming out. "I don't remember. They're big right now. These, like. Reconstructed religion stories. You know. Oh no, Jesus has developed an insatiable thirst for human blood! Or, you know. Buddha doesn't know what to wear to the ball."

Isidore is not entirely sure Lulu has just spoken English. She thinks maybe Lulu is running lines, the way she used to do. "Phone's ringing," Is would say, and Lulu would go, "I left no ring with her, what means this lady?"

"But if you're still Mormon by then," says River, managing to insult both Lulu's religion and her capriciousness at once. Lulu bounced rapidly from one thing to the next, blazing through a myriad of interests so that by the time she was eleven she could win a chess match, swim a triathlon, and debate the true author of Shakespeare's comedies while dramatically re-enacting the sonnets. Every day they expected to get news that Lulu had walked away from acting to become a war correspondent in Afghanistan or some stupid, made up thing like an interneteur or a comedienne. "How will you get the part? You won't be able to sleep with him."

Lulu forgets her line, tight-lipped. Anson mutters some quiet reproach. He and Isidore both disapprove of the savagery River sometimes turns on Lulu despite the fact that she seems to understand him more than anyone.

"Lulu Camper. Running around on a movie set, kicking some demon's ass," says Anson.

"Or narwhal's," Isidore reminds him.

"It's not about demons—" Lulu begins, and then catches herself. Squeezes her eyes shut.

"You look like you could go on Oprah," Isidore says.

"Would you stop saying these things, Isidore? It's creeping me out."

River sighs and fidgets in his seat. "Tell her why we're

here," he says. He doesn't understand why Anson is allowed to rib Lulu but when he does it, everyone fans themselves in shock.

"She doesn't care," Anson says.

"Why should I?" says Lulu.

"Because you're our sister," Anson says.

Lulu's eyes flicker guilty to Isidore. One time Lulu stormed out of target practice in furious tears, screaming that she hated Isidore and she wasn't even her real sister and that this—all of this—was Isidore's fault. They pretend it never happened, so of course it's always there, hovering just below the surface.

"It's about Dad—" Anson says.

"Can't you even pretend to care about my career?" Lulu erupts, cutting him off.

Isidore can't believe she'd follow a comment about Dad with a line like that. Except it's Lulu, so she can.

"I keep looking for you on Food TV," River says. No one can tell if he's serious.

"Can't you even pretend to care about Dad?" Anson counters.

Lulu turns away from them to the stove, flips a switch, and actual flames whoosh up. Isidore jumps. River snickers at her. Isidore worries that the brothers will upset Lulu before she gets her pancakes. She's willing to bet Lulu even has lingonberry jam hiding in that vast chilled food museum of hers.

"All right, Anson," Lulu says in a tone to let them all know she's playing nice. Like she's being so patient with them now, she deserves a medal. "What is it about Dad?"

"He's still alive. And we need to find him."

Sitting in their neat little row at the island, they all watch Lulu closely to catch her reaction. It is a vast pleasure, to for once know something that Lulu doesn't, something of this magnitude, and Isidore intends to enjoy every second. In her relish, she momentarily forgets the pancakes. Lulu's back is to them. Her shoulders are hunched in around her like protective wings, which means she's thinking. When she turns, her eyes are wide and delicately tearful.

"What?" she says. She looks from River to Isidore. "Annie—what?" Then, "You'd better not be messing around—"

Dammit, Isidore thinks. Just once, she'd like to beat Lulu. She can tell Anson is enjoying himself, and before he can open his mouth and make himself a fool, Isidore says:

"She knows."

"What?"

"You know," Is says to Lulu.

"No I don't—"

"Yes you do," Isidore says. "You already knew. I can tell by your face." When Lulu is truly surprised, she stays calm. Isidore is certain--it was a good performance, but a performance all the same.

Lulu looks at Anson, throws up her hands. "Of course Dad's not dead. What do you think killed him?"

"Angels," Anson says, clearly wondering if this visit is going to start with pancakes and end with them dragging Lulu to the mental ward.

"Angels," Lulu rolls her eyes. "Right." She turns and rotates the pan with her lovely wrist, spreading the butter around. Dips a ladle into the white bowl and pours batter into the pan. The scent of sweet almonds fills the room. Lulu looks like food porn. Isidore doesn't like it, not being able to take her eyes off her own sister.

"That right there," Anson says, and they can all feel his fury gathering, picking up speed. "That's exactly why we shouldn't have come. Because you act like our lives are some big joke. Pretending like the three of us haven't almost died a hundred times while you're sitting here in Hollywood, eating lemons and being Mormon!"

Isidore prepares to jump him. That same Christmas Lulu had toppled into the tree, Anson had gone fundamentalist over the reindeer decorations and pumped three quick rounds into a flickering plastic Rudolph that refused to remain upright. She doesn't want to owe Lulu for any China.

"What does it matter to you if I'm Mormon," Lulu says. She rounds on them with the pan in her hand like a weapon and their instincts kick in. They push back from the island, Isidore's hand getting all the way to her knife before reason returns and she sees her sister waving an expensive Swedish pancake griddle at her and not an angry angel with a rustic weapon. Lulu sees what's happened and shakes her head, lets out a bitter laugh. "I can't believe you three," she says.

"I can't believe you, Lulu," Anson shoots back. "I mean—I get you leaving us—"

"Oh, so that's why—"

"To come live out here and—go to the beach—"

"It's called growing up—"

"—and work on your tan. Nice tan, by the way—"

"It's not like you were orphans," Lulu sputters. "You weren't helpless kids, Anson. I didn't leave 'til I was nineteen. Nineteen," she says, her eyes are sad and pleading. Begging him to understand. "Do you know how old that is in actress years?"

"All the girls in the movies are nineteen," Anson says.

"Exactly. And now I'm twenty-seven," she moans. This means something to her that it doesn't to the rest of them. "They've just now started to give me the good roles. All that time playing murder victims and rape victims and strippers. Don't you see? I'm a year, two maybe, from my expiration date. I'm just arriving, and I'm too late."

"At twenty-seven?" River says. "You should pick a different career."

Lulu shakes her head. "You hate me for it if you want. I had dreams. I wanted a job."

"And did you ever think, maybe River wanted a job?" says Anson.

"Maybe Anson wanted a job," Isidore says, because she wonders sometimes, and wants to give him his chance at freedom.

"I don't want a job," Anson snaps at Isidore. A second later, he regrets it. Isidore's body springs to life, quivers like the flanks of a hunted deer. She tries to hide it, but she can't. They're like fairy lights strung along the same cord. One of them goes off, they all do.

"Why'd you come?" Lulu says softly. They all know Isidore would rather be ignored when she's struggling to stay more human than not, clutching empathy and compassion like a raw slippery heart in uncertain fingers, but unlike the brothers, Lulu is able to pull it off. "So you found out Dad's alive. I'm sorry. Why'd you come?"

It's only after no one answers that Isidore looks up from Lulu's countertop, the flecks in the granite in the shapes of tiny grimacing faces, and realize the brothers are looking at her. She's supposed to handle this, when she's already past her limit? It's like offering jaeger bombs to a man who's already drunk. Either situation promises paramedics and possible vomiting. They really are stupid.

"Minxy's dying," Isidore blurts and is immediately disappointed in herself. "Damn." She'd meant to coat it in sugar, ease it out gently. Anson pats her hand in commiseration. She regrets bringing him here. Anson's life is short enough on pleasure without her piling on misery like burrito toppings.

"So?"

"So, mom wants us to bring Dad home. To see her one more time. She says Dad'll be devastated if Minxy dies before he gets to say goodbye," Isidore says.

Lulu's eyes are genuinely teary. "Dad loved Minxy so much," she says. "They always used to go for walks, along the farmer's canal."

"Farmer's canal," River and Isidore whisper together. That was it.

Lulu's empathy is characteristically short-lived. "Well. Easy. I don't know where Dad is. He routes all his mail through Washington D.C. I think it's supposed to be some kind of a joke. Government interference or whatever." She looks at Anson. "Sorry."

Anson looks at Isidore for confirmation. She shakes her head. She's not buying it.

"What?" Lulu says. "No. I don't know where he is. End of story. I have an idea. Let's go out!" she proclaims with an embarrassment of cheer, plunging a pan to hiss in the water.

"Luluuuu," Isidore whines. "You ruined the Sven-cakes." She jumps up and goes to the sink. "They're all wet now," she says, turning off the water and staring at them sadly. Soggy pancakes at the bottom of a stainless steel sink. If she wanted, she could draw dramatic metaphors to her life.

"Now look what you've done," says River.

"You made it sad," Annie says. He's the only one allowed to call her it.

Lulu and Isidore stand shoulder to shoulder at the sink. Herbs grow in camera-ready white pots on the windowsill above. Isidore pictures Lulu, returning home late after getting head from directors and waking in the morning, smelling her herbs while brewing space coffee and going to auditions for paper towel commercials. She hopes her sister's life truly is so charmed. At times, it seems that the greatest riddle of Isidore's life is not god's unexplained wrath, but Lulu.

"When the hell did you have time to plant things in pots?" Isidore says.

"Huh?" Lulu looks up. "Oh. I didn't."

"Who did?" River says. Isidore is half-expecting a man to appear, possibly bare-chested, put his arms around Lulu, and call her lover in a porn star accent. She doesn't know why, but she imagines Lulu with an older man, accomplished, to whom Lulu can play muse and student. Either that or a stupid, beautiful actor who Lulu will keep in his boxers just for the fun of it.

"I can't leave," Lulu says.

"You have to," Anson says. It sounds like truth. He shares a glance with Lulu that Isidore has seen before. It means Isidore is going to die and everybody better give her what she wants. Isidore looks away. She's been ignoring this look all her life.

"No. I don't," Lulu says. Then she repeats it. "No I don't."

Anson is going to argue further, but Isidore interrupts.

"She doesn't. We can't make her." She wants this to be true.

"We could drag her," River says.

"Kidnap me," Lu says flatly, her characters all abandoning her. She's lifeless without them. Like pretending is to Lulu what sex is to Isidore. A way to wake up.

"Why?" Anson demands.

"I've got an audition tomorrow."

"Oh, well then."

"I have a life here, Anson."

Isidore isn't sure why she does it. She doesn't want to be Lulu's fate, and yet Anson looks so desperate. And even though she knows Anson is desperate to keep her happy, she still can't stand to let him down. "It's all right," she says. "It's fine. I remember—I'm pretty sure—Dad took Minxy for a walk along the farmer's canal—"

"Isidore," Lulu pleads quietly. But Isidore is merciless.

"A week or so, before he died. Or, you know. Faked his death and left. I'm almost certain they had a walk together, was it—what? Sixteen years ago? So, that's fine, then. That will have been their last walk together, and that's fine."

"Isidore—"

"Minxy will just have to understand."

"Goddammit, Isidore," Lulu sighs.

Isidore turns and grins at Anson. His gun is in his hand. He's still glaring at the lemons, but he sets it down.

SANTA MONICA CALIFORNIA

THEY LIGHT OUT from Lulu's house like midlife Midwesterners boarding a cruise, Isidore cradling Lulu's beautiful bowl of lemons against her chest. Once the decision was made, Lulu took to it like getting into character. She changed into a movie road trip outfit—high-waisted denim shorts from another decade and a silky blouse with a red bird on it. She let River load up her iPod while she packed, River calling out names of album after album and Lulu answering "Buy it," Lulu casual but River giddy like Christmas. It occurs to Isidore that despite Lulu's lack of commercial fame, she might very well be rich, or something close to it. It's possible this ridiculous house is actually hers, but no one is willing to ask.

Anson lifts Lulu's bag into overhead storage and teases her about the weight. She raises her eyebrows and hands him the second suitcase.

"You never used to have this much crap."

"Never had time to shop."

"Or money," Isidore says. She sets the bowl of lemons down on the dinette table with purpose and stands back to admire them.

"What's with the lemons, Isidore?" Lulu says.

"I thought it would make you feel more at home. Plus,

they look happy."

Lulu sighs and looks around the Airstream, taking stock, her wrists fiddling nervously with a white straw hat. Isidore wishes now that she'd cleaned it, but it's not too bad. She kicks the Xbox controllers over to the side and straightens the pillows on the sofa. She worries that Lulu will mention Trader Joe's—Lulu doesn't know about Anson and Trader Joe's—but for now, at least, Lulu doesn't.

Anson starts Pacey and they take their places, like actors on a set. Isidore in the navigator chair, River at the dinette. Isidore remembers this is Lulu's first time in the Airstream—she was gone by the time Isidore bought it—and wonders for a moment if she might do something unusual, like ask for the navigator chair or claim the bed. After a quick glance around, Lulu sits at the dinette with River. They're not sentimental; recognizing emotion other than irritation makes the Campers uncomfortable. So no one has any last words and no one even looks up as they drive out of Lulu's storybook neighborhood, headed for the freeway.

EAST L.A.

ANSON GASES UP at a Chevron and picks up the ten at the PCH. Lulu is moaning or grunting softly from the dinette, where River is showing her the touch tablet he's constructing out of used laptops and Starbucks' lids and Lulu is pretending to be interested. Just when Lulu mutters a question about when does craft hour end, they spot a sign for In 'n Out. Isidore commands Anson to stop. He thinks, at least it's not a Trader Joe's, and obeys. Anson remembers the first time they'd eaten at In 'n Out. Isidore was about five, like a rabid chipmunk with her blonde hair in pigtails and her fight technique improving. The family drove to California to visit one of their Mom's old hippie friends; putting things together now, Anson realizes his parents had spent the entire weekend smoking pot and eating food off their children's plates. Crammed backseat at the drive-thru, the siblings had doubted the ability of some place they'd never heard of to beat McDonalds. Isidore had finished both her shake and Anson's, had diarrhea, and ended the night in tears, terrified an angel would attack when she was alone in the commode. Anson holds many of Isidore's memories for her, but there is no one to hold memories for him. When Anson was five, Isidore didn't exist yet. He doesn't have a single memory of those years. It's as if, before Isidore was born, Anson didn't exist at all.

Anson says he needs to check the map, anyway. He won't use a GPS, he can't stand the way they tell him what to do. Like he doesn't already know.

They order four Double-Double's, two of them animal style, one with hot peppers. Isidore drinks Coke, River always a chocolate shake. Anson orders coffee and Lulu says what the hell was wrong with her coffee. She drinks a Diet Coke and Isidore reminds her that's not good Mormon. "Go fuck yourself", Lulu says, but not unkindly. When they're almost finished, Anson spreads out the map.

"So," he says. "Where's Waldo?"

"Where do they have art therapy schools?" Isidore says. "Maybe he went to college and never moved away."

"That's actually a very intelligent thought, Isidore," says River. "No seriously. You should—" before he can say, write it down, Anson punches him.

Lulu Googles "art therapy degrees" on her phone. She has kept her sunglasses on inside the restaurant, the implication being that she wouldn't want to be recognized, but they have reached a sort of truce and no one mentions it. "There's a ton of them," she says. "Arizona, California, Canada, Colorado, Connecticut. Should I keep going?"

"You said his mail comes through D.C," Anson says. "How do you know he's not just living there?"

"Dad? In D.C? Only if he's planning an assassination."

"Oh God," says Anson. "Mom was right."

"Look at this," River says. He's looking down at his phone. "A bunch of fish washed up dead in some river in Alabama. Like, thousands of them. They don't know what killed them all."

"Fascinating," Anson says. "Fish died, and this is news?"

"There were so many all at once. They think maybe it was firecrackers."

Anson rubs his face. Usually he can't believe what he

has to put up with.

"There were birds, too. In Georgia—" he is interrupted by Anson's impatient groan.

"San Antonio," Lulu says, before Anson can make some bitchy comment. "That's my best guess."

"Jesus," Anson says. "Dad, in Texas?"

"He's right," River says. "You know how Dad gets about armadillos."

"Still," Lulu says. "He made a few jokes about how River used to walk—remember you used to walk all funny, River? —and about walking down by the river. Both of those, together." She says this like it means something. Something they all should understand.

"I was bowlegged," River says. "It's cruel, Lulu. To make fun of that."

"We don't know what the hell you're talking about," Isidore says. She helps herself to the remainders of Anson's fries, eyes River's shake. He pushes it at her.

"The Riverwalk?" Lulu's voice is dripping with their stupidity. "In San Antonio? You know Dad and his stupid word games."

"All right," Anson says, doing his manning-up voice. Isidore doesn't know if he was born with this voice, or of he developed it because he had to, but it works well for them. It feels like somebody is in charge and like maybe they won't all die early deaths. "It's something. San Antonio it is."

ARIZONA

THEY HIT TRAFFIC headed out of the San Bernardino valley, taking nearly three hours to cross a distance that shouldn't have taken one. By the time they cross into Arizona, it's getting dark outside. The sun is dying bloody and the desert is cooling like a corpse.

"I can't believe I let you talk me into this," Lulu says to the window. She is sparrow-eyed and tragic, coming off like a Gothic heroine and aware of every inch of it.

"Already?" Isidore says. She has moved from her navigator chair to the dinette with Lulu, drawn by her sister's troubled energy. The Airstream, always roomy enough before, suddenly seems very small. Lulu's presence is bigger than any of theirs. She takes up extra room and makes Isidore feel small.

"What if they want to see me? For the show? And I can't get out there, because I'm stuck in," Lulu searches for the most absurd place she can imagine humanity existing. "Gary, Indiana. I mean, Jesus."

"If we have to, we can put you on a plane," Isidore says. She and the brothers don't fly, it would be a sort of passive-aggressive suicide. After a crash, there wouldn't be anyone alive to report seeing giant German man-babies with swords dropping from the sky. It would likely be safe, however, to let Lulu fly alone. Isidore just wants her to stop complaining.

There is no way not to take it personally.

Lulu seems not to hear, or is not at all comforted by the knowledge that, even in their world, it is still possible to get to L.A. from anywhere in the country in a day. "It's not just that," she says. Her leg bounces under the table. "I just feel. Like I don't belong here."

"You don't," says River from the sofa, thumbing furiously at the controllers.

"Shut up, Stump Hump," Lulu says.

"Jeez, Lulu," River says softly. "Why you gotta be so mean?"

"What were you expecting? A holiday special?" Lulu says darkly. Isidore knows what she means. Nobody wanted her here, and Lulu knows that. Isidore doesn't have anything honest to say to improve the situation, but she feels she should at least make an attempt.

She reaches across the dinette, past the lemons, and puts her hand over Lulu's. She gives her the wet-eyed look she's picked up from the women on the shows about doctors. She holds her chin in her free hand because she senses this communicates a certain feminine vulnerability.

"We're all really happy to have you here—" Isidore begins.

Lulu is revolted and jerks away. "Don't give me that crap," she says. Isidore tries not to be hurt, but it would be nice, to be the kind of sisters who could hold each other's hands and smile damply. Lulu stands up suddenly. "You still got any drink in here, or what?"

"Atta girl," Anson calls from the front. Isidore watches her sister frown at this unwanted brotherly approval, but notes it doesn't stop Lulu from searching for the liquor.

"Is today a cheat day?" River says. Lulu closes her lilac eyelids. Her restraint is a newly acquired trait. Isidore has seen her jump River like a trained monkey for less.

"Stop killing Lulu's buzz," Anson says. "Here."

A fifth comes flying down the galley. Lulu turns and catches it just in time. "Your reflexes are still pretty good," Anson says when he doesn't hear it shatter.

Lulu is holding up the bottle of expensive rye whiskey. "This better than the stuff you used to give Isidore, all those times you were sneaking down to the creek?"

Isidore senses malice but, like a bad odor, it's difficult to determine the exact source. River pauses his game.

"What are you talking about?" Anson says from the front, craning his neck, risking death to see them.

"You know," Lulu says, attempting to inject her tone with a lightheartedness she doesn't feel. She wants them to feel guilty for wounding her without appearing to actually be wounded. "You always used to sneak down to the creek with her, and give her whiskey—"

"After Dad died," River confirms. "Or—fake died. We could never find you."

"When Dad died Isidore was ten. I wasn't giving her whiskey." Anson doesn't get it. Are they actually upset about this? Do they think he wanted to be the one going to the woods alone with Isidore? "It was weird, anyway," he starts to say, before shutting his mouth for Is's sake. But it was weird. The things Isidore would do out there. The noises she'd make. The frantic running. Adolescence had been particularly odd on Isidore. Anson tries not to remember it.

"Annie didn't give me whiskey until I was at least fif-teen," Isidore says. She's trying for a joke.

River grunts. "More than I ever got."

"Yeah, River, you wanna know why? Why I wasn't putting back the hood and giving you strawberry wine—"

"All right," River says.

"It doesn't matter anyway," Lulu says. "It's—shit."

Lulu grabs Isidore, throws her to the ground and pins her there. "It is shit," Anson says vehemently. He hasn't caught on. Lulu and Is land with a hard oomph and glass shatters. The Airstream swerves. River rolls off the sofa, wedging in beside his sisters, half on top of them. Before anyone else can react, Lulu has drawn a handgun from the waistband of her well-fitted road trip shorts. She pumps three quick rounds out the window, in the direction that the spear, now resting halfway through the screen above the sofa, came from.

"River!" Anson calls. Their chain of command runs loosely oldest to youngest, putting Isidore at the bottom. Which at the same time makes no sense and all the sense in the world. River looks around to make sure no one is bleeding or mortally wounded.

"Yeah," he shouts. "Keep driving."

River's chest is pushed up against Isidore's face. She turns her head and gazes into her sister's eyes.

"Lulu Camper, you're my hero," she says. Lulu giggles.

"I'm glad we're having such a great time with the almost dying," Anson says. "Are we under attack? You think we could maybe—"

"Secure the perimeter?" says Lulu. Anson, always so uptight. For someone so sure he's going to die young, he seems unusually determined not to have a good time. "There do not appear to be any angels in the Airstream. Sir."

This just kills Anson. A giddy wrestling match springs up between his siblings and they ignore Anson's orders to clean up the glass, cut the lights, keep a look out. The desert is dark, there are no other cars. Anson drives through night to the symphony of his sibling's laughter, the sound of flesh slapping flesh. He has to remind himself about Lulu. She has no idea what it's like to be him, the one who has to decide which direction to drive every morning and which sibling should risk their life today by manning the Minigun. But he thinks she could at least be grateful. That she's not the captain and that, when the ship sinks, she won't have to go down with it. Anson decides to stop in Tucson. He wants to get out and see the stars.

LAS CRUCES KOA
NEW MEXICO

ANSON HAS WALKED down the highway to the liquor store because Lulu and River wanted to clean out the trailer and get it set up for the night and Lulu's swearing she doesn't want anything to drink, she's a Mormon now goddammit, never mind the twenty-two samples of wine she swilled like a pro at the winery outside of Tucson this morning. That was different because it was wine, or because it was morning, or because Anson doesn't know why and he doesn't much care. He knows she's going to end up drinking whatever he buys so he's bought extra; two six packs of pilsner, a liter of Jim Beam, and a bottle of Pinot Grigio. Lulu can drink that and see how she likes it. He's looking forward to sitting down and having a drink and doing nothing for once, but the moment his shoes hit campground, Lulu meets him halfway up the drive, heels of some expensive boots crunching in the gravel.

"We have to go," she says.

"Angels?" Anson's body assumes its familiar tension.

"Oh my god, no. No, it's not your stupid angels. There is more to life than your little game, Anson—"

"Where's Is?"

"She left."

Anson can see it has wounded Lulu that Isidore has given up the chance of a sleepover for sex. Again. "Listen, Lu, don't take it personally. It's just her thing."

"Shut up. I don't care about her sex life. How did she even have time to—never mind, I don't care. We have to go because of me."

"Are you secretly a Scientologist?" Anson has wondered if this is the reason for Lulu's paranoia.

"No. Scientology is over. It's all Mormon now. My agent just called, I have an audition. You're taking me to the airport, what's the closest airport? Albuquerque?"

Anson groans. This is terrible news. Not that he personally would mind unburdening himself of Lulu's presence. But for Isidore. If Lulu leaves, Isidore will be crushed. And then Anson will have a depressed supernatural thunder-being on his hands.

"When's the audition?"

"Tomorrow. Come on." Lulu turns and starts toward the Airstream. "Maybe we can find a flight tonight."

"It's after eight," Anson says, stalling. "The flights to L.A. are probably done for the day."

"Then I'll get a flight to Dallas."

"Now you're just being wasteful."

"Anson," Lulu says. "Don't do this. We are leaving right now to go to the airport. You promised."

Anson can't remember if he actually did promise. He can't remember saying much at all from Lulu's bungalow by the sea. Lulu takes the arm that's holding the six-pack and begins to pull. Anson doesn't move.

"Anson."

"Can't we talk about this, Lu? I mean—" he raises his arms, indicating the campground, the drinks, the desert. "We're on a mission. Remember? Operation Minxy's Last Stand?"

"Bullshit. It's Operation Make Isidore Happy, and I won't—I can't—"

"I mean, would it kill you to just—I don't know. Could you phone it in?"

Even in the twilight, Anson can see Lulu's eyes flash like meteors. "No. I can't just phone in an audition you dumbass." She slugs him. "It's for that pilot I was telling you about."

"The narwhals?"

"Damn you," Lulu says, and shoves him backward with both palms. Anson makes the mistake of laughing. Lulu goes rabid. "Don't do this to me. This is important. I am important, my career matters." She shoves him again. Anson loses his balance and stumbles backward. He knows what is about to happen an instant before it does, but not soon enough to stop it. While Anson is fighting for his balance, Lulu snakes one slim wrist into his jacket pocket and swipes his keys. She is off running before he can figure out how to stop her without dropping the alcohol.

"Unforgivable!" he shouts. He runs after her. She has a head start. She is fast.

"Lulu! Come back here!"

"I'm going to my audition," she screams over her shoulder. Anson unloads his liquor onto a picnic table as he passes it. Lulu is nearly to the Airstream and he has no doubt she will lock him out and drive away, abandon him and Isidore here in the night. Just before Lulu reaches the steps, he catches her. He goes into it full force, tackling her and pitching her to the right so as not to bash her against the Airstream. They land hard in the gravel.

Lulu swears at him. "Let me up. Let me up, you giant penis hat."

Anson is too wise for this. "Give me the keys."

"They're beneath me. Let me up and I'll give them to you."

Against his better judgment, Anson warily pushes off her, giving her room to rise. Immediately Lulu flexes onto all fours and aims her boot right at his nuts. Anson lets out a kind of scream and manages to get mostly out of the way before Lulu can drive her designer boot heel into his future children. Still, she clips him and he hisses in pain. He slams his palms

94

roughly into Lulu's back, shoving her down harder than is necessary. Lulu makes a pained noise as all the wind is smacked out of her. She throws her elbow hard into his sternum and makes Anson gasp before rolling over onto her back, panting and surrendered.

"What the hell, guys?" River says from the entry to the Airstream. "Anson? I thought you were gonna get beer? I can't get the satellite to work, could you go down to the office?"

Anson moans and Lulu spits gravel from her mouth. "Were you guys playing the secret game?" River says. It takes Anson a second to catch up. The girls had taunted River about the secret game, growing up. Tortured him because they were allowed to play it and River wasn't. He used to spy on them for hours, give up, and finally return to Lulu's eyes glittering. "We were playing the secret game, but you missed it," sending River away crying. The truth was, there was no secret game, it was just another ploy to tease River. Nothing Anson said could ever convince him of this.

"There is no secret game you dummy," Lulu says. "Anson's trying to end my career."

"I'm not asking you to end it, I'm just asking you to delay it. We're eight hours from San Antonio. Can't you just wait a couple days?"

"No," Lulu says. "I have to go now, or they'll find someone else. Auditions are tomorrow."

"But can't your agent tell them you're out of town? You said this director guy wanted you, right? Won't he wait two days to see you?"

"Why don't you just release a sex tape?" River says. He holds out a hand to help Lulu up. Anson climbs to his feet, bracing for Lulu to take another swing.

"Anson," Lulu says. "I know this is all important to you. And it matters to me too, it really does. But I have to make it to this audition. I have to—"

"Look, you're right. This isn't about dad, or freaking Minxy. It's all about Isidore. I mean, what if there's a reason? She knows things sometimes." Lulu looks at him confused.

"What if she wanted you here because she doesn't have—doesn't have—"

Lulu is furious and tearful. Her eyes cut like carat diamonds. Anson doesn't think she's acting, because the part she would want to play right now is that of an overly sensible British woman who would say "Nonsense" and firmly call a travel agent. It is unfair to her, he knows that. To ask her to put her life aside for the sake of perpetually almost dead Isidore.

"Doesn't have what, Anson?" River says, desperate, unraveling. "Doesn't have what?"

Lulu pulls out her phone. "How many hours to San Antonio?"

"Twelve."

"You said eight."

"Safety net," Anson says.

Lulu dials and puts the phone to her ear. "Vern? It's me. Lulu. Lulu Camper? Jesus Vern. Look, I should have told you this before but I'm in Texas for my Grandma's funeral. I need you to tell them I'll see them in three days. All right? Three days. Thanks." She ends the call and stares at Anson. "If I miss this audition I'll never forgive you," she says. Anson nods and goes back to retrieve his Beam and beer. He feels light as a cloud. Lulu is not the sister he cares about disappointing.

LAS CRUCES
NEW MEXICO

ISIDORE TUGS HER JEANS up from around her ankles where they remained during the act, because the hotel room is dingy and damp and she had no will to remove her boots. She waves a cheerful goodbye to the redhead with elegant fingers who is lying on the bed in stunned silence, tears in his eyes. He looks up at Is, mouth agape, then holds his palms at eye level and stares like he's seeing them for the first time. Isidore wonders if he's been on drugs. She doesn't envy him. A trippy lay with her has got to be a real doozy.

Isidore walks from the motel to the KOA even though Anson is always telling her cabs are safer. She keeps an eye out for Gabriels. The night is clear and full of stars, and she feels full and sated like a summer moon. At the KOA, Pacey is the only one with his lights still on. Inside Isidore finds them awake despite the late hour. Anson is at the dinette and Lulu is leaning on River on the sofa. Beer cans and takeout boxes and the scent of cheap whiskey lend the ambiance of saloons.

When they spot Isidore they cheer and raise their cups like people who've seen the twice-come Christ. "You made it out alive," says Annie. He's closer to drunk than to tipsy. Isidore doesn't like him getting drunk without her. Anson only truly relaxes when he's drunk and Isidore gets to see glimpses of what she thinks of as the real him, the person he might have been had Isidore not happened to him. So far the real Anson is jovial and weepy and horny for brassy female comedians.

"You all look happy without me," she blurts, a nice piece of inadvertent truth telling, and her siblings freeze for a moment before Isidore giggles falsely to try to soothe them. River's hand goes toward his weapon but Lulu unfolds her legs, gracefully unwrapping the gift of herself, and rises from the couch. She's dressed like she's about to film a slumber party movie, but not for a male audience, in pink silk pajamas with blue piping along the hems. She takes Isidore's wrist and pulls her to the sofa. She tugs hard and they land heavily, Isidore half on top of Lulu. Lulu's grunt is dainty and her laugh like Burgundy. River takes the opportunity to slam his fist into her thigh. Lulu panics, sitting up too quickly and spilling her whiskey in Isidore's hair.

"How was it?" Lulu says.

"How was what?" says Isidore. She is preoccupied with gratitude that they are still here, and annoyance to see them carrying on so well without her.

Lulu looks at her like she's disappointingly dim. "The motel décor. The sex, Isidore."

"Don't," River says. "For the love of God."

"Jealous," says Lulu. She throws her fist into his gut, yet somehow he doesn't go ape shit. "Have you always been such a prude, or only when the talk turns to vaginas?"

"River hates a happy vagina," Anson says, and finds himself hilarious.

To Isidore this is an unwanted illumination. Them here without her, bourbon buzzed and fancy free. She is about to shift away from Lulu when Anson offers her a plastic cup of golden drink. He's filled it to the top with ice and poured the liquor over it, the way she likes.

"Come on," Lulu says. "Was he cute?"

Isidore and Anson bump cups and go bottoms up, eyes locked together. Even now, through a drunken haze, he is watching her for signs of danger. The liquor is hot in Isidore's throat. She winces.

"He had red hair."

Lulu is disgusted, but tries valiantly to cover it. "Well—like Prince Harry? He's cute. I just kinda thought he was the only one."

Isidore is almost ashamed of her sister's ignorance. "Don't you know anything, Lulu? Redheads make the best lovers." She thinks a moment. "The men, anyway."

"Shut up, women," says Anson. "It's back on."

On the TV, a disheveled blonde is sending longing glances at Hugh Grant. "Jesus," Isidore says. "She's a mess. They should have hired you, Lu." Lulu begins to giggle thickly, her drunken laugh rich in her chest. Isidore likes this incarnation of Lulu. Here was the sister who had taken Isidore hitchhiking down to Mexico where they drank cerveza and tried on sombreros, laughing and dancing with much older boys until Anson had arrived in the old Chevy Citation, his eyes lit up with the angry fire of an Aztec god. Even River, always a low-level threat, does not at this moment appear to be on the brink of taking up a knife and pressing it to his own throat or quoting Bon Iver lyrics. Despite feeling left out, Isidore is pleased. She had hoped this would be good for them. Being united, the Campers four. Having a mission other than remaining alive another hour, or twelve, or twenty-four. And at the very least, she thinks, it has brought them this. A brief moment together when the angels, if not forgotten, at least hover meekly around the edges of the room, attending passively rather than waging attack. As if maybe not a savior, but at the very least a life vest, is being born.

LAS CRUCES
NEW MEXICO

ANSON WAKES on the floor of the Airstream, where he crashed last night atop piles of rancid laundry and an accumulation of grime. River is snoring above him on the sofa. Anson climbs to his sleep-weak legs and punches River in the arm. "I get the couch tomorrow," he says before River's eyes flash terror and he buckles oddly around his own groin. "I almost wet myself, Annie," he says, pathetic and harassed. Anson feels guilty and apologizes as River's eyes roll back and he returns to sleep. In the bedroom is a two-headed she-dragon, filling the trailer with guttural snores. Isidore and Lulu are tangled in the sheets, Lulu forming the little spoon. Isidore's arm is thrown across Lulu's shoulders, their knees locked together. He shuts the door.

Outside the Airstream the desert morning is a relief, a great expanse of thin air and sharp colors that scours the frantic working of his brain. He feels safer here than he does passing through New England or the south, where everywhere there are hills that Jesus himself could be hiding behind. Driving into the campsite last night they had passed a diner, and

Anson means to get a cup of coffee and a plate of eggs and bacon before facing the day. He will read the paper and get a warm-up, just like everyone else.

"Annie! Wait up!"

He maintains his pace. In a moment she catches up anyway. The brief run does not wind her.

"I saw you watching me and Lulu sleep."

"Dammit, Isidore. You don't say things like that."

"Inflection or content?"

"Both."

"Does it matter? I only ever talk to you guys. It's not like some waitress is gonna be all, 'Your sister's inflection is weird, are you guys being hunted by angels or something?'"

She has a point. It occurs to Anson that the only beneficiaries of his attempts to normalize Isidore are her motel-room conquests. Perhaps all along he should have been teaching her to be less approachable.

They are seated at a red vinyl booth along the window. It smells of syrup and sausage and the past. Anson is filled with nostalgia before realizing that the odor he has identified as his childhood is merely smoke. People are smoking at the counter, something Anson hasn't seen since he was a teenager. He grabs a paper off an empty table and hands the comics to Isidore for her to puzzle over. The front page is a story on a recent rodeo, a photograph of a little girl dressed like John Wayne imposing her dominion over a wild-eyed calf with futile horns. The determination on the little girl's face reminds him of Isidore.

"Morning," says the waitress. "Coffee?"

"My brother was watching my sister and I sleep this morning," Isidore says before Anson can reply. She has altered her inflection, stressing the words my, this, and morning. Anson laughs nervously.

The waitress cocks one red-penciled eyebrow. "That's the least weird thing I've heard all day. Mr. Moore over there's taken up with his daughter--in that way--and Mona Ray lost her son to a woman who knocked on their door dressed like a carnival barker. You know, with suspenders and the hat? They don't know if he's dead or in love. So now you wanna tell me your brother here watching you sleep is the worst of your problems? Count yourself lucky. You want coffee or not?"

"I could look into that—" Isidore begins, forcing Anson to break his silence. "Two coffees and the John Wayne. She'll have a tall stack of pancakes and two eggs over easy. Chocolate milk." The waitress collects their menus and leaves.

"Am I dreaming?" Anson says. "Did that just happen?" Anson's grip on reality feels looser than usual. Isidore just shrugs. It takes a lot to shock her.

"I could look into the missing guy—"

"No," Anson says. They've been over this. Isidore has occasionally entertained the idea of becoming some kind of gumshoe, traveling the country finding runaways, lost girls, cheating husbands. She insists it would give their lives meaning. Anson tells her staying alive is meaning enough. That the kind of meaning she's talking about is reserved for people for whom survival is not a constant pressing concern. She doesn't understand that the three of them being detectives—Isidore Camper, Private Eye—is a TV show life and not a real one.

Isidore is displeased. She watches him for a moment before saying, under her breath, "I could make it happen and you'd never know."

"What?"

"Nothing." She asks for a pen and starts the crossword puzzle. Anson goes back to his paper.

It isn't until Isidore says "Switch," and hands him the funnies that Anson glances at the date on the paper and gets a tilt-a-whirl pitching in his center. The dizziness is overwhelming and he sways in the vinyl booth. The diner drops away and goes silent as Anson tries to reconstruct his fractured reality. Isidore snatches the paper but it's too late.

"June 29th. Yesterday, when we left Tucson, it was June 29th."

Isidore hums noncommittally.

"Why does the paper say July 1st?"

"Maybe you got the date wrong."

"I didn't get the date wrong."

"Oh my god Anson. Oh no." Isidore attempts to appear shocked and concerned. "The angels have stolen our time! Oh sweet Jesus, this is cruel!"

"Isidore."

"I found a red-headed lover," she surrenders. "Dammit, Anson. I've taken a lover and I did not wish to leave. Is that so wrong?"

"So you—brain raped us? Made time just go away? How many times have you done this?" How much of his life has been lost to Isidore's devil tricks?

"Calm down," Isidore says. "You're being really intense."

"Intense? You know what's intense? Losing a day of your life."

"Why are you in such a hurry? Once it's over, it's over. Lulu goes home. River loses his sense of purpose--"

"River has a sense of purpose?"

"You must have noticed. This whole 'finding Dad' thing has been good for him. There's life in his eyes now."

Anson considers this. There is a yawning gap in his memory. Yesterday they left Tucson, intending to push straight through to San Antonio but stopping instead at a winery, waylaid by the siren call of fermented grapes. They pulled in to Las Cruces mildly buzzed and Lulu panicked about an audition. Then he woke up and came to the diner. The moments do not fit together properly. Now he understands that this is because an entire day has been surgically removed from his brain by Isidore's libidinous scalpel. "Maybe I did notice. I wouldn't know because I've forgotten the last twenty-four hours of my life."

"Sorry," Isidore says, looking like she might cry. "I shouldn't take from you what's already so limited."

This simple truth leaves him flustered and speechless. He makes her promise not to do it again, pinky swear, because there's no way to be sure she isn't doing it right now. "What am I like when you're doing it? Some kinda zombie?"

"You're the same as you are now. I don't change you. I just wait until you're asleep, and then." She snaps her fingers. "I take the day out of you."

He looks at Isidore across the table. It's a terrible circus act, learning to live with someone who is going to die young. He wants her life to contain as many pleasures as possible without taking unnecessary risks. The waitress offers a warm-up and Anson says yes. Emphatically, yes. Then he leans across the table.

"You do whatever you want to River and Lulu, okay? But don't do it to me. Don't you know I'll take you anywhere you want?"

"But you won't let me linger. Because of the angels."

"The angels," Anson says, catching up. "Why haven't they attacked?"

"I think they don't like Las Cruces?" Isidore shrugs. She looks nervously out the window and he sees it—there is an egg-shaped bruise on her neck.

"Have you been fighting angels?" he says, rage beginning to boil. "Alone?"

"What? No. They haven't come—"

"There's a bruise on your neck." Anson squeezes his eyes shut and sighs as realization comes. Her redhead. She fingers the bruise and smirks.

"Love hurts," she sings.

"We're leaving."

It is late morning when they pull out of Las Cruces, the desert the closest thing to heaven that Anson will ever know. The Organ Mountains tower in the east and remind him of home. He's got a bottle of water and a green drink in the cup holders, a paper cup of hot coffee in his hand. Isidore hums next to him, cradling her gas station hot chocolate. A drowsy type of well-being has descended upon them, and Anson blames this for what happens next: his phone rings, says

'MOM' on the display, and he answers it.

"Hey," he says. He hands Is his coffee. She puts it in the holder, taking out his water, which she opens and drinks. Anson swats at her. The Airstream veers. Anson checks his mirrors. There's no one behind them except for a purple sports car a ways back.

"What's wrong?" says Mom.

Anson is immediately annoyed. "Nothing," he says, unable to keep the irritation out of his voice, which furthers her cause.

"Anson. What is it? Is someone hurt?"

"No one's hurt," he says, glancing at Is. She can tell by his tone that he's talking to Mom, and rolls her eyes in sympathy.

"How's it going with your sister?"

"Which one?" Isidore has drunk half his water. He grabs at the bottle and she surrenders it.

"Lulu."

Anson wishes she wouldn't even ask. He doesn't have the vast amounts of energy required to assure his mother that he's okay. His resentment is only deepened by the fact that, at this very moment, she is probably sitting on her lush back patio drinking her coffee, surrounded by exotic flowers and the wafting scents of cinnamon and mango, or whatever they have down there in the nice parts of Mexico. Anson can smell the inside of the Airstream, which is funky like mold or socks. He takes both his hands off the wheel to lower the window and the Airstream swerves again. His water spills into his lap. He swears. "Jesus!" Lulu calls from the back. Isidore doesn't blink. She knows damn well Anson won't let them go out in anything so mundane as a trailer crash.

Mom launches into one of her speeches. Anson doesn't remember her carrying on like this when he was young. He wonders if she's actually getting worse, or if he's just getting better at spotting crazy. " . . . I've been in situations like that myself. When you're really dreading . . ." Anson looks at Isidore and does the Mom face, with the wide rolling eyes and flapping mouth. Isidore pretends to hang herself, her tongue lolling out to the side. River says something about autoerotic asphyxiation. In one swift movement Isidore removes her shoe and whips it at him. From the sound of River's choking, Anson guesses she got him in the throat. Lulu laughs madly.

Anson thinks Mom is aiming to break a record. "So anyway," he says, urging her along.

"Anyway. Well I don't want you to get upset. I'm absolutely not calling to make you feel pressured or worried in any way, and if I thought that was what I was going to do, I'd rather just keep it to myself. I'd rather just not have you thinking about it. Because it's not worth it."

"Okay," he says. He's gripping the wheel too hard. Isidore senses his agitation and turns down the radio.

"I guess what I'm waiting to hear, well what I want to know is, if you think you can handle this right now or if maybe the stress is too much and you'd just rather not—"

"What is it, Mom?" Anson snaps. He ignores the glance from Isidore.

"See, Anson, I've upset you and this is exactly what I was hoping to avoid. I think I'll wait and just call back when you've calmed—"

Anson snaps his phone shut. It's not as satisfying as slamming a phone down onto a receiver but damn, it feels good. Isidore looks at him, eyes bright, and he tosses the phone over his shoulder. It thumps on the ground somewhere behind them.

"Did you just hang up on Mom?" she says.

"Yup."

"Well done you!" she says, quoting the British people from the movie, he thinks, and holds out her fist for a bump. "How's that feel?"

"Feels good," he says. Indeed he is swelled with pleasantly aggressive energy. He rolls his shoulders.

"What's going on?" calls Lulu.

"Anson just hung up on Mom," Isidore says.

"No way?" says Lulu,

River's phone rings. "It's her," he says. "Declined."

This is a great deal of fun. The wheels spin fast and the highway is a blur until Lulu says, "Fuck. She's calling me."

"Don't answer it," says Isidore.

Anson's triumphant feeling is slinking away with its tail between its legs. Mom can hold a grudge. Sooner or later he will pay for this.

"I have to answer it," says Lulu. "Or she'll know we're ignoring her."

"So?" says Is.

"So. You're the only one who can get away with that."

"Because Mom loves me most," Isidore says.

"Yeah," Lulu says. "Because that."

"Don't answer," Isidore says. Lulu pushes answer.

"I don't know. Fine. How are you?" A pause. Then: "Well—he's driving now, Mom. He shouldn't talk while he's driving. He's very careful not to, actually." Another pause. "Can't you just tell me? . . . I don't know, I think he lost reception . . . well we're out in the middle of nowhere, Mom, he just . . ." Lulu thrusts her head into Anson's personal space and he startles. She covers the mouthpiece with her hand. "What am I supposed to say?" she hisses.

"ANSON HUNG UP—" Isidore says loudly.

"Stop," he says. He wants Mom to know he hung up on her. He also doesn't. "Just tell her I can't talk. Tell her it's raining."

"It's raining," Lulu says, like that explains everything. "Just tell me."

They all wait, listening.

Lulu sighs through her nose. "Well what are we supposed to do about that Mom—no, I'm just . . . MOM. It's not like we can make this go any faster. We're doing the best we can . . . it is raining—it's BOTH, MOM, can't it be both? We don't have any idea where to look . . .San Antonio. Because of something he said. Because of SOMETHING HE SAID . . . never mind. NEVER MIND, Mom . . . Do you have any idea . . . well, neither do we—Mom. Mom. MOM. Goddammit. She hung up on me."

"What'd she say," says Isidore.

Lulu takes a deep breath. "She said Minxy's worse." Lulu tries to say it matter-of-fact, but all her anxiety comes out. Her measured voice—the one she developed out there in L.A., trying to sound like someone more sophisticated, Anson guesses, or confident, than she is—is abandoned and the real Lulu voice comes through. "She said Minxy took a turn for the worst and if we don't hurry she's afraid," Lulu shrugs. She doesn't have to finish.

"Well that's just great," Anson says. "What the hell are we supposed to do about that?"

"Why would she even tell us that?" Isidore says. "That's only going to make things worse."

"She probably thinks she's helping," says River, coming to Mom's defense. "She just wants us to know what we're dealing with—"

"So we can totally panic? It's not like we can find Dad any faster one way or the other," says Lulu.

"Minxy," Isidore says softly.

"I'm hungry," says River. "We need groceries or something."

"Dammit, River, we just ate."

"We don't have time to stop now," Lulu says bitterly. "Minxy is dying."

"We'll stop in El Paso," Anson says, and then he turns the volume up too loud and ends the conversation.

108

WEST TEXAS

STANDING IN THE CANDY AISLE, Isidore watches Anson through the gas station window. She's worried that, after the news about Minxy, they will finally abandon her, leaving her to hitchhike and spend her remaining days killing serial killers.

"Circus Peanuts," says Lulu.

"Sick," says Isidore. What is it with her family and Circus Peanuts? She's not sure, but she's always sensed herself as something eternal. If it weren't for the angels, Isidore thinks she'd live forever. But they sure wouldn't. They'd all be dead at forty from sugar poisoning.

"Oh yes. You used to always pick Circus Peanuts," says Lulu.

"That was you. I always picked Peanut M&M's," she says.

"No you didn't," Lulu says.

They are at a Chevron outside of some town in West Texas. Everything, everywhere, is flat and brown. If you believe God formed the earth by hand, you have to admit he got lazy on this part. Smashed it down flat with his palm like dung Play-Doh and moved on. Anson is gassing up Pacey and, Isidore can tell from here, muttering about the goddamn tanks, goddammit. River stormed out and slammed the door behind him, mad at Anson, because somehow, Isidore doesn't know how, a conversation about the true cause of the Civil War turned into a competition over who has the bigger dick, and she and Lulu stuffing socks in their jeans and thrusting their hips at them while River denied the sub-divinity of Abraham Lincoln didn't help. Then Lulu had whacked Anson in the face with her sock penis and suddenly Anson thought they all needed gas and coffee.

"Yes I did," says Isidore. "I always picked Peanut M&M's because you didn't like them and then I wouldn't have to share." Nothing has ever mattered more to Isidore than Lulu admitting it was she who picked the disgusting Circus Peanuts. Her initial excitement has waned in the days on the road with Lulu. Not only does she have Anson agitated, she is giving River ideas. "River's a genius," she said yesterday, after River had spent all night fiddling with his computer program and then wouldn't get out of bed. "He's a depressed genius and you don't even know it."

"You bitch. You never shared," Lulu says, laughing. A shrewd change of tactics. The Texas boy at the counter, who has combed his hair forward and dyed it green, determined to prove he is not a cowboy like the rest of these assholes, glances at them—at Lulu—and lets his eyes linger. Isidore flips him off. She's accidentally given Lulu exactly what she wanted.

"Yeah well. Should have shared your Circus Peanuts," Isidore says. She checks again for Anson. There are only two other cars in the lot. A station wagon with luggage strapped to the top and a purple Mustang with fuzzy dice on the mirror. It's pretty, and somehow familiar.

"Yeah," Lulu says. "I'm the selfish one."

"Trying to stay alive isn't selfish," Isidore says without enthusiasm. Really, it's Anson's line. He says it and Isidore nods. She can't make it sound right in her own mouth.

She feels the wings on her neck before she realizes Lulu has drawn her sawed-off shotgun.

"Duck," Lulu says, and Isidore does. Lulu blows the

110

angel's head off. The soda fountain behind it explodes all over the pink and purple signs for Mexican pop and the red badge of Coke. Lulu's bullet snags the orange and it sprays, coating both of them sticky, spilling across the floor and dyeing the angel's wings fluorescent. His blonde head rests in a pool of blood and Fanta.

"Jesus," Isidore says. She turns to her sister in rage. "Were you going to let it take my head off before you warned me?"

Lulu smirks. She holds her elbows out and does an awkward dance, singing the Fanta jingle.

"What the fuck," cries the emo boy. He has fallen down beneath the counter and is now peeking over it, only his eyeliner and pierced nose visible. "Don't worry. We got this," Isidore calls to him. Then she turns to Lulu. "You're being a dick," she says. Lulu only smirks, and the Gabriel grow another head. This tempers their anger for the moment.

"Huh," says Isidore.

"They ever done that before?" Lulu says.

"No. Kinda freaky."

"You'd think re-growing a head would be on their list of unnatural activities. Right up there with screwing goats and wearing your hair uncovered."

The new head is blinking. It appears to be slowly coming to. Isidore fires three shots into it, shielding her eyes from the spray of blood and soda.

"You're wasting ammo," Lulu says, and Isidore swears to God, she would kill her sister if it wouldn't saddle Anson with the task of killing Isidore herself.

"Don't hurt me. Don't hurt me," eyeliner cries, his terror sparked by the two Teutonic, diapered angels headed toward the gas station window. They hover like they've been posed for a photo essay on the Book of Revelation.

"Why don't you get out of here," Isidore says. "I'll handle this alone."

Lulu rolls her eyes. "If I could, I would."

"Yeah," Isidore says. "We know." She doesn't know

why she says this, she's never resented Lulu for leaving. She knows Lulu was only doing what made sense to Lulu, like River building radios and Anson following rules.

"You know what? Screw you, Isidore."

Isidore thinks she should apologize because they might die here and isn't she supposed to be living life with no regrets? Then the glass, with the perky red stripe and the words "coffee popcorn beer cigarettes" scrolled across it, implodes. Lulu and Isidore turn in unison, draw a second weapon each from the waistband of their jeans, and begin firing at the Gabriels, who advance through the gap slowly, like maybe they are afraid of cutting themselves on the glass. The green-haired boy is expressing disbelief that they are real. Some movement to Isidore's left catches her eye. In the corner by the post cards and the shiny neon rocks is a wide-eyed little girl and her father, who is hovering protectively over her. These families, the roads are crawling with them now. It used to be mostly truckers but lately everyone's hit the highway, decided they need to see the Grand Canyon and Mount Rushmore and Shakey's Pizza with their kids before the world ends. The father is trembling. The little girl is holding it together.

"Get out," Isidore shouts. "I'll hold them off."

The man doesn't move. The girl sucks two fingers ferociously, like gnawing them off is necessary for survival.

"Everything was already a mess," Lulu screams over the sounds of gunshots and breaking glass. "It had been a mess since the day you were born. What the hell, Isidore? That poor OB/GYN. I couldn't ruin anything because you'd already taken care of that for me—"

"Shut up, Lulu," Isidore screams. To the man with the little girl, she roars. "Get the hell out of here! What's wrong with you!"

The man gazes at her in awe and terror. Finally, the respect she deserves.

"Good job," Lulu mutters at just the perfect volume so it's nearly a whisper under the cracks of gunfire. "Excellent—what would you call that? Bedside manner?"

"Let's see you do any better," Isidore says, forced to yell over the sounds of their own gunfire. She doesn't know how Lulu remains so calm, some sort of Hollywood witchery. Despite the noise, she hears Lulu's aggrieved sigh. "Can you cover me? For like, forty-five seconds? Can you do that, Isidore?"

"Maybe I'll just let you die," Isidore says.

Lulu ignores her and rolls, tumbling past the Abba-Zabbas and the Nerds they're blowing to oblivion. Isidore is almost out of rounds. She considers throwing down her weapons and going hand to hand, but there are four angels remaining and a good chance more will come. She glances to the corner, expecting to see Lulu ready to usher the father-daughter trip from hell out the side door, and sees nothing. "Lulu!" she screams. She hears a thin clicking sound and realize she's out of ammo. Even though she has always known this would come, it's difficult to process. Okay, she thinks. All right now.

Taking cover behind the Hot Cheetos and Funyuns, Isidore pulls another magazine out of her back pocket, drops the old one, slams the new one in. She will do this alone. She must.

"Got any more?" Lulu says, suddenly at her side. Isidore startles and immediately starts to cry.

"Where the hell were you? Here." Sobbing, she hands Lulu her second backup magazine, her last.

"Why are you crying?"

"I thought you left me. You stupid whore."

"Yeah, well," Lulu says. "Not yet, anyway. Where the hell is Anson? What's he doing? Jacking off? Is he even allowed to jack off now?" she says, referring to Annie's uptight girlfriend.

Isidore wipes her nose. "Are you?" she says. She's not sure what hurts more: Lulu abandoning her, or Lulu returning like this, breezily shrugging off the only fear that haunts Isidore in her sleep.

"Shut up. God Isidore, it's like, I swear. You're just jealous. You're jealous I'm a Mormon now because it's something you could never be."

"I could be a Mormon!" Isidore cries, and she is staring at Lulu indignantly when they rise up from the depths of the obesity aisle, guns blazing like Butch Cassidy and the Sundance Kid, only with better hair. And better outfits. And just generally better. Because they're real, and because Robert Redford was not that attractive. There are five Gabriels now, or six, brandishing their flaming swords in the vaguely erotic way they always do. Their blond locks beckon in the gasoline-scented wind. Isidore tries to ignore a growing arousal.

"No you couldn't!" Lulu screams. It looks like a ticker tape parade. Doritos bags, chocolate donuts, Doublemint gum wrappers flying around them. Cheetos land in Lulu's hair and she brushes them away, licking her fingers.

"Why the hell not?" Isidore says. She's only got a few rounds left.

"Because, you idiot. Angels want to kill you. I don't know what you are, but you are definitely not righteous." A Gabriel thrusts his sword at Isidore and she side steps it, grabs the hilt, and disarms the angel, glaring furiously at Lulu.

"And Mormons are?"

"We try to be," Lulu says, so high and mighty that Isidore drops her gun, draws back her foot, and kicks a bag of Red Vines at her sister. She did not suffer through four years of parochial school for this.

Lulu shoots an angel through the wing, one-eyed, distracted. She is too busy glaring at Isidore to watch the thing totter off balance and flop towards her. Isidore slices its head off. "I could be a Mormon if I wanted. They wouldn't know. How would they know?"

"Trust me," Lulu says, dropping her arm. Her magazine is empty. "They'd know."

To Isidore's dismay, tears fill her eyes. "You haven't changed, Lulu," she says. "You're exactly the same as you were when you were eight and I always had to—"

"Clean up the dog shit?" Lulu recites with a truly epic roll of her eyes. "Really, Isidore? Are we going to go there again? The dog shit was not my fault. You drew the shit straw out of the chore jar."

"You rigged it!" Isidore says tearfully.

"How would I possibly?" says Lulu, but Isidore is convinced.

Two Gabriels advance and Isidore spins, shaving off wings. Feathers flutter down and land in their hair. "Oh Isidore," Lulu says, pitying. Shaking her head. "Annie always did it for you, anyways."

Isidore bends down and picks up one of the Red Vines she has liberated from its blue plastic bag. She whips Lulu with it. Right across the shoulder. The pained surprise in Lulu's eyes is a true victory. Isidore whips her again.

"Ow! Isidore!"

"How could you be so mean to me? How do you think I feel? You think I like this?" Isidore licorice-whips her with every question.

"It's not my fault you were stupid enough to draw the shit straw, Isidore. It was brown, for chrissake." Lulu grabs the Red Vine out of Isidore's hand and throws it down. "Blue for dishes, green for lawn, black for trash. Every single time. This is why you never had any friends—"

"I never had any friends because I'm a limitless freak, Lulu. And I smelled like dog shit," Isidore is screaming when the bells jingle and Anson comes through the door. The angels shift momentarily toward him in defense, then back toward Isidore. She's the one they want.

"Why'd you use the door?" Lulu says, pointing to the gaping threshold where the windows once were.

"Leave him alone. He's here to save your ass," Isidore says.

"You guys fighting about dogshit duty again?" Anson says. He wields his Gurkha knife and splits their sides open, severing the thigh muscles of the ones who hover high. The Gabriels can take a few bullets; the knife is a riskier but faster way to slow them down. "Come on," he says. An angel moves toward him and Isidore jumps and runs it through. "Behind you," she says. Anson whirls, knife out, and an angel's sword hand thumps to the ground.

Lulu is still furious with Is. "You always do this," she says. "Whatever I'm good at, whether it's school or getting out of dogshit duty, you make it feel like it's some sort of short-coming."

"You weren't better at it, you were better at cheating," Isidore spits. It can't really have been because the dogshit duty straw was brown. Lulu can't be right about that.

"Guys!" Anson shouts, whirling in battle. He splits another Gabriel, meets a sword with a resounding clang. "Little help here?"

"I was better at everything," Lulu shrieks, ignoring Anson, who ducks to avoid losing his head. For some reason Lulu is pointing at her own chest with all of her fingers at once. Isidore doesn't understand this gesture. She looks to Anson for translation. The expression on his face as he parries with the Gurkha is furiously determined. Isidore just doesn't know if he's intent on killing the angels, or silencing his sisters.

"Isidore—dammit—Lulu—" he grunts.

"I'm sorry," Isidore says. "I'm sorry that my entire life, angels have been dropping out of the sky to try and murder me. I'm sure that was really hard for you."

"This is exactly what I'm talking about," Lulu says. "You can't possibly understand. Everything revolved around you, always. Anson could have flown to the moon. River could have run for president—"

"You got that from *Full House*—"

"Isidore," Anson roars for help, giving up on Lulu. "Battle! Battle, now!" Isidore easily beheads a Gabriel bearing down on him. Anson dislodges the Gurkha knife from the belly of the one he has just finished off and levels his gun at his sisters. Neither of them spares him a glance. So he's threatening them with a bullet to the brain, well, it isn't the first time. He fires three rounds into the Icee machine. Carnival colors spray out, dribbling onto Lulu's jeans, and she screams. The tiles are slick and sugary and Lulu slips, goes down hard. Her hand shoots out and she pulls Isidore down with her. They land hard on their asses on the sticky floor. The Icee machine spews and coats them in slushy and they wrestle there a moment, arms locked, before mutually surrendering and climbing ungracefully to their feet. Lulu begins upbraiding Anson but Isidore interrupts.

"Who always picked the Circus Peanuts?"

Anson frowns. "Lulu," he says, like it's the most obvious thing. "You always got the Peanut M&M's." Isidore screams, thrusts her hands up in victory, and goes down again into the slippery slush. Neither Anson nor Lulu moves to help her. River lays on the horn.

"You hear that?" Annie says.

"River being a douche?" says Lulu. "I've learned to block it out."

"No," he says. His voice is flat and terribly calm. Like he's abandoned them all to whatever fate Lulu and Isidore choose, and if they get arrested here for blowing a service station to all hell for no apparent reason, fine. "The sirens. The police are coming, Lulu. So what do you want to do?"

ANYWHERE
WEST TEXAS

ANSON IS TEARING down the road too fast. "Slow down, Annie," Isidore shouts from the cabin, where she and Lulu have their hands braced on the overheads, trying not to fall. Anson has a gash across his upper arm and Isidore feels guilty. "Get away from the couch, Is," Lulu says. "You're dripping."

"So are you," Isidore murmurs, but she obeys. Red and blue Icee is falling off her like bright gore onto the gray linoleum. "River, get a towel," Lulu snaps. Isidore stands in the commode, where there's nothing to ruin. "Bring me some clothes," she says.

"Everything's dirty," Lulu says, digging through their duffle. "Dammit. I told you we needed to do laundry."

"Didn't we do laundry in Las Cruces?" says River. Their memories of the place are hazy, everyone's but Isidore's.

"Um," says Isidore, and they all groan. "It's not my fault you're out of clothes! Didn't you pack like six suitcases?"

"I packed two," Lulu says, "and you burned through all my clothes because yours were dirty."

Isidore must admit this is true. "There has to be some-

118

thing. Just give me something dry. River."

"They're all dirty," he says, but he hands her a navy towel. She puts it up to her hair, which is sticky and smells really good. But the towel stinks, like pee or onions. "Gross," she says, toweling her hair anyway. "Where the hell has this been?"

Lulu's eyes are bright with outrage. "Seriously? Every single thing is either filthy or moldy. I can't believe you guys. I can't believe you live like this."

She's getting herself worked up. Isidore sends River a look. He's the only one that can deal with her when she's like this.

"We'll stop somewhere, Lu. Go shopping." Out the window behind him the desert is merely a brown-tinted blur. Lulu's reply is the dirtiest swear word any of them know. River gasps.

"Can't you three hold it together? Just for once?" Annie shouts, and then he pounds the steering wheel with his hand. "What does it matter what you're wearing? Why the hell does it matter?"

"You're driving too goddamn fast," Lulu says. She heaves the massive duffle bag off the sofa, throws it to the ground, and kicks it. "If you had just," she kicks it again, "listened to me,"—kick—"this wouldn't be a problem!" And then, for emphasis, she tears off her shirt and throws it at River.

"Dammit Lulu!" he says. She's standing there in her bra and jeans. He turns away, which gives Lulu some satisfaction.

"You're dripping on the couch too, Lulu," Isidore says. Lulu screams at her to shut up.

Anson is doing his deep breathing, rolling his shoulders, and River is muttering about siblings and nudity and boundaries, when they hear the siren.

Anson swears under his breath. River moves to the bedroom, peeks out the back blinds. "State trooper," he shouts. Then he reaches under the bed and pulls out the mess kit that they keep stocked in case they need to get out of the Airstream fast and flee into the wilderness. It has a small tent and three teeny squished up sleeping bags, collapsible cups, chlorine drops to purify water, and astronaut food. Isidore loves it. It's the closest thing she's ever had to doll furniture.

From the mesh bag, River produces two pairs of ratty beige long johns—his and Anson's. "Here," he says.

Lulu and Isidore don't argue. Somebody has probably reported the gunfight at the OK Convenience Store by now, and if the trooper sees them covered in slushy, they'll have a lot to explain. They wiggle out of their sticky clothes and shrug on the long johns. River hurries to the navigator seat, pausing to hide his knife in the lockbox beneath a trap door in the floor. Isidore tosses him her guns, he stows those too. Lulu holds out her hands for the dirty clothes. Isidore gives them to her and she shoves them into the tiny garbage can beneath the sink, moving coffee grounds and banana peels on top of them. "No dry heaving," Lulu scolds, because she knows what bananas do to Isidore, but it's too late. Her diaphragm clenching, Isidore rubs the onion-scented towel through her hair the best she can, and then she and Lulu slide into the dinette just as the Airstream comes to a complete stop.

"Lulu!" Anson calls, a whisper-shout, and his Smith and Wesson .45 comes sliding down the length of the cabin. Lulu tucks it in the storage beneath her seat. Isidore plucks a deck of cards out of the clutter on the table, shoves Lulu's lemons aside, and begins to shuffle. She dry heaves again.

"Oh, Isidore," Lulu sighs, almost maternal.

"Bananas," Isidore says, eyes watering.

The Airstream has a driver's side door, installed by River to no acclaim, but most trailers don't. The state trooper doesn't know, so he goes to the passenger side. Isidore hears River roll down the window. "Hi there," he says.

"You've got a tail light out," the trooper says. A man, so there's little hope of Anson and River charming him. "Broke up. Like it was shot out."

"Really?" Anson says. "I didn't know. Sorry about that."

"Where you boys headed?"

"San Antonio, sir," Anson replies. "Little vacation. Wanna see the Riverwalk and eat some brisket."

"You've got Colorado plates."

"Yes sir. On a return trip from Los Angeles."

"Listen, son," the state trooper replies. "We had some kind of massive, illegal alien drug gang warfare violence back at a gas station not seven miles from here." Isidore wonders if he possibly could have fit in one more newsy noun. Satanic, maybe. Cult. "And now you've got a tail light looks to be shot out by a weapon. I'm sure you understand—"

Before Isidore knows what's happening, Lulu levels her eyes at her like a prayer and slides out of the dinette. She bounces to the front cabin, feminine and lively.

"Howdy, Officer," she calls, leaning forward between Anson and River. "What's this about gang warfare? Are we talking illegal immigrants here? Has anyone notified the border patrol?"

She's smiling, talking like an idiot, and showing her boobs. Except she isn't, Isidore realizes. Because even though she's bent forward to offer cleavage, she isn't wearing one of her usual low cut, snug white tees. She's wearing River's dingy long johns.

Officer Drug Cartel isn't charmed. "Ma'am, I'm going to have to ask you to have a seat," he says, and Isidore can tell by his tone that this has gone south. "How many you got hidden in there, son?"

"Four, sir. None hidden," Anson says, testy now. He despises being called son. Why did the officer have to call him son?

"Where's the other?"

Isidore can practically feel Anson gritting his teeth. "Isidore?" he calls.

She goes up to the cabin and pushes in next to Lulu. "Hi," she says, and then, because Lulu did it, "Howdy."

Her siblings let out a collective sigh of dismay.

The officer is wearing a straw cowboy hat and the beige trooper uniform. He's got a fat blonde mustache, and

Isidore can't see his eyes through his aviators. He's kind of fat, but he's a man, so you wouldn't really notice. His shiny badge distracts her. The pin on his right man-boob reads Officer Tidwell.

"Son," Officer Tidwell says, his voice taking on a tone Isidore can't interpret. "I'm about to ask you a delicate question, and I need you to answer as truthfully as possible."

"Sir?" says Anson. Isidore can tell he's as confused as she is.

"The delicate question I find I must ask you is this. Son. Are you a polygamist?"

Lulu chokes on something. "What?" Anson cries.

"Are you a member of the Fundamentalist Church of Latter Day—"

"Gross—no—they're my sisters. He's my brother. We're not polygamists."

Isidore smiles brightly at the trooper. He's eyeing her and Lulu in a way that Isidore mistakes for lusty.

"You're wearing that funny underwear," he says. "Them FLDS holy delicates." Isidore sees that he is taking them for freaks, not for sexy, and loses all hope that she can get her siblings out of this with her amazing sex powers.

"Oh Jesus Christ," Anson groans. "How could we be polygamists? There's two each of us."

"This little one here," he gestures to River. "Looks like a girl in man clothing."

"What?" says River. Lulu makes the sound she makes when she's trying very hard not to laugh. "No. I'm a dude. There's only four of us. That's not enough for a plural marriage."

"So you admit you are married, then?"

"No!" River and Anson say together. Isidore grins blankly.

Officer Tidwell flutters his hand over his head. "Their hair is funny. Like them sister wives," Officer Tidwell says.

"It's the style in L.A.," says Lulu. Her hair is matted on top of her head like a ratty beehive. Isidore finds herself in danger of giggling helplessly.

"I'm going to need you all to step out of the vehicle," says Officer Tidwell. "Plural marriage is a felony in the state of Texas."

"I understand that," Anson says. "But we're not polygamists—"

"I said I need you to step out of the car, son. If I have to say it again, I will remove you by force."

Isidore thinks they are screwed. They are so totally screwed, because there was a shootout a few miles back, and they are sitting atop a funhouse of illegal, unregistered, automatic and semi-automatic weapons. It is her fault. She has to save them. "Wait!" she says. "Look. If we were polygamists, would I do this?"

"Isidore—" says Anson.

"No!" says Lulu.

But it's too late. One movement is all it takes for Isidore to yank up her shirt. She's wearing a bra, but it's quick work to hook it with her fingers and flip it up to expose her breasts. She can feel her nipples pointing at him like the tips of vanilla ice cream cones. She really does have nice breasts. Lulu tells her she shouldn't say this, Isidore can't fathom why.

River cries out in horrified dismay. Anson says that he's going to be sick. "Oh Isidore," Lulu sighs, like she knows they're done for; like despite the fact that they have a Chinese army's worth of illegal weapons and police scanners hidden in Pacey, it's somehow Isidore's breasts that have screwed them completely.

"Ma'am, I am a Methodist and a Republican, and I do not wish to see your bosom. Kindly put it away."

"Religion and politics got nothing to do with it. A man wants to see a breast. Unless he's—"

"God!" Anson interrupts her. "A man of God!"

There is a pause in the dialogue during which all four of the Camper siblings attempt their most winning smiles. River thinks he is suave, in fact his leer is condescending and vaguely predatory. Anson goes for self-assured and reaches dope-eyed druggie. Only Lulu hits anything close to winning; Isidore, for her part, is ridiculously, overtly, sexual. She might as well be shooting a music video, albeit an odd one.

"I'm going to need you all to step out of the car," Officer Tidwell says. "Immediately."

They know better than to try anything. Still, River shoots a brief glance at Isidore—like there's something she, of all people, can do about it. Anson's glare quells any thought of shenanigans. They tumble out of the car into the thick Texas heat. It's a wonder, this heat. Like God is attempting a batch of human biscuits, and he wants them hot and now.

"Put your hands against the vehicle," Officer Tidwell says. "Keep your legs spread. Don't move, now."

They do as they're told. A chorus of colorful curses is bursting in Anson's brain. They're going to be arrested and he's going to get life. The angels will likely come for Isidore, but the rest of them are going to rot in jail. He hears a wet sniffle and turns his head, expecting to find Lulu sniffling. Poor Lulu. Anson sees her mug shot plastered on tabloid covers and feels responsible. There is only dull surprise when he realizes the crying is coming from River.

Escape must be attempted. There are four of them, after all. They could knock this officer out—leave him alive but take his weapons, his keys. Ditch the Airstream fast and lay low for a while. It's possible, with their training and with Isidore, that they could flee into Mexico and live on the lam. He's trying to catch River's eye for a signal when he hears a strained squeal, and then a grunt. Anson swivels his head, thinking one of his sister's has already made a move. He can't believe what he sees instead.

Lulu and Isidore are laughing. Trembling in silent laughter. Maybe it's not just Isidore who's deranged. Maybe it's everyone, all of them except him. They have their hands braced against the shiny silver of the Airstream, their heads down, their hair hanging in sad sticky strings around their faces, but he can tell. They're both shaking. River looks at him wildly. Officer Tidwell is headed for his vehicle, probably to call dispatch.

Lulu does a fake, whiny cry.

God help him. They are mocking River's terror.

"Knock it off," Anson hisses. "You don't know what it was like for him in prison."

Raspberries of laughter force their way out from Lulu and Isidore's lips. River cries harder.

"Hey!" Officer Tidwell shouts, one arm reached awkwardly through the passenger side window. "I said keep your heads down!" He draws his weapon.

"I hope you two get arrested," Anson says. Without meaning to, he has raised his head and pulled his feet in toward the Airstream, no longer in submissive position. Lulu and Isidore look up just in time to catch it. Anson doesn't see it coming. The sisters watch, their anticipation simultaneously giddy and terrified. Officer Tidwell raises the butt of his pistol in the air and brings it down across Anson's shoulders. Anson goes down hard. He immediately and forcefully vomits.

Lulu and Isidore cry out, sympathetic, but they can't stop laughing. They break position, move toward Anson, but Officer Tidwell has his gun trained on them. Anson is curled in the dirt, moaning. The sound of River crying rises above it all.

"Be strong, River," Anson mutters from the ground. Isidore realizes she is going to get shot because she can't stop laughing. Tears are rolling down her cheeks.

Officer Tidwell is highly aggravated. He's got his two-way in one hand, his pistol in the other, and is screaming something at Lulu and Isidore while trying to call for backup. Lulu and Isidore put their hands back against the Airstream, promising to be good now, watching Anson on the ground. Anson's vision is blurry. He feels seasick. From inside the trailer, the heat meter sings a hymn.

"Oh, shit," Anson says.

Officer Tidwell expresses similar sentiments. He expresses them again, and again. Isidore glances and sees he's turned away from the Campers, has forgotten them completely. He's got his gun raised and trained on a huge Gabriel who is descending from a cloudless sky, smug like Jesus come with the good wine.

"Move," Lulu commands. She tugs River's shirt. He wails and then follows her like a lost child. Isidore scrambles to Anson, curled in the dirt. Officer Tidwell fires at the Gabriel. It deflects his bullet with its sword. Isidore helps her brother to his feet. He's shaky, he puts his weight on her but she's feeling strong, at the moment, and doesn't sway. "Come on, Annie," she says, moving for the sweet shelter of Pacey.

"Officer," Anson moans. Isidore flinches; he doesn't smell great.

"Give me a minute," she soothes him, proud of herself for overcoming her disgust for a human being in need.

Officer Tidwell is firing at the Gabriel, missing every time. The Gabriel is smiling. Officer Tidwell is screaming like a blonde in a horror film. The sound sends Lulu helpless with laughter. She manages to start the engine, doubled over at the waist. Isidore apologizes to Anson for laying him on the floor, then urges Lulu to drive.

Lulu hits the gas. The back of the trailer fishtails, searching for traction, and finds it. Isidore forces down the window. As they pass Officer Tidwell and the angel, she fires two shots. The first hits the Gabriel in the head and he flops in the dust like a dead heifer. The second takes the patrol car in its front tire. Man, Isidore thinks, she is good. Breasts, sex, battle. She should be her own franchise. Lulu whoops in victory.

SONORA
TEXAS

THEY STOP AT a gas station in Sonora. Lulu waits
with the engine running while Isidore goes inside. She returns
with white chocolate mochas for herself and Lulu, Cokes for
Anson and River, and packages of bright orange crackers with
peanut butter in them. She knows how much they enjoy un-
naturally hued foods. Lulu hits the highway while Isidore sits
Annie up at the dinette—he has lain unmoving on the floor
since Officer Tidwell, occasionally singing something Isidore
doesn't recognize while grinning at the ceiling. She won't try to
heal him, she doesn't trust herself with a head wound. Fat and
tissue are one thing, the brain is another. One day Anson is
going to lose it completely, and if she's gone poking around in
his brain, she'll always wonder if it was her fault. She pops the
Coke open, tells him to sip it slowly. He stares at the can for a
moment, then Isidore. He nods and does as he's told. He's got
a spray of red wounds on the right side of his face, from hitting
the gravel when Officer Tidwell took him down. At his hairline
a swollen goose egg has formed and is flushed red and purple.

River sits across from Anson, staring at his hands and
sniffing intermittently. Isidore gives him the same instructions,

though perhaps, if she is being honest, with a bit less tenderness than she afforded Anson. She opens a bag of crackers and tells them to get some food in their bellies. She says she has brought them something nice and salty.

"Psalty wants you to be fishers of men," says Anson.

"Praise the Lord," says River.

Isidore doesn't like the sound of this. "Just drink your Cokes," she says. She decides she should put some ice on Anson's head wound, but just as quickly realizes they don't have ice and Lulu has already pulled away from the station. Isidore goes to the bedroom and riffles through piles of dirty laundry for a washcloth. Not finding one, she selects a tube sock and takes it to the sink, running it under the cold water. She drapes the sock across his forehead. "Here you go, Annie," she says, thinking herself soothing until Anson sees her and flinches. She goes back to Lulu before the brothers can make any further disturbing comments.

JUNCTION
TEXAS

IN THE LATE AFTERNOON, near Junction, An-
son comes to. It's like waking up from a dream, his brain drags
a moment behind reality. Lulu and Isidore have comman-
deered Pacey—the Airstream, dammit, the Airstream. They're
blasting some song in which a robotic voice keeps declaring
itself a Barbie girl, and a spooky demon man keeps asking her
to party. Anson doesn't think Barbie should go with the demon
man, whose intentions are obviously dubious. He suspects he's
snapped to because he's registered the demon man as a threat
that must be eliminated.

River is curled into a ball and staring listlessly out the
window. Anson hopes it's just the music. "River," he says.
"Hey." He snaps his fingers in front of his brother's face.

River turns slowly. His brown hair is mussed in a bed-
roomish way that Anson finds repugnant. River frowns, his
eyes fixed at Anson's hairline. When he speaks, his voice is a
dry croak. "Dude. Are you okay?"

Anson fears he has lost an ear and doesn't know it. "I
think so. Do I look okay?"

River shakes his head. "You've got a sock on your
head, man. A sock."

Anson reaches up. Indeed, there is a damp sock at his

brow. He grabs it and flings it away. This is why Isidore can't be alone. This is why he can't leave her. He might be concussed and she has treated him with a dirty sock.

Anson takes a sip of a warm and syrupy Coke on the table before him. Then he makes his way to the front of the Airstream. "Pull over," he says, his voice low and thick.

Instead, his Barbie-blonde sisters sing wide-eyed at each other. Lulu has her eyes off the road completely, she and Isidore croon earnestly into each other's faces. He thinks Lulu should keep her ingénue eyes on the road.

He reaches forward and punches off the stereo. Lulu and Isidore startle.

"Jeez," Lulu says. "You scared me."

"Put it back," says Isidore.

"Pull over," Anson says.

His sisters share a glance and agree to humor him. Lulu takes the exit for a country road that leads to nowhere and pulls over next to a barren field where black cows are grazing in the angry sun. Anson has intended merely to take the wheel, but now he stumbles out the door, overcome by a need for fresh air. He wonders who the cows belong to. There is nothing but sky for miles. He pulls out his phone and pauses, considering a call to Martha, but he has no idea what he'd say. Certainly he can't tell her he was pulled over after being attacked by angels at a Chevron.

Anson begins to pace along the side of the road, next to a ditch overgrown with high weeds and yellow flowers. His siblings have followed him out of the Airstream and huddle in a pack, watching him. He throws his hands up at the Texas sky.

"What the hell are we doing here, guys?" he says. "Huh? What the hell is this?"

"Texas," Isidore says.

"I think it's Saturday," says River.

"A fucking joke," says Lulu. She's ribbing Anson, but he points at her and says, "Exactly."

"I'm sorry," says Isidore.

Anson moves into the shade of the trailer. Pulls his

shirt up and uses the inside collar to wipe his face. They are headed to San Antonio, he tells himself. Like talking River down from a bad high, only now it's his own heart racing, his own death breathing down his neck. They are going to find their father. They are not going to die in an angel attack, they will not go to prison, they will not kill each other. This must be true. He will hold them together and make it true.

Isidore looks small, worrying they might decide they've had enough and leave her here. He knows she worries that. They're so short, she and Lulu. Perky blonde munchkins. For a moment, at the gas station, he'd thought they were both dead. His foremost regret was that now he was stuck alone with River.

It is habit mixed with desperation that causes Anson to lunge at Isidore, looping his arm around her neck and forcing her face toward the ground. He has caught her by surprise and she starts to lose her balance. They spin to regain it and Anson gets her into a full nelson. Isidore goes for his feet while driving her elbows down and back, but Anson remembers their training and he twists. He manages to get her pinned to his side in a noogie-ready position.

"Stop it Annie," Isidore says. He can tell she's not in a killing place.

"Quit messing around," says Lulu. Anson growls, wrestles Isidore to the ground and sits across her hips while Isidore giggles and swears exuberantly.

"Isidore," Anson scolds. He pins down one wrist, ignores her other hand beating at his chest, and grabs her rib skin between two fingers. "Language." She flops beneath him, a laughing fish.

"Anson," Lulu says. In her voice is calculated strain. "This isn't the time to be messing around. I've dropped my life for you three, you know."

Isidore tries to roll and get her leg up behind him. It's useless.

"You'd be dead, girl," he says to her. He slaps her belly once for good measure.

"Anson—" Lulu says.

"Lulu, you stupid whore," Anson says. "We're alive—"

"We're in Texas—"

"We're alive, and we're not in jail. Doesn't that strike you as something, I don't know, not to bitch about?"

Anson has to hand it to her—he doesn't feel it coming. One moment he is enjoying himself, batting away Isidore's flimsy, very human wrists as they attempt to hit him, and the next he is forced down on top of her by Lulu, who pounces him like a lioness from behind. Looking at her, you'd expect frenzied nail raking and hair gripping. You'd be wrong. Lulu takes his head by the temple and chin and twists it hard right, a painful reminder that she is a spray-tanned starlet still capable of snapping a neck. It's so absurd that Anson is tempted to laugh. But that would be unwise, as perceived mockery would make Lulu want to kill him. And Lulu could.

Lulu bends low to whisper something in his ear, threats undoubtedly, but no matter how well she was trained, she's still Anson's little sister. He drives an elbow up into her ribs and rolls. There is a brief scuffle, and then he is planted atop Lulu on the side of the highway, in the dirt.

"Come on, guys," River whines. "I'm really hungry."

"Who do you think you are? Buffy?" Anson says, grinning his victory over his tiny, panting sister. "Thought you might stab me with your high heel for a second there."

Tears flood Lulu's eyes. If it's a performance, it's an impressive one. Anson is baffled. Why can't a wrestling match ever be just that? "We could have gone to prison," she says.

"You know how hard it is to get Food TV in prison?" River says, shaking his head. His eyes are haunted. "Or risotto?"

"Risotto? Shouldn't you be more worried about the rape?" says Lulu.

"No one's getting raped," Anson commands, the way he commands everything. Like his words can make it so.

"Guys try and rape me all the time," Isidore says, standing and brushing dirt off her ass. They stare at her a moment, then decide collectively to take this for one of those times when Isidore doesn't mean it exactly how she says.

"What are we gonna do," says Lulu. Her blonde hair is spread in the dirt beneath Anson, rocks and gravel driving into his knees. "Guys. What are we gonna do?"

"I always kill them," Isidore says. They ignore this too.

"This is the biggest mistake. God, River, you're so pathetic," Lulu snaps. River is staring at the ground, rubbing his arms, memories of prison clearly playing in his mind. "I just almost died at a gas station in the middle of nowhere, I'm supposed to be in L.A. but instead I'm going to San Antonio because of some joke Dad made about River's birth defect, and we keep, like. Almost dying."

"Hey," Anson says. Lulu is feigning defeat beneath him. She learned it young. The best defense under a brothers' onslaught has always been to go limp. Anson could let her up. He doesn't. This primitive dominance feels important somehow. Anson doesn't know what to do with his own panic. But he knows how to manage theirs. "Hey," he repeats. Lulu looks at him.

"It's gonna be okay. Okay? It's gonna be okay."

Lulu snorts and rolls her eyes. A sound explodes from Pacey like a canon. Anson rolls off Lulu. His hand goes to his weapon even as he remembers he isn't packing, that all their weapons are still stowed in the trap door. Instinctively he shifts to cover Lulu, and realizes what he's hearing is music. What he's hearing is "Barbie Girl".

River kicks the tire, displaying the frustration and rage they all succumb to. "I thought it would help," Isidore says, wincing. "I'm sorry." Her eternal refrain.

SAN ANTONIO
TEXAS

SOMETIMES IT'S DIFFICULT to believe that this life is his own, the one he was intended to have, and not some terrible mistake on behalf of the universe. Waking up with a first aid sock stuck to the forehead tends to jolt a person's sense of harmony with the world. Anson is still feeling one degree separated from reality when he pulls into San Antonio around 8:00 p.m. this sultry evening. Lulu and Isidore, freshly showered, sit on the sofa with their hair damp and fluttering long wheat tendrils across their faces in the open wind. Between them sits a tin of Lulu's almonds and a giant bottle of water. They take turns drinking the water and throwing almonds for River to catch in his open mouth. Anson navigates to the Riverwalk, where lights and candles glitter in the dusk and illuminate a fat, lazy river dotted with boats in carnival colors. Lulu and Isidore ooh and ahh. Isidore urges Anson to hurry up.

"All right! You wanna find somewhere to park a trailer in all this?" he says.

But Isidore is bright with excitement. "Smoothies!" she says. "Gelato! Tony Roma's!"

"We're here to look for Dad," Anson says half-heartedly. If they find Dad tonight, Lulu will probably be on a plane home by morning. Dad will fly to Mexico to see Minxy and make comments about how Mom has finally started taking care of herself, leaving him and River and Isidore to hit the road again. Probably they'd head to Seattle for River's Space Needle fix, and then they'd be where they were two weeks ago. Wandering aimlessly around the country like con men without the romance, cowboys without the poetry. Anson can't admit even to himself that he doesn't want this to happen.

"We gotta eat first," River says. "And not at Tony Roma's."

"Yeah, but—Minxy," says Lulu.

"I'm sure there's a phone book or something, down there," Isidore says. "What?"

"That's your plan?" says Lulu. "To look him up on a phone book?"

"How else are we supposed to find him?"

"Isidore. Dad doesn't want to be found. You really think he's in the phonebook?"

"I'm more worried about the fact that you thought we had to come all the way to San Antonio to look him up in a phone book," says River. "Those things are online now, you know. We could have Googled him from anywhere. From Mom's living room."

"Why didn't we?" says Anson.

"Didn't think of it 'til now," River says.

"Do you honestly think," says Lulu. They all groan. But Lulu persists. "Do you honestly think that I would come all this way with you asshats and not think to Google Dad's name? I'm an actor. Not an idiot."

"There's a difference?" says Anson.

"We'll all feel better once we eat some Tony Roma's," Isidore says, at which point she is informed—in what she believes is an unnecessarily harsh manner—that they absolutely will not be consuming any Tony Roma's.

They stroll along the Riverwalk, watching the languid tourists. They don't know if it's the crowds, or the lights, or even just their shower-damp hair, but they find themselves in an optimistic mood, all of them at once, which is rare. They are discussing the idea of getting on a tour boat, Anson is actually considering it, and the fact that he's willing to do even that makes it seem like a ridiculously good idea. Anson, who never considers much beyond pizza and whiskey and lately, female driven comedies. River is asking if they think they sell beer on the boats, and Isidore says what, like a booze cruise? pleased to know a cultural reference at the appropriate moment, for once, when Anson's phone rings.

Lulu's mouth puckers and Isidore sighs. Only River is stoic.

"Don't answer it, " Lulu says, but Anson does. He doesn't know why. Don't ask him why.

"Hello?"

"Hi, honey! God it's good to hear your voice. Where are you?" She's a little long on her vowels. A little soft on her r's. Anson knows his mom's drunk voice from years of experience. She sounds like a valley girl on Adderall.

"San Antonio," he says tersely. He swears she's not as stupid as she acts.

"Oh. Any particular reason? San Antonio?"

Hadn't Lulu explained this to her already? "We think Dad might be here? Remember?"

"Did you tell me that already? I'm sorry. I've been so distracted thinking about Minxy. Which is why I'm calling, actually. Just a minute." She speaks a few muffled sentences, and Anson realizes she's with Raoul. "No baby, the daikon—the daikon—well I don't know. Shut up! You just shut up!" She's laughing. Her voice is giddy, like a girl's or a pig's. "Honey? Anson? You there?"

Anson can see it now. The martini in his mother's hand. The jar of olives. Her boozy eyelids. His siblings have given up on him and the boat. They turn their backs and move on. He follows them down the walkway, through the crowd, the river on his left, the storefronts and restaurants under glowing lights to his right. He casts a regretful glance back at the tour boats; he could never say it but it sounded pleasant to him. To sit for a few minutes and let someone else do the steering.

"Yeah. Okay."

"Are you—where are you? I hear lots of people, are you at a concert somewhere, Anson?"

A concert? What the hell? "No. We're at the Riverwalk."

"The what? Anson, are you smoking pot?"

He won't answer that. "The Riverwalk. In San Antonio. It doesn't matter. Does it matter?"

"I can't hear you very well. I just wanted to get the address of your nearest post office so I can have these t-shirts overnighted to you."

Isidore and Lulu have stopped in front of some kind of Latin gypsy's lair. It's dark inside. Blue-tiled tables with votives, and fairy lights strung overhead. They are examining a menu tacked up by the door while River hangs back, managing to look like a delinquent just by putting two steps between himself and the girls. He's slouchy and greased. Anson can't believe they're related.

"I hope you'll keep an open mind," his mom is saying. "About the t-shirts."

He is going to kill himself. He is literally going to open a vein here along the Riverwalk.

"I just thought it might be a nice idea. A gesture. And Anson you never know—"

"What did you do, Mom?"

"I just had some t-shirts printed up. For the occasion."

Anson has a memory of his mother. He was in his early twenties, Isidore was about thirteen. He can't remember where they were headed, though he has a vague feeling it had to do with one of Lulu's adolescent demands. They'd met trouble on the road, as they so often did. In his memory his mother's hair is long and blonde and spilling out of a ponytail. It is whipping about in the wind as she drives the Chevy Citation at 90 miles an hour down a country road. Her arms are muscled and tan, she is holding an Uzi in one hand and the steering wheel in the other, screaming at Anson to back up his sisters, who are turned in the backseat and have shot out the rear window. Then his mom hits the brake, spins the wheel, her eyes blazing the frenzied focus of a warrior queen. The car rotates 180 degrees and now Anson and his mother are blowing out the front window, aiming at a flock of twenty Gabriels, Isidore and Lulu safe with Anson and their mother between them and certain death.

He knows this memory is real. But he can feel his faith in its truthfulness slipping, as his mother gets older. As she buys haciendas, takes lovers, and prints t-shirts. He can feel the truth of his mother becoming a story someone once told. Then he wonders about himself and Isidore. Who will tell their story when they're gone? Maybe Lulu will sell it to Hollywood. Maybe no one.

Lulu and Isidore approve the restaurant and head in. River glances at him. Anson holds up a finger, and River goes ahead.

"Anson? Are you there?"

"The occasion. What occasion?"

"You know. Minxy's last walk." Anson would like to do a lot of things, none of which include pretending this is in any way okay, but it is this moment his mother chooses to make her voice go teary and he can't very well act out his fantasies of matricide or a good death when his mother is weeping.

"It's going to be her last hurrah," his mother says. "You know. Her last walk with your father."

"If we can find my father," Anson mutters.

"What?"

"Nothing." He's getting testy now. "Have another drink, Mom."

She doesn't hear, or chooses not to. "So I just thought you kids might like to. I don't know. And if it's a bad idea, you know, I'm not going to force you to wear them."

Anson doesn't understand. The best he can tell is that

his mother has lost her mind and nobody has thought to restrict her access to a credit card. He wonders what else she may have ordered. Commemorative Camper family coffee mugs. Family portrait sittings in which they will all be asked to wear white and khaki.

"We're at the Marriott. The, uh," he fumbles through his wallet, finds the card. "The Rivercenter Marriott. Just send them here. You need the address?"

"Why are you at a hotel?"

"Lulu. She won't sleep in the camper."

"Oh. Well ok. Just a minute."

You knew you needed the address. You called specifically for the address, Anson thinks. So don't pretend like I'm doing something wrong by—

"All right. I'm ready."

He reads her the address and then, when she shows signs of starting up again, says, "Mom? I gotta go. It's really crowded and I'm trying to keep up with Isidore." He hangs up before she can come up with further questions.

It's a relief to duck out of the crowded walkway, with the wet heat and all the people pushing past him, everyone meandering like because they're on vacation they have the right to do whatever the hell they want, and into the dark cantina. His siblings are in the bar, at a high table with stools, and he reaches them just as the waitress is leaving. He raises a hand but she pretends not to see him.

"It's okay. We ordered a bunch of shots," Isidore says. Their spirits are high. His spirits are low.

"What's wrong?" Lulu says. "Was it Mom?"

"Again? She bugging you about Dad?" Isidore says.

"No. Kinda, I guess. She needed our address so she could overnight us some shirts."

Lulu and Isidore are smiling like this is hilarious. "Shirts? She thinks we're out of shirts?"

"She had t-shirts printed up," Anson says, and—this is the great relief of siblings—suddenly it does seem funny. "For Minxy. Minxy's Last Stand, or something."

Lulu's mouth drops open while Anson grins. "Oh my god," Isidore laughs.

"You're kidding me," says Lulu.

"Nope."

"And she thinks we're going to wear them?" Lulu says.

"Sounds like it," says Anson. The shots arrive. They haven't lied. The waitress unloads nine little glasses of white and gold onto their table.

"It's a tequila bar," says River. "But they have food too."

Anson is pleased. There is nothing he wants more in the world right now than some warm, salty chips and the burn of tequila. And what do you know, but here they are, being dealt from a bar tray like communion wafers at church.

"All right," says the waitress, a broad with black hair and tattoos. "For the blanco you've got the Milagro Reserve Silver, La Certeza, and Patron Platinum. These are the reposados," she points, "the El Mayor, El Reformador, and the," she checks her notebook, "Hijos de Villa Rifle. And for your añejos we've got the Cabo Wabo Uno, the Don Julio Real, and the Patron Burdeos." She grins. "Easy on that stuff. Get you anything else?"

Anson orders nachos and asks for another drink menu. Isidore and Lulu have pulled the two Patrons to themselves, grinning like they did over blue snow cones at the ages of six and eight, and it is clear they are not going to share most of this. He has already forgotten the names she rattled off and will not be aware until three hours later, when the waitress brings the bill, that they have just ordered over three hundred dollars' worth of premium tequila.

"This is delicious," Isidore says. The evening is fine, the music is cheesy, she feels like a bumblebee drunk on flower and sun. "Amazing. Try it." She holds it out to Lulu, who pretends to hold it on her tongue and consider the flavors.

"Wow," Lulu says. "That's amazing. You can really taste the vanilla in there. And uh, raisins."

"Shut up," says Anson, and she hands him the glass.

He shoots it back. His siblings cry in simultaneous dismay.

"What?" he licks his lips and sets down the glass.

"I wanted to try that," River says. "Fuck!"

"Why? It's tequila. It's all tequila. Try one of those. What, you gonna pout? I'll order you another one, sweetheart."

"You're supposed to sip them, you barbarian," says Lulu.

"Let's get some guacamole," Isidore says, savoring the very idea of it, and they do. A nice-looking man comes and makes it at their table with fresh tomato and purple onion, and the chips are hot and wet with grease and salty. Isidore picks up another shot and wiggles her shoulders to the beat of the salsa music overhead.

"Remember that time we drove to the Grand Canyon," Lulu says. She's put a clever little braid in at her temple. Isidore tries not to stare at it.

"Worst idea ever. Worst idea ever," River says, and orders four more shots. "Patron," he tells the waitress. "Patron Patron Patron Patron." It doesn't matter, really. Their mother has a mysterious source of income. Money rolls into Anson's account every month and he's never asked to explain where he's spent it. A small price for her to pay for freedom from her own children.

"Why?" says Isidore.

They look at her incredulously. The salsa music feels like a soundtrack to their movie life. "You don't remember?"

"No. Why? What?"

"Seriously you don't remember?" says Lulu.

"Seriously. The Grand Canyon? How old was I?"

"Eight," Anson says, doing the calculations. He was sixteen that year, his dad had made him drive most of the way, and Anson had pretended not to be afraid of it, the big SUV and the high speed limits. When it began to rain, he'd finally claimed he was too tired and his mom had taken over. Isidore and Lulu chewed bubblegum and knotted lanyards in the backseat, they'd fought relentlessly and then Isidore stole Lulu's diary, and--

"Remember? You took Lulu's diary and read it out loud to us while Lulu was sleeping."

"Yeah," says Lulu. "And nobody stopped you. Not even Mom and Dad. What the fuck?"

"Dear diary," River says. "Today I thought about Jonathan Taylor Thomas and got the special feeling—"

Isidore snorts tequila up her nose but Lulu just quirks an eyebrow and says, "Jealous."

Anson takes a sip of something clear. It's harsher, this stuff, than the gold. "Let's get more of that . . . that . . ." he points clumsily.

"Añejo," Lulu says. Her smile is a flower, pink lips around perfectly whitened teeth. "You're drunk."

"I'm not drunk," Anson says, and orders more añejo.

"Why was it the worst idea ever?" Isidore says.

"Because there were about ten thousand angels in that place," says River. "We hit 'em like a swarm of locusts. They smashed up against the windshield."

"No way," says Isidore. She has no memory of this. Anson is nodding.

"We were about ten miles away from the park," he says. "We thought we'd be all right, on the major highways. Never saw them coming. Then they were splattering all over the car."

River starts laughing. "Mom wasn't even scared. She was just like, 'Goddammit! Can't we ever—'"

"No way," says Isidore. Their mother does not say goddammit.

Lulu and River nod. "Yeah. Like, 'Goddammit, can't we do something nice! Even once!'"

"'Can't we just have one nice fucking vacation!'" Lulu says in her mom voice, which is wobbly, like a cartoon goose. "'One nice day without God trying to murder us!'"

"Then she pulled out the Uzi," River says.

Anson laughs now, which feels good, because it had been terrifying at the time. He'd been driving again, angels slamming into the car like a plague of Egypt, his dad pretend-

142

ing to sleep in the back and wouldn't open his eyes and take up arms, his mother cursing and upset which made him feel like they'd never be happy again. He'd glanced at them in the rear-view mirror, the kids. Lulu had her headphones on and her arms crossed, righteously ticked off. River had handed her a Colt and she'd grudgingly taken it, slid the magazine in with her pink sparkly tipped fingers, and pulled the safety. Isidore had her eyes squeezed shut, rocking. Another family event ruined because of her. They'd fought off the angels and turned back. That night he'd taken her for ice cream and not yelled at her like Mom did when she swallowed all the bubble gum.

"How'd we get through them?" Isidore says.

"We didn't," says Lulu. "We turned back."

"We never made it to the Grand Canyon?" Isidore says.

"Nope," River says, and does a shot. "Ended up in a grungy motel with a bunch of real polygamists. Mom figured God would spare them."

"Well. That's why I don't remember it."

This strikes them as hilarious. They request another basket of chips. "Two baskets," says Anson, and it goes on like this for hours. They recall event after event from their past, things that were horrid at the time, things that almost killed them. The time they'd had to flee a burning house and Lulu's white kitten, Sugar, had been left behind to the flames. The move from Pueblo to Colorado Springs, the nasty white gang at the Lutheran high school that Anson had allowed to beat him badly because he couldn't reveal that he was, in fact, skilled in ways that would have enabled him to fend off three kids easily, hands behind his back. The time the angels had swept into the Starbucks in Albuquerque and the old woman there who was huddled under a table, terror painted on her wrinkled-canvas face, had soiled herself. They recall events and then they rewrite them, over tequila and guacamole and hot salty chips. The memory of Lulu praying to the very God who sent the angels, who started the fire, to please save Sugar and she'd never spy on her male classmates in the locker room again, sends Isidore forward over the table, snorting tequila out her nose, eyes watering. The kid taking his chained wallet out of his pocket and whirring it over his head, like a portly Indiana Jones, the look of constipated concentration on his sweaty marshmallow face, the memory makes Anson laugh until he cries. The old woman clutching her Frappuccino, covering the straw hole to protect her frothy coffee beverage from shattering glass. Lulu pounds the table. River's laugh is loud enough to draw looks from other diners. They rewrite their stories so that the past is no longer haunting, but hilarious. It's a power none of them possesses alone. The only have it together.

SAN ANTONIO
TEXAS

THE MORNING DAWNS a sour-breathed, temple-searing, leftover scab of a modern Bacchanal. His stomach oily and flinching, Anson remembers that the world is a cruel place and he will never feel good in it again. Although he has purchased them two rooms to the tune of almost six hundred dollars, they're all in the same one again. Isidore and Lulu in one bed, River in the other, Anson on the couch. Why do they always do this? He gets that they're accustomed to the noisy chaos of each other, the press of bodies and flurry of sounds a primal comfort. But you think four adults would be capable of spending one night in separate rooms. And why does Anson always agree to take the couch? He's the oldest. Shouldn't that count for something?

"Morning." Isidore is cheery. She's sitting up with her legs folded, her hands in her lap. She has spent the night entertaining fantasies of angels and is still gently aroused. With one arm Anson reaches over his head and shoves open the curtains, squints across the room at her. In the air is the peanutty smell of all hotel rooms, cheap or pricey. "We know you don't sleep, Is. You can stop pretending." His voice is husky and cracking, the effort of speech painful punishment.

"What do you mean?" she says, twirling her hair around a finger.

"Jesus, shut the curtains," River groans. Anson pushes the curtain open even further. River tugs a pillow over his head.

"What time is it?" Lulu says. Anson can hear her tongue sticking to the roof of her mouth.

"Ten-fifteen."

Lulu lets out a dainty moan. She sounds like a Smurf dying bravely.

"You okay?" Anson says.

"I think I'm gonna be sick," she mutters. "Everything's still spinning."

Anson heaves himself up and out of the couch. He is stiff and sore everywhere, his loins throbbing with the need to pee. He goes into the bathroom, and the release of his bladder is a holy pleasure. He brushes his teeth with a tube of all natural paste the hotel has provided, then fishes in his bag for the jar of ibuprofen and swallows three pills with three glasses of water. When he's done, he picks up the small plastic waste bin and carries it out to Lu. "Here," he says, setting it on the floor at her side. "Lulu." When she doesn't look, he takes her hand and touches it to the bin. "Use this if you're gonna puke. Drink some water."

"Stop talking," she says.

"Sorry I got up in the middle of the night for water."

"You know it makes me have to pee," she murmurs.

"Man," says River. He tosses the pillow aside but his arm remains draped across his eyes. "What did we do last night?"

Anson opens his mouth to answer River and this is when he realizes he doesn't know. He can't believe it's not coming, that he actually drank enough to black out. Or did he, he thinks, eyes falling on Isidore. She catches his gaze and smiles nervously. "Isidore? Did you—what day is it? Is it to-morrow?"

"We drank," Lulu says. "It's not her fault."

"Tequila," says Is. "Lots and lots of lovely tequila."

"Please, Isidore. Never say that word again," Lulu's voice is muffled in her pillow.

"So it's not—I don't remember anything because of the tequila?"

Lulu lets out a chuckle that turns into a pained moan. "Yes Anson. The angels didn't wipe your memory. That was the Patron."

"We ordered Patron? Shit." That stuff is expensive. Anson rubs his palms deep into his temples. He is comforted to know that at least he hasn't been brain-wiped.

"Boobs," River blurts. "I remember boobs."

This is not fair. Anson does not remember boobs.

"Did I get boobs?" he says.

"No," says Isidore. "You were offered boobs. But you kept saying, 'Maa-tha. Maw-tha.' And the girl kept saying, 'My name's Shelley'." Isidore blinks and cocks her head, an imitation, Anson's assuming, of Shelley.

"Awww," says Lulu, rallying now to tease Anson.

"Yeah. It was sweet," Isidore says.

"Shut up," Anson says. He doesn't know if he's proud or irritated with himself. He figures they have until about noon before they risk getting heat. "I need food. Something greasy. Lulu?" Even River has sat up, swallowed painkillers, but Lulu isn't moving. No wonder. She's too tiny to be keeping up with them. Like giving pints to a hummingbird.

"I don't know. Give me a minute."

"She needs a Bloody Mary," says River. "No, seriously. That's the best thing."

"Shouldn't we start looking for Dad?" Isidore says.

"Awww, Isidore," River groans. They all join in and start throwing things at her. Pillows, shoes, even Lulu manages to grasp and toss a pair of underwear. "Come on!"

Outside the window of this expensive hotel, Anson sees, they have a beautiful view. They're on the thirty-first floor, though Anson doesn't know how he knows this. He presses up close to the floor-to-ceiling glass. It makes him woozy but he knows he's safe, behind the glass. San Antonio is silver and green below him, wavering heat in the late morning sun. He can see the Riverwalk. It looks empty from here, the river small and brown. Then he yells, he actually yells it, "Incoming!" like a massive douche, and throws himself to the ground, taking Isidore with him.

The glass shatters inward, raining down over their heads. His gun is on the couch, which is up against the window—or the place where the window was—and he thinks he is actually going to piss his pants when he registers three things at once: the beating of wings, the lack of "Oh When The Saints", and a hot Texas breeze across his legs and neck, like Anson's being creeped on by the devil himself. The only thing certain in the world is that they are on the thirty-first floor and there is no longer any blessed thing between them and the ground almost four-hundred feet below.

"Stay down!" Anson shouts, chest down and half on top of Is. Lulu's already out of bed. She's got her weapon and she pumps off four rounds fast. Isidore turns and Anson releases his grip around her waist. Drawing her Colt, she rolls to her back and aims, shooting from the ground. She meets his eyes. "Stay down, Annie," she says. He's not stupid, he knows she's trying to protect him from his certainty that he will, somehow, manage to plunge off the edge.

"How many?" Anson shouts. He is on the carpet with his arms around his head. Isidore doesn't answer. River is firing away, edging further and further from the glass and toward the door. "Move, I'll cover you," Isidore says. Anson rolls, slowly so he doesn't panic himself and plummet. Not three feet away from him is a great toothy gap in the face of the hotel, nothing but air, angels, and sky. He's going to vomit. He turns away before he passes out and begins to crawl on his forearms deeper into the room, carefully so as not to slice himself to ribbons on the glass. Lulu fires into the air behind him, then steps over him and toward the death plunge. Anson cries, "Lulu, no!" but she marches to the couch where he was sleeping and stops just inches away from the edge of the world. Seeing her stand there, her pajama-clad silhouette against the sky and the murderous angels, her hair flying in the breeze, Anson wonders for the first time if perhaps both his sisters are less than human.

She fishes under the cushions and Anson knows she will fall to her death and he will go with her. Yet somehow she withdraws his Glock, shooting at the Gabriels all the while, aiming with her peripheral vision. She turns back to him, a smug smile on her face and a pistol dangling from her finger. Everything is dreamy. Anson is lying on his back on a carpet covered with glass and just inches from his bare feet there are six or seven angels, he's too nauseous to count, hovering over the precipice with the breeze in their locks and their swords raised for war. Isidore aches to engage them hand-to-hand, but she can't until they come into the hotel room. Their swords whirl, deflecting bullets.

Lulu says, "Oh no," and hurls near the hole in the luxury hotel, the void aching to reach up and swallow her. River covers her with a round of gunfire until she stops heaving, then grabs Anson by the shirt and drags him backwards into the room. They scramble over to the bed and crouch behind it. Cautiously Anson peers across the sheets and sees Lulu. She is repeatedly retching over the side of the building, like it's a toilet and not a wicked mouth screaming with hunger for them. Isidore maintains the front line, firing at the Gabriels to keep them away from Lulu. Anson curses under his breath and shouts "Cover me!" He pulls Lulu back, away from the edge, ignoring the fact that she's still—yep, it's still coming up—and drags her back to their refuge behind the bed.

"Thanks," she says, catching her breath and slapping his weapon into his palm. "Anson? Oh no, Anson. Oh no. It's okay, honey. We're safe here. We're—"

Then she shuts up and thrusts the waste bin at him, the one he'd brought out for her, and Anson pukes into it. "It's so high!" he says miserably.

"I know honey. I know," his sister says maternally, which is the last thing Anson wants or needs, and then she reloads her magazine and pumps eight rounds fast into the angels hovering in the entryway. "It's all right. We're holding them off. You're gonna be okay."

"Shut the hell up, Lulu! Shut up or I swear to God, I will push you!"

"Why are they just hanging there like that?" River says.

"Maybe it's the puke," says Isidore. "Keep puking, Annie. It's keeping them away."

"It stinks," River calls from across the room where he's crouched behind a desk.

The angels are gathered at the gap, like gangly girls in braces waiting to be asked to dance. Later, sometimes, after they've made their escape and they're safe, speeding away from some one-horse town in the Airstream with the screens still down and the path clear ahead, Anson can conjure up the image of the Gabriels and laugh. They're righteous in every sense of the word. They brandish swords and toss their hair like high-spirited ponies. Their eyes are filled with the holy light of their godly cause, so blue and blazing that Anson is surprised they don't shoot lasers.

"I'm out," Isidore says. She doesn't have another magazine. Anson tells her to pull back, but she doesn't. She stays between the angels and her siblings.

"What are we going to do," says Lulu. "Just sit here?" She fires lazily at one of them. He blocks it with his blade. The bullet ricochets and slams into the wall behind them. Lulu is right, a plan is called for. It's up to Anson to come up with a plan. They had their guard down because of the hotel. The angels have always avoided public places before. It occurs to Anson that they've been trapped. That the lizard brains of the Gabriels have, for once, formed a plan that goes beyond fly softly and carry a big sword. Anson would think they've evolved, except he knows God would send them to hell for that.

He is about to tell his siblings that they need to run when the angels surge into the room. Anson hears someone scream, high-pitched. He knows it isn't Isidore and suspects it isn't Lulu. He lunges for the Gurkha knife in his bag, behind him. He comes up swinging. He shouts at them to run. Run.

But he can't let into the Gabriels with the knife. Isidore has thrown herself into the fray and they've all gone after her, all six of them, together. They were waiting, he realizes. Waiting for the Campers to run out of ammo.

SAN ANTONIO
TEXAS

"DAMMIT ANSON, GO!" Isidore says. There is no time for romance. No one swears they'll go down with her, it would only ensure their death. There is nothing to do but run for the Airstream on adrenaline and hope.

There are five Gabriels now. That's two over the sweet spot. A sword swings at her ankles and slices her like a shaving mishap before Isidore yanks her feet up and out of the way, just in time. They were trying to hobble her. It worms into her brain, an unsettling distraction. Isidore is accustomed to dealing with angels who don't think.

They're fast. One of them gets ahold of her neck with his meaty palm and thrusts her down toward the bed where he falls atop her, squeezing. He is flawless and pouty and empty-eyed like a male model. "You know," she gasps. "There're a lot funner things to do on this bed." If he understands her, he doesn't show it. His pressure around her neck increases and Isidore feels a sick and ferocious pounding. If heads could have orgasms, hers would be about to blow.

She reckons last night wasn't too bad, as far as last nights on earth go. There are too many angels and she is still her human self. It's like a sneeze, Hulk mode, and she can't choose when to do it. Just when Isidore is sure she's not going to, sure her head is going to burst and some poor maid will have to mop up her brains, she snaps. Loses all hold on her humanity. She becomes bone and instinct only, all her flesh turned to weapons. Whatever it is that has made God hate her enough to sentence her to death and eternal torture, it comes out. Something hungry for blood, raging for destruction. If she were to stay in Hulk mode she'd begin to ache for the end of the world. The explosive power she unleashed the time they were trapped in the canyon in Arizona, surrounded by angels, had saved their lives. It also created a rockslide that blocked off four highway lanes and Isidore had fought ferociously to stop it there, keep it from breaking loose like an unstoppable tide.

Isidore's mind goes silent. There is nothing beyond what her body knows. There are five angels now and when she's drunk on desecration, five is nothing.

While Isidore is upstairs pulling the wings off angels and hurling them to their deaths, Lulu is in the pristine lobby, giving the performance of a lifetime to the lulling background music of Bach.

"Everything was lovely," Lulu says, leaning against the white marble counter. "The views especially." She's managed to pat her hair down and coax it out of its wild nest so that it lies fairly smooth. Running down the stairs, she pulled a lip-gloss out of a pocket and smeared it on. Still, there is no accounting for the fact that she has not brushed her teeth. And that she's wearing a white t-shirt with no bra and blue and white striped pajama pants. And that she's barefoot. Luckily, the clerk can't see that. She hands him Anson's credit card, his wallet was in the back of his jeans. "We just—unfortunately—have news about our father. He's not doing well, I'm afraid. We only just found out." And she chokes up. A stroke of sheer brilliance, way to work it, Lulu Camper.

The clerk makes a sympathetic face. He's a lovely young man. Bright eyed and endlessly polite, a thick Texas drawl. Normally Lulu likes a good drawl; like every vagina-equipped humanoid, she has a thing for accents. But this time it seems that the drawl is just making it take ten times longer to communicate. She hides her irritation. She is on her stage. "I'm real sorry to hear that, ma'am. Real sorry. We'll get y'all taken care of as soon as possible." It takes him three years to get out all those vowels.

"Thank you," Lulu says, and takes a tissue from the box he offers up to her, dabbing at her eyes. "I'm sorry. I must be an awful mess. It was just so sudden." His accent is starting to creep into her voice, as often happens, but she figures it can only benefit her now.

The man shows pity and terror. "How awful for you, ma'am. My sincere condolences. Let me just . . ." he clicks furiously at the keyboard in front of him and returns the credit card. "There you are ma'am. Will you be requiring any assistance to your car?"

"No, thank you. You've been a real help. A real help." Lulu is selfless in her frailty, a hot mess Pollyanna. Jesus, but she's good. She glances over her shoulder to see if River is getting this. He's over by a fountain with his back to her, dammit.

"Your luggage, ma'am?"

"My brothers have seen to that. Thank you," Lulu says.

"Of course. Oh—I'm sorry to bother you ma'am. If you have a quick minute—"

Lulu's fragile smile freezes. The clerk turns and lifts something from under the counter—a package. Lulu quivers with adrenaline like a cowboy-roped calf. What the hell is this? Some kind of sneak attack? Angels going around as slow-talking men, now? Her hand goes to her knife. River turns in time to see his sister drawing weapon on the polite young desk clerk and startles, jerks forward, unsure whether to stop her or help her. He goes for his piece, too, and then the young man sets a box on the counter and Lulu's knife comes up and River says,

"The t-shirts, Lu. Thank God, the t-shirts."

Lulu thinks the stress has finally taken sweet River. Then she remembers, and manages to get her knife back into the waistband of her pajama pants before the guy looks up. The Minxy t-shirts. She has launched into a refrain of tearful god bless yous, the boy just eating it up, when a noise makes her turn to the elevators.

"Sweet mother of Christ," she says, falling completely out of character as River visibly braces himself and starts slowly toward Isidore, palms raised.

It's Isidore. They're pretty sure. It looks like Isidore, but it's of course both more and less than Isidore. Isidore in Hulk mode. Isidore, harbinger of the apocalypse. She comes out of the elevator like a thunderstruck ballerina, graceful and fire-alight at once. She is so bloodied that, for a moment, Lulu thinks she's been flayed alive. There is a blood-thirsty energy wafting off her that destroys all other concerns, like the fact that she's dressed only in a white shirt and gore-soaked underwear.

Lulu is afraid to approach her.

"Oh no," says the nice young man. "Oh dear. You know, I thought I heard a commotion upstairs." He picks up the phone to call for help.

"No!" Lulu snaps. "That won't be necessary." She says it in her most commanding tone. She's doing broad now, and she knows she'd better do it well. The clerk looks doubtful, but he pauses. "What's the matter with you?" she scolds. "That's my little sister." And then, because she must, Lulu starts toward Isidore, to intercept her. Isidore turns her head in Lulu's direction. The look in her eyes stops Lulu cold.

"This is just her grief," Lulu calls over her shoulder. "It's not how it looks. It's a Hindu ritual. A very sacred—all right, it's not working," Lulu gives up when the clerk lifts the phone. "Let's go. Go go go."

They rush Isidore out the revolving door. Lulu is terrified. She has a perverse desire to needle Isidore, just to see what she might do. She opens her mouth, then shuts it.

"Just get her in the Airstream," River says through his

teeth. Luckily that appears to be where Isidore is headed, because neither one of them is willing to touch her, much less ask her to do something she's not already intent on.

"Ma'am," the hotel clerk cries. "Your package!"

Lulu runs back for the box, says thank you, and they're off.

Anson mutters a curse the moment he sees Isidore. Turning the steering wheel over to River, he grabs his knife and sheathes it in his waistband in case Isidore snaps. "Make sure we're not being followed. Head out of town," he commands. Lulu scrambles out of the way and Isidore goes straight to the back room. Anson takes a breath and follows her in.

"Here," he says, handing her a pair of jeans. Isidore doesn't look at him. She steps into them.

"Is that blood yours?"

Isidore nods.

"Where?"

It's a moment before she can answer. "Ankles," she says. Her voice is ragged.

"You still . . . super strong?"

"Don't know. Yes."

Isidore has never actually hurt him. Bloodied his lip, broke three ribs once. Nothing life-threatening. But the possibility has always been there. He bends to look at her wounds, but Isidore's voice stops him.

"Don't touch me."

From a crouch, Anson freezes and turns his eyes to his sister's face. "Ok," he says softly. The knife is for mild protection. He also has a loaded gun in his shoulder holster but is hoping it won't go that way. "In my pocket," he says. "I've got a bandage. I'm gonna hand it to you. For your ankles."

"Whiskey."

He jerks his chin. "Next to you."

She picks it up. She has such a hunger on her he imagines her smashing the neck against the cabinet to drink her own blood-tinged whiskey from a jagged glass edge. She unscrews the top and drinks long. Gasps. Drinks again. She takes a ragged breath and Anson can see her fighting with something.

Finally she nods.

"Ok. I'm not going to kill you now."

Anson is glad to hear it. "Is a little Neosporin going to change that?"

"Probably not."

He takes the first aid kit from the cupboard, pours bottled water over the lacerations and presses what is probably the only clean cloth in the camper over the wounds. She fumbles with the bandage but she's still shaking and it drops to the floor.

"I got it." Anson unrolls the bandage and wraps it around one ankle. "Achilles heel, huh," he says. "I wonder if you have one."

"What?" says Isidore. She is watching Anson, her own hands gripping the sheets for traction, something to keep her in this world. Her chest is still fluttering earthquakes across her ribcage. She caught a glimpse of her face in the mirror as she stumbled in and had to look away. She didn't recognize anything there.

"Have I always been—this bad?"

Anson glances up from her ankle. "You sure you're not going to kill me?"

"No," she says. "But like—sixty-five percent."

Anson toggles his head, considering the odds. "Well. As a baby, I mean, you couldn't break my neck. But don't go thinking you were normal. And once you hit two, it was pretty much minute-to-minute with the near death experiences."

"Are you trying to make me feel better?" she says.

"You're not getting worse," he says, securing the bandage and raising his gaze to her forehead, scanning for wounds. Isidore wipes blood from her eyes. "If that's what you're asking." He wets the cloth again and runs it across her hairline. Isidore regularly reminds herself that he could abandon her, to stay prepared for the worst. But the truth is, she's pretty sure he won't.

"Why can I do these things?"

Anson's eyes show deep exhaustion before he cocks a grin. "So the angels don't kill us all," he says. "Want some donuts?"

OUTSIDE AUSTIN
STILL TEXAS

LEAVING SAN ANTONIO feels like leaving a war-ravaged countryside. Lulu imagines the camera on her face, up close to register her conflicting emotions of sadness at what has passed and triumph at having overcome it, as she stares out the window at a smoldering landscape. Except it's only the endless suburbs of San Antonio, treeless and post-apocalyptic. The giant Cineplexes and Applebees make it hard for Lulu to feel her motivation. She tells herself that the day after tomorrow, she will leave as planned. She will go to her audition and let the three of them sort this out, this Dad mess, as they certainly always have. Lulu knows that she has to stay clear of their emotional messes if she is going to evolve as a person. She just doesn't seem to be able to. They are written all together, like a series. They don't make sense without each other, their plot lines are all tangled up, so none can ever be extracted from the others, not really. Lulu feels them like claws at her ankles, pulling her down into their dysfunctional mire. Which smells like canned green beans. Distance is her only hope. She has always known this.

Meanwhile Anson has other plans. Unlike his siblings,

he is aware of the fact that they almost died today, all of them. First by angels and then by Isidore. All right, so maybe Isidore's episode wasn't exactly dire, this time, but it wasn't good either. He can bandage her flesh wounds but not the ones that really matter. He will never have those answers, she will never have peace in the night. It's best not to think about it. Anson has a deep need to see something good, salt of the earth-good, some reminder that in America there exist families who sit down to roasted chicken dinners and don't almost kill each other, and for him that means Martha. He imagines what Martha might be like when she's mad. The fact that he's never seen her angry doesn't strike him as a problem. He can't imagine her swearing or shouting, and thinks that Martha might be one of those people who never gets mad, but disappointed. Still, he knows she'd never kill anybody. Not even by accident.

River listens to the scanner to see if police are searching for an Airstream, but the disturbance at the hotel is being blamed on a flock of seagulls and weakening building infrastructure. The feathers have thrown the law off the Camper tail once again. "We can probably turn around now," he says to Anson. "They're not on to us. Maybe we could get some lunch."

"Turn around? Are you crazy? We're not going back there."

River is confused. They came to San Antonio to look for their father. The prospect of seeing him fills River both with dread and a terrible urgency. It was one thing to hate his father for dying and leaving them like this, it is another entirely to hate him for being alive. The thought of seeing the man who had taught him, a sensitive boy with a knack for staying indoors, how to survive this life and then abandoned him to do it alone is weighted in so many emotions that River feels like he's drowning every time he tries to dwell on it. It makes him restive, makes him want to pull off his shirt, run outside, hit something. And hungry. River is so very hungry.

"But Dad--"

"Dad wasn't in San Antonio," says Anson. "Too many

tourists."

River is worried about Anson's reasoning, about all the myriad ramifications of every action they might take. He has always had the sense that they are writing the story, that every decision matters, that even the small ones will have consequences that they will be forced to suffer. Without permission his brain teases out every narrative thread and follows it to its worst possible conclusion, rendering him dizzy with terror, and what about Lulu? She's going to miss her audition, surely, and Isidore can't last long either way, no matter how many prayers she offers or rapists she slays. He can't speak any of this, he never does. Every thought rushes at once to his throat and creates a logjam, allowing nothing to come out. "Just a beer, Annie?" he says, weak under the pressure of everything pressing in. "Can we please just stop for a beer?"

"We have to get out of town," Anson says, certain as ever. "Those are the rules. Leave the location. Then comes beer." River has no strength to argue and after all, there is comfort in submission.

After sitting in traffic for two hours, River says, "Someone's following us." Off-handedly, so that at first Anson doesn't really hear it. He is wondering if he should hop on the 290 East, and keeping a wary eye on Isidore. He managed to coax her down off her carnage high with whiskey and black coffee and a sugary fried donut, but the attack has left them all feeling harrowed, the noisome scent of death still lingering in the air. Isidore is overly chatty in an attempt to compensate for the side of her everyone has just seen. Like if she rehashes enough new age affirmations they'll all forget death was wedded to her at her birthing. It is deeply embarrassing for her, to lose control of her world-ending impulses. "Tori Amos and I are on the same spiritual frequency," she says now, and Anson says, "Uh-huh," like he knows what that means.

"Shut up for a second, Isidore. Someone is following us." River is uncharacteristically persistent.

"Another Gabriel?" Anson says, still thinking about

the side roads. He doesn't like how long they've been sitting here. It's important to change locations fast. He didn't used worry about being ambushed in public, but the angels have grown unpredictable.

"No. A person."

Anson cranes to see the highway behind them in the big side view mirrors. It's not that he doesn't believe River, it's just hard to understand why a human would bother following them. Isidore perks up and searches with him. "Who?"

"Purple Mustang, four cars back."

"Man," Anson says. "What a douche." He's offended to be followed by someone driving this obscene vehicle. Like it cheapens them somehow.

"Yeah. They're good, whoever it is. They've been keeping a good distance. I just keep seeing that same car."

"Doesn't exactly blend in," says Anson.

"I've been seeing it since Las Cruces. And it passed us, on the way out of town. When we stopped for gas."

"Well there you go. It passed us, it can't be following us."

"But it's behind us again."

"Ok." Anson flexes his grip on the steering wheel. Obviously he is going to have to humor River before his mind can be his own again. "Why would a human be following us?"

"Maybe mom put a tail on us," says Isidore.

"You serious?"

"You know. Like that one time she told me the rat poison was candy. Only it didn't kill me, because I'm me."

"I'm sorry," Lulu calls from the back. "But I can't keep my mouth shut anymore. Rat poison, Isidore? What are you guys—you know what? Never mind. I don't want to know."

"Yeah that's right, Lulu," Anson calls. "You just sit back there in your fancy clothes showing us how functional you can be."

"I only have to be a little bit functional to beat you guys. You're nuts. You're all out of your minds."

"You're the one drunk on a Monday morning," River

162

says.

"It's called a collective hallucination," Lulu says, in her Lulu voice. Anson hears the whiskey bottle slosh. "I've looked it up." This has always been Lulu's coping method, pretending the dangers of their life aren't real but a story the other three made up. They let her have it.

"Good for you, Nancy Drew," says River.

"Maybe you're the one with the hallucinations, Lulu," Anson says. "You ever consider that? You're the one living in Hollywood, screwing some D-list writer, trying to be somebody—"

"Leave her alone," Isidore mutters. "I don't want us to die fighting."

"At least I'm trying," Lulu spits.

"What the hell is that supposed to mean?" Anson says to Lulu. To Isidore he says, "We're not going to die. Today."

"Can we all just calm down," says River. "Pull over and think?"

"I am calm," Anson says forcefully. "Think about what, our tail?"

"It's human," says Lulu. "Who gives a shit?"

"Because, Lulu," Anson says in his I am being very patient now voice, "Even if it's a human, a tail's a little weird, don't you think? Just because the thing following us is not supernatural doesn't mean it isn't dangerous."

"Yeah," Lulu says slowly, dragging it out, in her now I am being even more patient with you but I can't keep this up for very long voice. "But it's a human. What's the worst they can do to us? Cut us off? Fail to signal?"

Anson must admit this is a good question. It's hard to imagine any flesh-and-blood person doing real harm to the Campers, who have a Minigun in their roof and enough weapons to power the ragtag civilian armies of the post-Armageddon. Unless, of course, they're talking FBI. River occasionally gets drunk and hints darkly that he knows things they don't, that maybe the CIA is after them, or something even more covert. The CIA's CIA. A black ops unit operating out of an unsuspecting town like Sheboygan, Wisconsin. Holed up in a paper supplies building for cover, sitting up nights tracking the Campers.

"It's probably the brother of some pervert I've killed," Isidore mutters, her face toward the window so that Anson can't see if she's joking or not. "Seeking revenge." She does have an uncomfortable feeling about that purple Mustang. She considers telling Anson, but doesn't want him to know the way her lovers all blur together, a long and rapid-firing stream of abdominal muscles and sandalwood.

"Wouldn't that just figure," Lulu says darkly. "All this effort to save you from the angels, only to have you killed by some poor murder victim's grieving brother—or sister, in a catsuit, who's taken a secret identity to protect her dead brother's savant child—does someone have a pen?"

"Save it Lulu," Anson raises his voice and bangs the steering wheel.

"I thought you said writers were mole people," River says to Lulu even as he hands her a pen and a liquor store receipt to jot on. Lulu winces, suddenly self-conscious. She goes to the bathroom to write down her script idea in private while Anson rests his forehead on the steering wheel and lays on the horn. Not because it will get them anywhere. Just because it feels good.

WACO
TEXAS

IT'S ALMOST SEVEN by the time they pull into
Waco, edgy as the members of any weak-ruled cult. After Isidore goes Hulk they all go out and unless Isidore feels like harassing River, nobody mentions why. Lulu thumbs 'bar' into her
phone. The nearest turns out to be an old honky-tonk and sits
plum on the prairie quite proud of itself, nothing around for
miles but water towers and sky. Anson is grateful Isidore goes
for the kind of men found in bars, and that he doesn't have to
spend his evenings hanging out at art galleries or poetry read-
ings. Lulu declares that there better not be any fucking square
dancing. Anson says, you think I want to square dance? I look
like the kind of person who's into that? River says Annie, we
don't really know a thing about you, do we, and Anson swears
to end him the minute he gets the chance.

He parks the Airstream in the far reaches of the lot
and his siblings light out of the trailer without sparing him a
glance. They don't even ask for money, certain he'll follow
along and pick up the bill.

"Have fun," he calls. "Enjoy yourselves. Don't worry
about me." He still needs to shower, get cleaned up. River's
extended middle finger is the only reply he gets.

Lower back and thighs aching, Anson opens the door

to the commode and swears. It's filthy. Humid with water still clinging to the walls and shower door. Five or six wet towels on the floor; how the hell do three people ruin six towels? The mirror is dripping with perspiration, his siblings' essence wet and thick around him. He just knows they'll be out of hot water. Worked up into a good rage, he gathers up the towels and dumps them on the bed, spreading them out, where they'll leave it damp and cold. He doesn't know who will be sleeping there tonight, he only knows it won't be him.

After his shower he unplugs his cell and calls Martha. Isidore and River both have smart phones, he's still on a flip phone that has no internet access and sometimes shuts itself off when he's trying to send a text. It seems that every time Anson sets aside money for a new phone, somebody has always ruined a pair of jeans or is fresh out of ammo or wants a three-hundred dollar hotel room, and he hasn't been able to upgrade his own phone yet.

Martha answers on the first ring. "Are you okay?" Her voice is tense and aggressive. She doesn't even say hello, just this question that manages to sound more like an accusation.

"What? Yes. Are you okay?" Has she heard of the hotel attack? Has it been connected to them, is Anson's face being broadcast on TV like a Wanted poster?

"Sorry," Martha says, and she sighs with such pure relief and, Anson thinks, embarrassment, that he can't be angry anymore.

"What's wrong? Are you okay?"

"Me? Of course. I'm fine. I mean, I've been worried sick about you. But other than that."

"Why?" he asks, trying to figure out if she's worried because he hasn't called in a few days, or because he is now an official fugitive.

"I guess I'm overreacting—Mom says I'm overreacting. It's just, when I heard the news about San Antonio, and I knew you were headed there—"

"What news?" Anson says sharply. Oh God, oh God. There's going to be a manhunt, and Martha is going to betray him—she's probably wired right now—

"About the poodle flu. There was a huge outbreak. Like thirteen people have died. Or—have been hospitalized, or something. You seriously haven't heard about this? It's been all over the news."

Anson thinks the stress must be getting to him. It is not possible that Martha, with her good horse-sense and her old Protestant pragmatism, is in a tizzy over a dog cold. "I'm sorry—the what flu?"

"Poodle flu," she says impatiently. "They don't have vaccines for it yet—they say it'll be six months, at least, until they can make one. They didn't see this one coming. Thirteen people, calling in sick to work. Tragic."

"Poodle flu?" Anson repeats. Martha makes the sound. The thin exhale through the nose. She thinks he's being a wise guy, now. "I'm sorry, I'm not trying to be—I just can't be-lieve—" he tries hard to hide the laughter from his voice. "You're worried about a flu for poodles? I mean, when have I ever been near a poodle?"

"It isn't funny," Martha says.

"Well," he says. "It is kind of funny."

"No it's not," she protests lamely, laughing now too. "Anson. It's very serious."

"Poor poodles. Just little guys."

He smiles at her laugh. "Oh, jeez. It's just been all over the news and I guess I got. Swept up. It's just hard, you know. Anyway."

They talk for a while about things in Martha's life, a half marathon she's training to run and what's still growing in the garden. For a moment Anson fears he will be pressed to invent details about his last few days, but Martha doesn't ask. She doesn't ask much about him ever, really, which is a relief for anyone running a con.

"Hey," he says. "I should be up there. Couple days, at most."

"Yeah?"

"Yeah. Long as, you know. Nothing goes wrong."

"Long as you don't get the poodle influenza."

"Long as I don't get Influenza P."

They say that they love each other and get off the phone. Anson steps out of the trailer into the embracing heat of the Texas evening. Every time Anson leaves Texas, he forgets what a beauty it can be. They sky is electric blue with pink jellyfish clouds, and there is so much of it, shimmering in the lambent light. Music is throbbing from the honky-tonk, the pulse of the living earth.

He checks the safety and slips his gun into the holster around his waist, securing the piece at his lower back. Inside his boot is a knife. He considers bringing another gun, no doubt River and Isidore forgot theirs. But he figures he can at least count on Lulu to be packing, and anyway, it's a dance hall full of God-fearing people. The angels are unlikely to endanger their own. The incident at the hotel room just has him edgy.

The place is packed. He stands in the entry for a moment, scanning for his siblings, payday Texans raising a weekend ruckus on the floor. First he spots Isidore. From behind he can only see her white-blonde hair hanging down to her waist. She's sitting at the bar with a man on either side of her, clearly in her element. Isidore doesn't have to work for what she wants, she just plants herself at a bar and lets it come to her. There's a dance floor in the middle where people are, indeed, dancing in unison. Clapping their hands and slamming their boots under strings of gold lights. He spots Lulu sitting alone at a table in the back, in a dark corner that is not dark enough, as a wiry cowboy with tight jeans and a big white hat is leaning in toward her, beer in hand, smiling like he's God's gift and well-wrapped, too. He's not. If he'd stop looking at her breasts and look at her face, he'd probably get the hint.

In general, Anson finds, these things can be done more delicately than people believe. He starts toward the table. Lulu sees him coming and sends a sibling SOS signal, but he already knows she needs a rescue. It's subtle, in his shoulders, probably, but he makes it known that he will be coming in between the cowboy and Lulu's table, and the cowboy moves back, allowing him to pass. "Hey," Anson says short and flat, in the cowboy's direction but not actually to the cowboy. He takes the seat next to Lulu, glowering down at the table, and doesn't say anything.

"Thanks," Lulu says after a moment, and Anson knows the cowboy is gone.

"Was he prettier than you?"

"I'm not available," Lulu says.

"Right, " Anson nods. "But you're not talking about that." He catches the eye of a waitress in a red tank top and jean skirt. Cowboy boots. She holds eye contact for an uncomfortably long moment, making him wary.

"Howdy," she says. "You two movies stars or something?"

Anson frowns, confused as hell, while Lulu perks right up. "I—yes," Lulu says. "I'm an actress, yes."

"A real actress? Like, a Hollywood type?"

"Yeah," says Lulu, trying to play it cool. Anson lets Lu have her moment. He has the sad thought that this may be the first time she's been recognized in public, after eight years in Hollywood, and pushes it away.

"No way," the waitress says. She snaps a coaster down onto the table. "I mean, I thought so. We've been taking bets, me and the guys—"

"The guys?" Lulu says, glancing at Anson.

"The bartenders," the waitress says. "We don't get many Hollywood types in here. Not any, actually. What are you doing here, now you mention it?"

Lulu remains flattered but Anson's intuition is sounding a half-aroused alarm. Is it just him, or is this buxom waitress pressing them for information? She's being sly about it—which, he realizes, is probably a sign that his instincts are good. Someone who was merely curious wouldn't bother trying to come off subtle, would they?

"Family reunion," Lulu lies smoothly. "Real pain in the ass." Anson thinks that her delivery, for that last line in particular, is actually pretty good. Then it hits him.

"Can we get some drinks?" Anson says too roughly. Lulu kicks him under the table.

"What kinda movies you do?" The waitress says. "You ever do a movie with Bill Murray?"

She's asking about Bill Murray now? This is too weird. "Look, lady—" he says. Lulu cuts him off.

"I'm a television actress, actually," Lulu says. She straightens her back but Anson can tell this is a cross for her to bear. Poor Lulu. Another ten years, she'll probably have a reality TV show or a tantric sex-therapy practice.

"Oh!" It's clear the waitress is trying to hide her disappointment. "So then—then you don't know Bill Murray?"

This is too much and if Lulu thinks Anson is going to sit here pretending this is a normal question to ask a pathetic unknown TV star, she's wrong. "All right, lady," Anson growls, leaning in toward the waitress. "Who sent you here?"

"Oh no," sighs Lulu, slumping back in her seat. She smiles at the waitress apologetically.

"What?" the waitress steps back. Anson leans in, as intimidating as he can be without actually grabbing her. His hand has gone to his knife but Lulu clamps her fingers around his wrist, and he allows her to hold him there, for now. Lulu isn't any more surprised than she would be if Isidore was diagnosed with chlamydia or River relapsed and was found donut-eyed in a gutter. Anson is the direct result of testosterone combined with physical prowess and an overdeveloped sense of responsibility. A display like this was only a matter of time.

"Who sent you? Hmm? A Gabriel, or God himself?"

"A what?" the waitress cries. A few people around them have turned to look, but the music is too loud and the place too packed for there to be a real commotion. Yet.

"It's nothing, Annie," Lulu says. "She was just curious. Some people are."

"Why is she asking about Bill Murray now?" Anson says. "That seem normal to you?"

"I just really liked What About Bob," the waitress says tremulously.

"I'm very sorry," Lulu says. "He has a disorder. Todd, take your meds, honey. Did you take your meds?"

"Don't call me Todd," Anson growls. He hates it when Lulu calls him Todd, and she knows that. She fucking knows that.

"You see what I mean?" Lulu says, shaking her head. "I'm so sorry. I'm going to give him his meds now, he'll perk right up. Let's get a drink in him, he'll be right as rain."

A drink tray is dangling from the waitress's fingers and Anson considers grabbing it and breaking it over her head. Then we'll see, he thinks. Who we should trust and who we shouldn't. The waitress is eyeing him up and down. He doesn't like it. He starts to pull back his jacket so she can see the weapon strapped there, but Lulu stops him.

Anson thinks he is about to get kicked out, but the waitress has come to a different decision. "Will he dance with me?"

This stuns even Lulu, but only for a second. "I'm sure he would love to—"

Anson opens his mouth to protest and Lulu grabs the skin on his ribs and pinches, pinches hard, until he's practically rising in his seat with the effort not to cry out. "Could you just—could you bring us a couple drinks? Please? He'll be good. You'll be good. Won't you Todd?"

The waitress eyes Anson appraisingly. "I'll bring you some of the good tequila. On the house."

"Great," Lulu says. "Thank you. Thank you so much. I'm sorry I don't know Bill Murray."

"Well," the waitress says. "Not your fault, I guess."

Lulu doesn't release Anson's rib skin until the waitress has disappeared.

"Maybe next time I'll know Bill Murray," Anson says in his whiniest Lulu voice and slams his fist into her thigh.

"What the hell is the matter with you?" Lulu says. She aims a closed fist at his upper arm. He flexes in anticipation but it's a fake and she gets him in the ribs. It hurts. Damn sisters with tae kwon do training. "That is a cocktail waitress. Not an agent of the Lord."

"You never know who is a vessel for the wrath of God," Anson says with too much conviction. He takes a deep breath and attempts to get ahold of himself.

"Jesus," Lulu sighs. "This is just like that time you were sixteen and you pistol-whipped that guy for saying he liked Cole Porter."

"Nobody at sixteen actually likes Cole Porter," Anson erupts. "It was shady—"

"All right," Lulu says.

"You have to be careful—"

"All right," Lulu says again, holding her hands out flat over the table. "Let's just. Can we just?"

Anson takes a deep breath, rolls his shoulders, trying to release the weird energy. He is not usually like this, paranoid and confrontational. He doesn't think he's usually like this.

"Hey Lulu, can I get your autograph? Can I get your autograph, Lulu?" he says.

"Shut up." She says it like a good sport.

"It's not that you weren't famous enough for her," Anson said. "It's just 'cause you're ugly."

"Your Mom's a pilgrim whore," says Lulu. After a moment, another waitress drops off two Molson Golds and two shots of clear tequila with a little white ramekin of lime wedges. Anson ignores the lime. Lulu swipes it around the rim. They clink the glasses together and knock them back.

"Where's River?" Anson says, smacking his lips. Lulu sighs and jerks her chin toward a dark corner. River is next to the jukebox, his eyes closed, singing earnestly to "Faithfully" by Journey. Anson rubs his hands with his face. "Jesus Christ," he says. "I can't hear Journey without worrying he's going to relapse."

To Isidore, the room is full of opportunities. Cowboys are like chick flicks. There is one type, but many variations. One might make her laugh, another might make her feel inferior and disheveled. Her favorites are the ones who make her feel hopeful. The kind that end with tears and dopey smiles.

She is aware of all their exact positions. She always is. River is over by the jukebox thinking about the day she and Anson picked him up from prison, Anson and Lulu are in the corner commiserating. Isidore swills a rum and Coke too fast and gags. She hates rum and Cokes, wishes she could erase whatever stain makes men invariably buy them for her. She knows she looks classier than rum and cokes. The cowboy in the K-Mart bolo tie who sent her this one raises his glass at her from down the bar, his eyes full of pornographic intent. This man has no mind to ask for anything. Isidore holds the glass out over the bar like she's requesting another, then opens her fingers and drops it. "Oops," she mouths, her expression flat, before turning and apologizing to the bartender. She asks him for scotch, neat. She loves the caramel sweetness that follows the burn.

A good lover is hard to find, but Isidore has all night. Unless of course she dies. The siblings will eventually retire to Pacey under Anson's command, Isidore only knows she can't be with them. She's embarrassed of everything that happened this morning. The attack and her unfortunate slide into her otherworldly animus, her not-best self. It's difficult to look her brothers in the eyes and see their fear, even worse to look in Lulu's and see pity.

Isidore is sitting at the bar waiting to see who will buy her the next drink when a man approaches. He's not Texas, she can tell immediately, though she's not sure how. Maybe it's the skin, which is pale and smooth, or the belt buckle, which is a reasonable size. There is something alarming about his energy. Not like the men who attempt to rape her in bathrooms and parking lots, it's not nearly that dark. But it's different, still. Unlike the good cowboys, telling themselves they're just out for fun when really they're imagining slim-hipped wives in the shower on Sunday mornings. Unlike the bad cowboys, out to cause something pain.

He sits at the barstool next to her and Isidore ignores him. Looks at the barkeep and points to her glass for another.

She knows it's coming because he clears his throat, like clinking a glass before making a toast. "I will buy you an Appletini." His voice is thin, cadence clipped like this is a line he has rehearsed. His delivery is poor.

Isidore groans and lays her head on the bar. As if the order weren't bad enough—Appletinis, what is she, four? — but the way he's said it. Like Isidore's about to die and this single Appletini might save her life.

"No you won't," she says. She doesn't look at him, and the bartender brings her the scotch she ordered. She picks it up and stands to leave, and that is when she feels the unmistakable cold prick—of a knife—pressing into her side.

POOL TABLE
WACO

"HE'S WAVING A GUN at her now," Lulu says.

Anson turns to look. "Huh."

The redheaded elf-man has been harassing Isidore for some time. Sidling up too close to her, putting his hand on her ass and her thighs. Isidore's letting him, which is not the most pleasant thing for her siblings to witness. It was entertaining at first but then they got bored. They've all seen it before.

River glances over his shoulder. The crowd hasn't caught on yet, it's too loud, but off to the side of the bar a man is indeed brandishing a pistol at Isidore.

"Ex-lover?" River guesses. He was about to play some Meatloaf when Lulu came and dragged him here instead. She had said she "can't watch this anymore", but River knew she was just trying to cover for desiring his company, which she often did.

"Isidore doesn't have lovers. She has conquests," Lulu says. This is true of course, and it wounds River to be, as always, so out of sync with his siblings. He turns back to the billiards, where Anson is setting up his shot. "Six ball, corner pocket," he says. Anson makes the shot, then aims beyond his ability and misses. "Your turn," he says to River.

Lulu and Anson lean against the pool table, heads identically cocked to the right, watching Isidore. They can't see their sister's face, but the man with the gun is impressively pissed. He shouts something, his mouth flying wide, and Isidore flinches.

"Ew. Spit," says Lulu.

There is the satisfying sound of cue balls knocking together and then River says, "Dammit." He takes a long pull off his bottle of Shiner. River sucks at pool, but for anyone to point this out would be more than he could handle and he'd likely end up breaking a stick over someone's back or trying to turn the table over in rage, so no one mentions it.

"Tough shot," Lulu lies, and chalks her cue.

"What's he saying?" River asks Anson.

"I don't know," Anson says. "It looks like he's yelling, though."

"People are starting to freak. Oh man." The thought of what could ensue makes River start laughing.

"If we get killed in a stampede, I'm gonna kill her," says Lulu. She takes her shot, puts away two balls, and swears. She was going for three.

"You're up, Annie." She glances at Isidore. "That dude is seriously pissed, you guys."

Anson takes the cue but doesn't move. "What do you think she did?"

"Could be an angel," River says.

"Don't be an idiot. You ever seen an angel with red hair?"

"Just because I've never seen one doesn't mean they don't exist," River says.

The music stops in mid-song. There is a small creek of cowboy hats streaming toward the exit. Somebody screams. Lulu sighs and swears in resignation.

The Campers look on as a real scuffle begins. The redheaded man sees the ruckus he's raising and looks caught between panicked and pleased. Isidore's head is curved to the side, like she's confused, or maybe bored. Red seems encouraged by the panic. He cocks back the safety and levels the gun at Isidore's forehead point blank.

"Yep," says Anson. "He's gonna kill her."

"What do we do?" Lulu asks. Anson shakes his head and chugs his beer. His siblings take his cue and do the same. No one wants to waste the beer. It's on a tab. Anson wonders how he's going to settle the tab. Mayhem possibly followed by murder is about to break out and he can't return later for the card. They'll know, by then, that he had something to do with this. He'll be wanted in all fifty states and end up in prison after all.

"Excuse me," Anson says, wiping his mouth, and begins to fight through the crowd. The people around him are panicking. He smells urine. "Oh, come on," he mutters. "It's one skinny college boy with six rounds." Then he raises his voice. "You should get on the ground," he says. "Get down. That's right. Yep, hide behind the table, just like that. Nobody panic. Just stay down."

"Don't be a hero!" someone shouts. Anson turns around. River and Lulu are smirking.

"Fuck off," he shouts at them, causing the poor woman next to him to startle and spill her beer into her orange cleavage. "Sorry," he says. "Not you."

As he pushes past Isidore and the ginger, he hears some of what is being said. It's typical nonsense. He thought they had a connection, but she's just a whore, isn't she. And now she's going to pay. Pay for her dirty whore sins. This gets old. God himself wanting to kill you for your sins really takes the thrill out of a religious zealot. "Excuse me," he says, leaning far over the bar. The place is clearing fast. The bartender has mascara running down her cheeks and now she thrusts her hands into the air, like this is a stick up.

"No, no," says Anson. "I just want my check. My check? We started a tab." He mimes writing in the air. Isidore looks like she can't decide if she wants to end this now or let it go on because rarely is life so entertaining.

"Um," the bartender's eyes dart nervously. "What

name?"

"Shirley," he says, figuring Isidore opened the tab. "Anne Shirley."

"One moment, please," says the waitress. As she rises to a crouch before the register, a shot explodes and nobody remembers to stay calm. People scream, wetting their pants and running toward the exit, crushing each other along the way. Everyone heads for the front doors, putting themselves closer to Red and the gun even though there are at least three emergency exits. Anson is forced hard against the counter. Red shoots the ceiling again and Anson gives up on the tab to go hurry Isidore.

"Is? What do you say we wrap this up?"

"I can't kill him," she hisses. "There are security cameras everywhere."

Anson hasn't thought of this, and he realizes now how deeply this guy has screwed them. There are probably cameras in the parking lot too, which will capture the four of them heading for the Airstream, which Anson parked within camera range, even though he knows better. Isidore's not the one wielding a gun, but she's the one it's being wielded at, and once they spot her on video the cops are going to want to talk to her.

"Are you one of them?" says Red. He's got the gun on Anson now, which isn't a great feeling, though Anson's lived through worse. "Are you sleeping with her too?"

"No. I'm her brother. Why does everyone keep saying that? Who is this guy?"

"We did it. Back in Las Cruces, I guess."

"You guess?"

Isidore shrugs. "I don't really remember. It's possible."

"This guy? This is who you memory-wiped me for?" Anson remembers Lulu laughing. Something about Prince Harry.

"There were a few. In Las Cruces. There's something about that place."

"She doesn't even remember," says Red. Anson wonders why the hell Isidore picked this one. Then realization dawns.

"This is our tail, Is."

"No way."

"Yeah. He's been following us ever since your seven minutes in heaven at the Backwater Motel."

"It was more than seven," the ginger says wildly.

"All right," Anson says low to Isidore. "Look, we gotta get outta here."

"What does it look like I'm doing?" Isidore snaps.

"It looks like you and this guy have settled in for the night, actually," Anson says. "You might as well be in a trailer home with a case of Pabst."

River and Lulu arrive behind them. River takes up two abandoned, almost-full beers from the bar and hands one to Lulu. "Who are these people?" says Red. "Get them out of here, bitch, or I swear, I'll—"

"Hi," River says, offering a hand. "I'm River. You are?"

The guy stares at River for a moment, then fires another round into the ceiling. It hits a light, sparks shower down over their heads. That's three, Anson counts. It's a six-shooter he's waving. He only has three more rounds, and Anson would bet he doesn't know it.

"Ok," River says. "Well, anyway. This, I guess you know, is Isidore and yeah, she can be a real pain in the ass. I mean, you wanna shoot her, man, I get that. You wanna see her knocked to floor and watch her bleed out. Watch her die. Her little eyes going all fluttery and then blank. Yeah? Am I right? But see, here's the thing. Isidore's carrying a gun. Aren't you Isidore?"

"Yep," Isidore says.

Anson sighs. He's not in the mood to do this the long way tonight. He's hungry. Twenty minutes ago he ordered mozzarella sticks. He glances toward the kitchen. They still haven't arrived.

"And you know what? So am I. And so is she. And so

is he. That's four of us, dude. Four of us, packing heat. Between us? We've got about forty rounds. Maybe more. Maybe less. I don't know. Is, you brought your Colt tonight?"

"Brought my Glock," Is says.

"She brought her Glock. So yeah, we're in the neighborhood of sixty. Now—I'm sorry, I didn't get your name—"

"I think it was Wes," Isidore says. "Or—Chard? Something stupid like that."

"Wes," River says. "We'll go with Wes. Don't worry, man, I'm not gonna call you Chard. Now Wes. Do you happen to know how many rounds you have left in that six-shooter there? That's right. The one you're waving in the air. Hmm?"

Chard's eyes are wide, he's breathing hard. The saloon is practically empty, except for a few idiots crouching behind tables or vomiting in corners. "This woman," he says. "Belongs to me."

"Okay. Okay Wes. We get that." River's tone is soothing, but somehow River is not soothing. At all. Chard swallows hard.

"I don't want any other man to touch her. I want to watch her sleep. I want to take the engine out of her car so she can't go see anyone, anyone else. I want her to be with me all the time."

"Awww," says Lulu. Anson's sure she's joking. Of course she's joking.

"You sure about that?" says River skeptically. Isidore is offended and elbows him in the ribs.

"I want to buy her tiny shoes. Tiny little shoes, so she can't walk very fast. And then I can always make sure she's here with me. And she can't go anywhere without me, because, oh no! Look. I'm in my tiny little shoes." He makes a strange prancing motion. It's unsettling.

"Ok. That's weird," River says. "I mean, I was expecting weird but you just exceeded expectations."

"So delicate," Chard says, licking his lips.

"Think about it, Wes," says River. "That's a six-shooter. You've fired three rounds. Six minus three is?"

"I am the lion and she is the lamb!" Chard aims the gun at Isidore, and fires again.

"Holy shit!" says Lulu. Her shock enrages Anson. Like up until now, she'd been thinking this was going to go well? Isidore ducks. The bullet grazes her hair.

"All right," says Isidore. "That's enough. I mean, the shoe thing is sweet, but watching me sleep? That's creepy. Where did you read that, Stephen King?" Isidore is not a fan of Stephen King. Her life is scary enough. She pulls back her arm and is about to drive her palm into his nose from beneath, forcing the bone up into his brain, when Anson catches on. "Whoa, whoa, whoa!" he says. He grabs her arm and manages to force it downward before she has a chance to kill the guy.

"Oh, come on," Isidore cries. "Why not?"

"Do you want to be wanted for murder?"

"Why the hell not?" says Isidore. "If I can dodge God, I think I can dodge the Waco P.D."

Chard has the sense to look afraid. River pats his shoulder and shushes him. "It's all right, man. We won't let her hurt you."

"We should go," Lulu says. "Cops'll be here sooner or later."

"We can't just leave him here alive," Isidore says. "He followed us from Las Cruces. I don't want him following me everywhere, it's freaky."

River shrugs. "Could you pretend it's romantic?"

Lulu begins to laugh. Chard raises the gun again and Anson throws his elbow up, into Chard's face, and then brings his arm down over Chard's and twists, knocking the gun so it goes flying. Chard bends forward in attempt to stop his elbow from twisting too far and cracking apart.

"I'm sorry," Chard says. Fat slug tears slime lines down his face. "I'm sorry. I just want her to be with me forever."

"Jeez, Isidore, what did you do to him?" Lulu says.

"That thing where I—" her hands go to her breasts.

"Shut up," River orders. "Knock him out, man, we gotta go."

"How?" Anson says. "I'm not sure I can do it without killing him." It's never really been his goal to hurt something only a little.

"Here," Lulu says. She has seen this in the movies. She picks up a beer bottle from the counter and slams it down over the ginger man's head.

"Ow!" Chard protests. The bottle doesn't break.

"Great," Isidore says. "Now what?"

I-35 EAST
OUTSIDE WACO

"THIS IS A BAD IDEA," Lulu says. "This is the worst idea maybe ever."

"Shut up!" Anson cries, and pounds the steering wheel. "Shut up, Lulu, shut up!"

His anger frightens Isidore. To lighten the mood, River leans forward and pounds the dashboard hard with two fists. "Everyone remain calm!" he shouts. It is a perfect imitation of Anson. For some reason he is at his best when Anson is moments from losing it.

It works. Isidore forgets how frightening Anson can be when he's angry and remembers how fun it is to tease him. She pounds her fists against the cockpit floor, where she is sitting cross-legged between the two seats. "Nobody panic! I'm not yelling! Do you want to hear me yell?"

She and River are laughing now, which annoys Anson because they are in an emergency, and Lulu because she doesn't like to see them bonding.

"Maybe we should get off the highway, Annie? Try to hide ourselves or something?" she says dully. Lulu doesn't know what's wrong with her, that she has left her little dollhouse in L.A. for this. She thinks maybe she has issues with self-sabotage, or codependency on these parasite people who

183

have latched their angel-bait fangs into her neatly toned upper arms and refuse to let go. She pulls out her phone to text a friend for the name of her life coach.

"They're not going to be after us," Anson says. The crowd had been gathered in the front, consoling each other. Anson had led his siblings out an emergency exit and they'd looped to the Airstream from behind. "No one saw us leave. They're going to be looking for him."

"Who are you people?" Chard whines through his gag, which is pressing on his tongue and it comes out more like, "Who-aah-ooo-eel?"

"Shut up!" Lulu and Anson snap simultaneously.

"What are we going to do with him?" Isidore says. They've tied Chard facing the rear of the cabin so he can't see Isidore. His eyes like palms on her were making everyone sick.

"We'll dump him off the side of the road somewhere. Then we'll go where we're going, to the place he doesn't know we're going, and he won't be able to follow and maybe he'll even get arrested and tell the cops about us and then they'll know he's crazy."

"You 'oin 'uh 'ul-ha," Chard says.

"What?" says Anson. "What did he say? Lulu?"

Lulu leans down and rips the gag out of Chard's mouth She uses her nails because she is feeling fierce. She feels like she might be on the verge of a breakdown, which at this point could only help her career. She decides to hire a publicist. "What did you say, you little asshat?"

"You're going to Tulsa. To see his girlfriend. She told me."

"Goddammit, Isidore!" Anson yells, and pounds the steering wheel again.

Isidore flinches. "I didn't know! Guys sleep with me all the time, how was I supposed to know this one was a nut job?"

"Because he slept with you?" River says.

Anson reaches out wildly to punch River, who is just out of his reach. He pitches too far and the Airstream sways. Lulu makes a strangled noise in her throat. "Should you really be the one driving?" A breakdown is one thing. Facial disfigurement is another.

"If we're gonna dump him, we gotta do it now," River says. "We'll hit the suburbs soon."

He's right. They are speeding toward Dallas and they need to lose Chard before they get there; even in this state Anson can see that. He takes a deep breath,

"Isidore," he says. She stands up. "One—two—three." He slides over and she slides in, taking the wheel, but not before the Airstream sways again, dangerously close to the sloped median.

"Not our best," Isidore says.

"Not our best. Pull over as soon as you can."

Anson moves back into the cabin and goes to Chard. Yes, his hair is red, but he has a good head of it. A lot of men would be jealous of that thick hair. He glances up at Lulu.

"How are we going to do this?" she says. Lulu means business. Anson would never admit it, but out of all his siblings, he finds her the scariest. He could always tell when River was about to lose it, when he might quit messing around and take a real swing. With Lulu, you'd never know. She'd glitterface you, wait for you to sleep, then creep into your room with a screwdriver without thinking twice.

"Frisk him for weapons," Anson orders.

Lulu pulls back, crosses her arms righteously across her chest. "I can't do that. I'm a Mormon," she says, but Anson is teasing her. He takes a deep breath and performs the unpleasant task himself, prodding Chard under the arms and around his calves and ankles before, grimacing, briskly checking his thighs and groin area to make sure he can't put a knife in their backs.

"Get a room," says River.

"Shut it," Anson says. Isidore is pulling over, tapping the brake and jerking them all back and forth like she always does. For a minute Anson is sure she's going to turn the Airstream over into the ditch along the road. His belly rises up into his throat, but then the sway straightens out and they stop on solid ground, tilted to an unnerving degree.

"All right," Anson says. "This is how it's going to go-"

"Annie," Lulu cries. "For Chrissake. Come around this side. He's. . . ogling me."

Anson sighs but assents, moving around the chair they've stolen and strapped Chard into, putting himself in between Chard and Lulu's rack. He drops the act because he's exhausted. He is weary of this life the way he imagines sea captains tire of the sea. "We're gonna push you out the front door and drive away. And you're not going to put up a fight, because if you do, we're going to kill you. There's no one to see it now. Got it?"

"I won't stop following her," Chard says.

Anson is stunned into pity. "You on a suicide mission, here, man? You got someone you can call?"

"I know what she is," Chard hisses.

"What?"

"I know what she is. Your sister. Isidore."

This is it, Anson thinks. The climax. Everything has lead them here, to this moment, to this strange little Rumpelstiltskin man with whom his sister has indulged her evenings, who will turn out to be her true demon lover or a vengeful prophet of God. Here, on the side of a lonely highway in Texas.

Isidore cuts the engine. "Don't cut the engine," Anson yells. She starts it again. "Hurry up," Isidore calls. "I am starting to have regrets about this choice."

"What is she?" Anson asks. He's holding his breath.

The man's eyes are alight with something. It could be holy fire. It's hard to tell, they're a very pale blue. "She is Jezebel."

"Preach it, brother," says River.

"Shut up." Isidore sounds wounded. "Man, I was good to you. I think."

"All right," Anson sighs, frustrated mostly with himself for falling for it. "All right."

Chard's eyes are ecstatic like a preacher's at confession. "She's a demon-whore—"

"Yeah yeah. We know, Let's go, buddy." Anson and River kneel to cut the bindings.

"Maybe he's right," Isidore says. It's not as if the thought has never occurred to her.

"You're not a demon," Anson says. He can't have her going down this road right now. "But you are a whore."

"Maybe Mom was a succubus," says Isidore. She looked it up after watching an episode of South Park. If her mother was indeed a succubus, that would make Isidore a Cambion. Half human, half demon. All hot.

"Shut up you idiot," hisses Lulu. "If Mom was a succubus, we'd all be demons. And we're not. It's just you. Shit," she says, when she sees the look on Isidore's face. "I didn't mean it like that. Come on, Isidore. I'm a little distracted here."

They get Chard loose and jerk him to his feet. Anson hears the click of a safety and figures it's Lulu backing him up. He's going to dump this kid out the front door and then he's driving to Tulsa to see his girlfriend and maybe take her for sushi, dammit. They don't like sushi, either of them, but it feels like something people should do. Anson drags Chard toward the door and the heat meter goes off. Oh when the saints. Go marching in. Oh when the saints go marching in.

"No way," says Lulu. Isidore apologizes rapidly.

"All right, let's move, let's move," Anson says, shoving Isidore's stalker forward. Chard stumbles. Something slams into the side of the Airstream, pitching it in the direction it's already leaning, on the side of the highway. The driver's side wheels lift and slam back to the ground.

In his panic, Chard's facial muscles strain open like an alien is trying to break through his skin. "What's happening?" he cries. "Guys? What's happening?"

"You're getting your ass off this trailer, now," Anson says, pushing. Chard digs his heels in. He is whining don't do this to me, man, come on guys, over and over again, like Anson is his drinking buddy. River yanks him toward the door. The Airstream pitches again. Forward this time, like they've been rear-ended by a semi. The Camper's know they haven't.

"We gotta move," Isidore says. While she has always feared causing their deaths, she never imagined her sexual proclivities would be to blame.

Anson shouts for them to hurry and the angels body-check the trailer. The force throws Anson sideways and his forehead hits the sharp edge of the overhead storage. He grunts in pain. Lulu hears Anson grunt and mistakenly assumes Chard has struck him. Chard lurches, River stumbles, Chard appears to reach for Anson's gun and Lulu's had enough. She trains her gun on the hostage and before he can get his hands on Anson's weapon, she shoots. Outside, Gabriels rush the trailer and it pitches at the moment of gunfire. River screams in pain.

"Son of a bitch! Son of a bitch! What the hell!"

Lulu has shot him.

She hurries to River, catching him sort of, as he slides toward the ground. A velvety flower of blood opens in the region of his armpit, and Lulu backs away. She doesn't have another clean outfit. Anson pistol-whips Chard, who crumples to the ground, unconscious. Isidore gathers Chard's ankles and together they pitch him out the front door. He lands with a thump in the dirt, rolling a few times away from the highway and into the drainage ditch, everything yellowed by the highway lights. Gabriels hover in every direction. Anson slams the door and shouts at Isidore to drive.

"She shot me! She fucking shot me!" River is wailing.

"Would you shut up? I didn't mean to!" Lulu calls over her shoulder. She has opened the hatch and hauls herself up to the Minigun. River is bleeding everywhere and Lulu is cursing mightily. Speeding recklessly down the highway, Isidore is inexplicably half-sobbing, half-shouting, "Minxy! Miiinxy!"

"All right man, lemme see, lemme see," Anson says, ripping off River's jacket, looking for the source of the ridiculous amount of blood soaking his brother's clothes. "Where are you hit?"

"I don't know," River says, which worries Anson.

What does he mean, he doesn't know? He can't be losing consciousness. He doesn't look that pale. He's red, actually, with the righteous indignation of being shot by his sister.

"Where does it—here. It's your shoulder, man. Just your shoulder. Hold on."

"Minxy!" cries Isidore. "Miiiiiink-say!"

"Why'd she shoot me? Why'd she shoot me, Lulu!"

"Don't talk," Anson says. Not because he's worried about River over-exerting himself, but because he cannot take one more voice screaming at him right now. Isidore is swerving and flooring the gas like she thinks this is a video game and not a flight for life. Lulu has gone full-on blood lust and is hanging out the roof, screaming battle cries and wielding the machine gun.

"I think I'm gonna die, man. I can tell I'm gonna die."

"Then die now before I get so sick of hearing you whine about it I kill you myself," Anson says. He takes River's jacket, pulls River forward to get it under him, and ties a tight tourniquet over the wound. River hisses through his teeth.

"You're going to be fine," Anson says.

"You're just telling me that because—"

"These are our last moments together!" sobs Isidore.

"Would you fucking pull it together?" Anson snaps. "Come on, Is. Everyone is losing it on me. You can't too."

"I'm not losing it," screams Lulu, who has somehow heard them over the noise of the highway and the angels. "If you haven't noticed, I'm the only one killing any of your Goddammed Gabriels!"

Isidore slides open the driver's side window, which is screenless for this very reason, aims her Glock with her left arm while steering with her right, and fires away.

"I gotta move you," Anson tells River. "Sorry." River groans but allows Anson to haul him up and sit him on the floor against the sofa, where hopefully he'll be out of the direct line of fire. Anson returns to the navigator seat, opens the passenger side window, and fires at the field of Gabriels encroaching like zombies or Black Friday shoppers.

"Think I should pull over?" Isidore says. "Collateral damage could get pretty high." She is thinking about all the people they could kill, engaged in combat here in the middle of the highway. She doesn't want to be responsible for any deaths other than the inevitable ones.

"Where are we?" asks Anson. He can see lights ahead, he thinks, between the Gabriels. "That Dallas? They'll take off if we hit Dallas." He hopes they will, anyway. Other than their hotel room blitz, they have always avoided big cities and he needs this to continue.

"Don't think so," says Is. "Too soon. Isn't there something before Dallas? Hootenanny, or something. Some funny name."

Lulu fires the Minigun again, and the Gabriels fall back even further. River groans.

"How you doing?" Anson calls to him.

"I'm losing a lot of blood, dude. I don't feel good."

Anson doesn't speak, but something inside him clenches and doesn't let go.

"We gotta get him to a hospital," says Isidore.

"I know." Anson fires at a Gabriel gone brave, a rapidly advancing blur of white in the streetlights.

"Listen," Isidore says. "If they don't pull away once we hit—Whattahoochie—I'll just drive us to the hospital—"

"Is—"

"Shut up. Once you're outta the way, I can do my thing."

"I thought you couldn't do that on purpose."

"What do you know?" Isidore says. Anson thinks she's bluffing, but he doesn't ask. It's almost a good feeling, soaring down the highway with the wind in their hair, the starry sky above, fluttering and feathered celestial beings hovering in front of their old trailer, trying to kill them. Anson and Isidore pull off rounds into the flock, mercifully encountering no other cars, throwing down one weapon for another when they run out. There's a pleasure in doing what one is good at, trained for, even if it does involve violence and near-death experiences. Anson turns up the radio. "Here," Isidore says, handing him her phone. "I'll hold them off. Google map the hospital."

"I don't know how to use this thing." Anson has to shout.

Isidore looks down. "Slide to unlock, Annie! How hard is that. Don't stab it. Jesus. Treat it like a woman."

"Maybe I am!" Anson shouts.

Isidore fires into the night, glancing between the phone and the highway. "Maps. See the icon—maps!"

"Apps?"

"Maps!" Isidore says, frustrated, before she realizes he's playing with her. "Shit. Look at this."

Anson's eyes dart up. "Dammit. Lulu!" he shouts. The angels are drawing in. They seem to be increasing in number, multiplying or collecting like assholes on the internet.

"I got it!" Lulu screams. There is something disturbingly raw and wild in her voice. The carefully constructed Lulu is slipping.

"We're all gonna die," says Isidore. She's serious. Anson does not disagree. There seem to be hundreds of them, maybe—Anson doesn't want to even think it, but maybe thousands. There is no way they can fend off this many if Isidore doesn't do her thing. "Do your thing, do your thing!" Anson urges. He's planning on Martha and the sushi.

"I can't! I was bluffing!"

"I knew it," Anson says. "Never lie in combat situations!"

"Guys," River moans. "You gotta hurry." His voice is weak.

"Shit shit shit," says Isidore. Then she looks at Anson. "Oh. Oh my god. I'm so dumb—we're so dumb—"

Anson thrusts the phone back at Isidore. "On three," he says.

"One," says Isidore. "Two, three."

On three they stand. Isidore drops back and Anson slides over. It's a smooth transition. The Airstream doesn't sway at all.

"Man," says Isidore. "That was a good one."

"River," Anson says.

"Right." Isidore kneels down by River. She needs to do this fast. She doesn't know what kind of damage Lulu is capable of doing anymore, out of practice as she is, and she needs to get back to Anson to keep the angels at bay.

"Is," River groans.

"Hold on," she says. She puts one hand on River's shoulder, clutching her phone in the other. They hit a bump and it throws her into him. River groans in agony.

"What the hell—"

"Shit! Sorry!"

"Isidore!" Anson bellows from the front.

"Just a goddamn minute," she says. She needs to be calm to do this. She's never sure if she's going to heal them or kill them.

"Is," River says weakly. He is gazing up into her eyes and smiling now, which worries Isidore. "Is. You're gonna fix me, aren't you? Sweet sister. Gonna fix me right up."

"Shut. The hell. Up," Isidore says. She channels the energy that sits, always, like a hot coal in her belly and coaxes it up to her chest. Placing her hand on River's wound, she prepares to send it down into his flesh, where somehow—she has no idea how—this warmth will knit him back together. She takes a deep breath and sends the energy down.

"Shit!" Anson cries. The Airstream swerves. Heat like a glowing poker sears into Isidore's palm and she drops the phone.

"Did it work?" River says. He's still bleeding.

"Goddammit!" Isidore cries. "Goddammit!"

"What? Isidore? What the hell?" Anson is shouting.

Laying on the ground at Isidore's knees is a vaguely rectangular-shaped hunk of melting glass and steel. It looks like the Terminator burned in molten lava. It's going to stain the carpet.

"You swerved! You fucking swerved!" Isidore is nearly hysterical. Tears flood her eyes. She has gotten River shot and now she has failed to heal him. River is gazing up at her with his dopey eyes and it reminds her of his bad years.

"Isidore," Anson says in his warning tone, still clueless.

"I blew my load!" Isidore admits, pathetic. "I blew my load on the phone."

Annie says fuck and bangs the steering wheel. "Do it again," he orders.

"I can't. It's like an orgasm. It has to build back up."

"Isidore?" River says. He is childlike in his race toward death. "Sweet Isidore?"

Isidore can think of nothing else to do. She takes River's head in her hands and presses it toward her breasts. She begins to sing. "Ol' Man River", a song from an old musical she once saw at Grandma Ruth's house, Grandpa wouldn't ever let them watch anything else. She sings about River being an old man, and knowing nothing, and growing all wrong. She may or may not know the words.

River must be dying. Anson can comprehend no other explanation for Isidore's funereal intoning. Tears form in his eyes. He sings along. Powerfully in his smooth baritone. If they are going to lose River, they can send him off right, dammit. He belts out the chorus with feeling.

"You guys are the best brothers ever," River wails. "Oh God, Isidore."

Anson has started on another verse. Something about River eating taters that are probably rotten. "Oh Jesus," he says, and slams on the brakes.

The Gabriels have shot up into the sky like bottle rockets all lit off at once. Anson expects an ambush, imagines the angels will hurl themselves into his windscreen again. Last time that happened, he almost died. He takes a quick glance in the sideview, puts the Airstream into reverse.

Lulu screams a triumph followed by an ecstatic stream of curses. "Take that mother fuckers! You little assholes! Take that you fucking holy rollers!" Her screaming reminds Isidore of when they were young. Most of the time, Lulu seemed to be biding her time until she could be somewhere else. But sometimes, on shopping day or TGIF, Lulu would be insanely, in-fectiously giddy. And she'd sound just like this.

"Lu?" Anson says, foot hovering over the gas pedal. "What we got?"

"They're gone," she says, and Anson puts the Air-stream back in drive and starts forward.

"Is," River says, gripping her arm. "Don't stop sing-ing." Isidore tries to start again, but Lulu is climbing down from the hatch, screaming victorious. "Did you see that? It worked. I can't believe it fucking worked!" She shimmies her hips, her elbows bent out at funny angles. She looks like a Val-kyrie trying out for the cheerleading squad.

"What worked?" Anson says. Isidore grabs a bottle of water and presses it to River's lips. She slaps his cheek. "Hey! Come on, Riv. Eyes open."

"You know that TV show, about the people who have thirty-two kids?" says Lulu.

"What?" says Anson.

"They've got all these kids and they're like, really con-servative. Christian, you know."

"So?" says Isidore, slapping River absentmindedly. Has she changed the subject entirely? It's possible, with Lulu.

"So they have all these rules, about bodies and stuff. The girls can't show their arms above the elbows, or whatever, and if they see a girl coming who's showing her knees, they have this code word they say and all the boys look away. So they won't be—disenfranchised, or something. Dismembered. They have some word for it. So they boys won't be sent to hell for seeing a woman's knees and liking it, you know."

"Lulu," Anson says, a warning.

"That is such bullshit—" starts Isidore, but Lulu cuts her off.

"So they must be God's type, you know, those guys. And I figured your boyfriends—"

"They're not my boyfriends."

"—would be too. They wouldn't want to be disenfran-chised either."

"That can't possibly be the right word," River mutters. Anson fears they'll be his last.

"It's not. I can't think of the word. It's a funny word."

"So what did you do?" Isidore says.

Lulu grins. "I flashed them."

There is a moment of stunned silence, and then Isidore tries to wail a victory cry. It comes out all wrong, Isidore is all wrong, and at any other time the Camper siblings would feel embarrassed for her, howling like an orangutan in estrus, for crying out loud.

"You mean you actually—flashed—"

"I showed my boobies to the angels," Lulu says. "And the angels, they did flee."

"You must have," River draws a ragged breath. "A really awful rack."

"Shut up," Lulu says lightly. "They fled because they didn't want my beautiful body—my fantastic fucking body—to give them dirty, dirty thoughts."

Anson starts to laugh and shake his head. "Oh my god," he says.

"Exactly," says Isidore.

TEXAS

TO AN OUTSIDER it might have appeared that the Camper's didn't give River's situation the consideration it was due. Screaming and dancing with unchecked joy while their brother reviewed the best hits reel of his own life: moments of frenzied groping in basements and the sight of the Airstream arriving outside the prison gates where he was unceremoniously dumped on a hot summer day. But really, while Lulu was telling them about God's favorite family and prancing like a polio-stricken whore, she was also finding directions to the hospital on her phone. They pull up to the emergency room door and Isidore lays on the horn while Lulu and Anson get River out of the camper. The triage nurses put him onto a stretcher and wheel him through the doors. To Isidore's dismay, Anson follows them rather than returning to the Airstream to help her park it.

Parking Pacey proves an ordeal so trying, Isidore thinks she'd rather fight four Gabriels. The waiting room where she finally finds Anson is dimly lit, more appropriate for romantic dinners than waiting on news of life or death. In the corner, a teenager with heavy eyeliner and marshmallow-plump neon tennis shoes is pushing a fussing toddler back and forth in a stroller. The only other person there is a very obese man with an oxygen tank and tubes in his nostrils. He has his eyes closed and is breathing noisily. Two televisions show live coverage of a tsunami that hit the Puget sound while the Campers were dancing honky-tonk. A cell phone video shows people trapped in the Space Needle, where they are dining on Dungeness crab and awaiting rescue. This has replaced the twenty-four hour coverage of the Poodle flu and the weird thing in Namibia, where hundreds of African elephants simultaneously and inexplicably dropped dead. Isidore sits next to her brother on chairs upholstered scratchy like Grandma Ruth's house.

"The world's coming to an end," she says quietly.

Anson glances up at the screen. "Probably". He needs a shave. His eyes are empty and flat. Isidore doesn't think she's ever noticed the lines around them until now. She's unnerved by how weary he seems. Like maybe he is a floaty toy that can't be reflated. Maybe he has torn an irreparable hole.

"How's Riv?"

"They patched him right up. Had to give him a blood transfusion."

"Jesus," Isidore says, almost a prayer.

"Yeah. He's gonna be okay though. Just needs to rest. Lulu's with him. Says she'll do it again, if they get heat."

"Do what?"

"You know." Anson mimes, moves his hands to the bottom of his shirt, then up to his chest. "Free the twins. River made her promise to warn him so he can close his eyes."

Silently, Isidore asks Jesus yet again what she's done to piss off his dad. She wants to know so she can stop doing it. Is it the sex? She can't believe he'd really care about that, but she tells him that if he does, she'll quit. She thinks she can quit. "I don't want to lose River because I can't stop having sex," she murmurs.

"What?" says Anson. Isidore shakes her head.

"You hungry?" Anson says. He reaches for his wallet. "There's machines."

"I'm not hungry."

"Coffee?"

"Stop," she says. She doesn't deserve to be worried

over.

"I'm hungry," Anson says. "They never brought my mozzarella sticks."

"You want me to go," Isidore begins.

"Maybe we should both go. Bring something back. It could be awhile."

"Let's go, then," Isidore says."Lulu'll be hungry too." But neither one of them moves. They are showing terrible footage on the news. Someone on high ground, a shaky camera. The water rising and rising, unexpected debris—huge logs and garden sheds—swept up in it. A dog swims by, holding his head eagerly above water. Isidore turns away.

"What was your deal, back there?" Anson says. The dog has reminded him. "I thought I was gonna have to knock you out, for a minute. Pull an Aunt Nell." There is a famous story about their father's Aunt Nell. It begins with a garter snake and ends with Nell knocking their father out to save him from his own hot panic.

"Nothing," says Isidore.

"Okay," Anson says, relieved to be spared a heart-to-heart.

"It was Minxy," she says. "Thinking of Minxy. And how, if Minxy dies, before Dad gets to see her—and if Lulu accidentally killed River—it's all. You know. Because of me. I just couldn't handle it all for a minute. I'm sorry."

"If Minxy dies before Dad gets to see her, it's because Dad's an ass who abandoned his family," says Anson. His father has done something he could never, in a million years, even conceive of doing and he's worried that if he actually claps eyes on the old bastard, he won't be able to stop himself from shooting him. Not to kill, maybe not to kill, but through the kneecap at least.

"I keep asking him. To tell me what I did wrong."

Anson thinks he's too hungry. He doesn't comprehend. "Asking who?" Has she been talking to Dad, too? How mystifying, to be related to these people. People who speak over telephone to their long-dead father and don't find it worth

198

mentioning.

"Jesus," Isidore says. "I ask him all the time. I think I at least deserve to know. What I did to deserve all this."

Anson is absolutely apoplectic. There is sharp pain in his lungs where there should be air filling them. His fingers curl hard around the armrests and he gasps. God help him, he is going to kill his sister. He is going to pull a gun on his baby sister in Waxahachie, Texas, actually put an end to this mess and kill her.

"You talk," he says, in a strangled voice. "To Jesus?"

Isidore looks at him wide-eyed. "All the time. You hear me. I always say Jesus—"

"I thought you were cursing—"

"I'm praying to him. Or whatever. What's wrong?"

Anson can't believe it. Because of the events of their lives he is unfortunately unable to deny God's existence, but it would never occur to Anson to pray to him. "Isidore," he says. "Jesus wants you dead."

"No he doesn't," Isidore says. "Just God does. I think."

"Look," says Anson. "You wanna separate Jesus from the killing, and the wrath, that's fine. That's your business. But praying, Isidore? Do you really think that's a bright idea?"

Isidore blinks. She realizes she's done something wrong, she just doesn't know what. "What do you mean?"

"I mean you might as well be sending him text messages with our location!" Anson says. Isidore flinches. "You might as well put a giant blinking target on the Airstream!"

"It's God, Annie. I'm pretty sure to him, we come with a satellite signal. He doesn't need a prayer to find us."

The moment is surreal, even for Anson. People in the Space Needle are eating delicacies above an adjusted ocean like this is Water World and they're just the upper class. His sister, who damn well knows how to handle a firearm, has shot his brother in the back and his other sister, demon-spawn for sure, couldn't heal him because she blew her wad on a smartphone. And now she's telling him words that sound suspiciously like the words of a believer. Of someone with—

"Is," he says. "Have you found faith?"

Isidore makes a valiant effort to take this seriously, like a young mother whose two-year-old has dropped her first f-bomb, but in the end a laugh escapes.

She reaches over to him and takes his arm. Pushes back his sleeve, exposing the wound he got off the angel back in West Texas, a gash that Isidore herself sterilized and band-aged. "Anson," she says. "Are you asking me if I believe in God?"

The corners of his eyes crinkle. Before he can let out a full-blown laugh, a great racket comes from the explosively lit white hallway. They are both on their feet, expecting heat.

"What?" says Anson.

Lulu and River are running toward them, frantic. Lulu is laughing. Clutching her purse and an armful of River's bloodied clothes, she's bent forward, lurching with laughter. At first Isidore thinks it's a joke. Then she sees the intense concentration on River's face and knows that he is drugged, and that he's making a concerted effort to hurry anyway. He is barefoot. He is in a white hospital gown with faded pink and teal print. In his left hand, he's dragging an IV stand. With his right, he is struggling to keep his gown closed behind him. His legs are pale, sticking out from the bottom. Cords fly loose around him.

One nurse at the station drawls "Oh my Lord," like a scandalized debutante. The other barks, "What the hell—"

"Go!" screams Lulu. She's utterly useless, dissolving in giggles. "Go go go go—"

Isidore turns and runs. Anson waits for River to catch up to him. Then he takes his brother's IV stand in one arm and his elbow in the other. They rush for the door, River running like a stunt clown, up on the balls of his feet, his hand anxious at the gap of his gown.

"What's going on?" Anson says as they rush out the sliding door.

"Don't look at my ass!" says River.

"It's a fucking gunshot wound," Lulu says, and Anson gets it. Of course. A gunshot wound. They will have called the police. This is an incredibly stupid mistake, and all his fault. "River—come on, man—"

"They're gonna see my ass!"

"There's no one to see your ass, but if you don't get a move on, they're gonna be doing a lot worse than seeing it."

This puts a spring in River's step. In the back of the parking lot is the Airstream. Isidore's got it going. Lulu falls in the door. Anson shoves River in. There is a brief scuffle with the IV. Anson thinks of the needle tugging in River's arm and feels faint. He takes a deep breath and shoves the metal stand into the trailer.

TULSA
OKLAHOMA
JULY 3ᴿᴰ

THEY ARRIVE IN TULSA in the late morning, after having pulled over to give Anson a few hours of sleep on the side of the road. Isidore didn't offer to drive, happy to put off Tulsa for as long as possible. Driving into the city is like arriving on another planet, where people are struggling against an endless, devouring army of flag t-shirts and lawn chairs. There is the sense of battle, Anson thinks as he watches a father juggling a stroller and two crying kids across a street, the kids going boneless in the intersection. Just not the sort of battle Anson is familiar with. He doesn't worry too much about angels in Tulsa. The place is a religious Mecca, and he figures they wouldn't want to stage a snuff show in front of their best boys.

Next to him, Isidore is jittery. Her hair is a disorderly pony mane, pale and dry. She's twirling her fingers in it, her nervous tick. Occasionally one gets stuck and she struggles to dislodge herself. Anson can't muster much sympathy. She can rip the wings off angels. His tolerance for her anxiety over awkward family gatherings is low.

River is stretched on the couch, completely out of it. He's bogged down on Lulu's supply of barbiturates and is sniffing, intermittently, about getting swallowed by a tornado. Lulu, never one to let River suffer alone, has taken a handful of God knows what and is freaking Anson out. "I feel so good," she says, grinning sleepily. "Guys. I'm just so happy. To be here with you. I'm just so . . . happy right now."

"Drink some water," Isidore says for the fifteenth time. Finally Anson gets it.

"She didn't take ecstasy," he says. "She's not gonna die of dehydration." Isidore's street knowledge is limited. He once overheard a guy invite her to a rave. Isidore had frowned and said, "Can't we just talk about how much we like it right here?"

Isidore frowns. "Still. I think she should drink some water. Drink some water, Lulu."

"You take such good care of me," Lulu slurs.

"Shut up, Lulu," Anson says. Lulu laughs richly like it's a wonderful joke they share.

They weave through downtown Tulsa and head for the outskirts. Anson knows Isidore is flirting with her limit, her countdown clock ticking faster than usual, but resentment is keeping him from the preventative measures he would usually take. He needs to see Martha because he is losing his grip on normal life. He is starting to forget that there are people in the world who God isn't trying to kill. Isidore jiggles her leg and hums as he turns down the country road, the prairie gold and green and steaming in the heat around them. A herd of black cows in a scrubby field are indifferent as they pass, swishing their tails against the flies.

"This was the best decision of my life, you guys," Lulu drawls from the kitchenette. She picks up one of her aging lemons and tosses it at River. They both laugh when it bounces off his nose.

"Uh-huh," says Anson.

"No seriously," Lulu says. "The people in Hollywood are so much better than you guys, you know? But they're not my family. They're not my family." On the last word, she thumps her chest.

They come to the long gravel driveway and Anson breaks for the turn. Isidore braces against the dashboard like they're about to crash. Martha's family's ranch looms over the crest, a stately yellow farmhouse surrounded by trees. "Oh Jesus," Isidore says. She squeezes her eyes shut. "Oh Jesus."

"Goddammit Isidore," Anson says. "It's just people. Just a family. I know it's weird but come on. Your life is a lot weirder."

"I'm used to my life," Isidore says. "A yellow farmhouse? Totally absurd." She shakes her head. "The life got to you, Anson. You've finally cracked."

"I haven't cracked, but I'm about to if I can't spend five minutes doing something normal." He glances behind him, where Lulu and River are stretched like belly-scratching apes atop dirty towels and blankets.

"What did you tell her about us?" Isidore says.

"I didn't tell her anything, yet. Yesterday I told her I'd be here, and now I am."

Isidore realizes she might need to stage a mutiny. She speaks slowly. "But Anson. How are you going to explain us?"

"You're my family. What is there to explain?"

Isidore says nothing.

"Fine," Anson sighs dramatically.

"Pound it," Lulu says, and he pounds the steering wheel. "Shut up, Lulu!"

Anson has told Martha that he is, indeed, a traveling Bible salesman. Lying to Martha troubles Anson, more lately than it used to, but there's no way around it. One cannot simply inform a pastor's daughter that he travels the country hunted by God's choice creation, which he kills when he can. She knows he travels with his brother and sister sometimes, and Anson has let her believe they are some form of footloose missionaries, or youth ministers at the least. He has dropped vague hints about Navajo reservations and let Martha's tendency to assume the best lead her where it will. It hasn't escaped Anson that there is something borderline sociopathic about the lie he has chosen, considering his truth. Like so many before him, he is an evildoer who has styled himself as God's peddler.

"I'll say we're having a family reunion," Anson says, remembering Lulu's lie in the saloon.

"Lame," says Isidore.

"Yeah," Anson says, putting the camper in park. 'But she won't think so."

"Why have we stopped?" Lulu calls from the backseat. "What's the plan, my sister?"

"Annie's brought us to meet Martha's family."

"What the fuck?" Lulu says. She sits up abruptly, bangs her knees on the banquette, and debris goes flying. Playing cards and pencils scatter. All Lulu's lemons, now spotted brown and hardened, roll onto the floor where they bang more like cue balls than fruit. "No. No fucking way, Anson. I don't do meet the parents. It's not even my girlfriend."

"I knew it!" River says, pointing. "I knew you were a lesbian."

Anson ignores them all. He calls Isidore over to River. Together they haul their brother up. He clambers like a Sasquatch and snatches up an empty smoothie cup, sucking furiously on the straw. When his efforts yield nothing, he throws it to the ground.

"He needs more meds," says Isidore.

"Are you kidding me? That's the last thing he needs. He needs a clean shirt. And a shave."

"I'll shave him."

"She's not shaving me," River slurs.

Anson pulls open all four of the small drawers in the bedroom and looks in the closet. "There has to be something clean in here," he says. He needs a fresh shirt too. He hasn't changed since the saloon. Since then he has disposed of a pervert and battled an army of modest angels, wrestled his full-grown little brother into a tiny trailer, and driven for five hours. They are road-weary and dirty, grime in their skin, alcohol reeking out their pores.

"I told you we needed to do laundry. Again," Lulu

says. She is watching Anson closely for indicators on whether she is actually going to be forced to meet this bizarre family who lives out in the middle of nowhere on a farm. With cows and, from the sound of it, chickens. Lulu shudders. She has been terrified of fowl ever since Anson and River locked her in a barn with a particularly dominant rooster at the age of six.

"Don't be so smug," says Isidore. "You reek, too."

"So?" Lulu says, throwing open her arms. "What does it matter how I smell, Isidore? You think Oprah cares how I smell? She's too big for that. She's . . . " Lulu's eyes go bleary as she searches for the word. "Ascended."

"It matters," Isidore says. "Because you're coming, too."

"No," barks Lulu like scolding a puppy, her motivation all wrong. She rises half off the couch before losing her balance and flopping to the floor. To save face, she stays there and fumbles in her massive cream leather purse for her saucer-eyed sunglasses. She puts them on. "Why do I have to go in?"

"You don't have to," Anson snaps. "God forbid any of you do this one thing, this one thing, for me. Forget it."

"Listen up you dick," Isidore hisses, leaning down to Lulu's ear and pulling her up. "This matters to Anson." Isidore still thinks this is a terrible idea, but it's clear that Anson has made meeting the family a touchstone in his wayward life, however misguided or downright insane it might be. She decides the only way out is through.

"It does?" Lulu says, suddenly feeling very sorry for Anson.

"Of course it does."

"What am I supposed to do?" Anson says. He has not overhead them. "There's nothing clean and I'm not going in there smelling like this."

Isidore fumbles for the box, which has been shoved under the dinette and forgotten. "There's these," she says, holding up a shirt.

Anson turns. "No. No way. I am not wearing that."

Fifteen minutes later Anson is lifting the heavy iron knocker and tapping it against the big oak doors, his siblings hiding behind him. They are dressed in identical turquoise shirts, each with a picture of a sad-eyed, fluffy white dog, each with the script "Minxy's Last Stand" printed across it. Anson is bearing it with as much dignity as he can, his shoulders broad in the bright circus colors. Lulu appears to have pulled it together, though she's leaning heavily on Isidore's arm. Her chin is high, and she's managing to look chic thanks to the sunglasses and a sleek blonde bun. River is gazing down at his shirt, caressing the picture of Minxy. Anson smacks his hand away. River raises his gaze slowly, staring at Anson in outrage, but seems unable to form any words of protest.

Martha opens the door and surprises them all by looking like a sacred sight. After everything, this. A home on the range topped with sweet blue sky. Her upper-class blonde hair is a neat and respectable length. Not hippie and wanton like Lulu's and Isidore's. Anson breathes deeply, taking her in. Her shirt is pale blue and it buttons snugly over her breasts. She somehow exudes wholesomeness, femininity, and athleticism all at once. Lulu ponders her own wrinkled jeans and wonders how she has come to this. Just days ago, her siblings arrived on her doorstep and she was in the role of Martha. She was clean and cultured, they were dirty and gross. And now she is playing their role, the traveler, the godless filthy gypsy, and dammit.

"She's perfect," Lulu breathes. "She's perfect, Anson."

Isidore nods. She must admit this is true.

"She looks like a dryer sheet commercial," Lulu says. "Tell her she looks like a dryer sheet—"

"She can hear you," Isidore says, smiling fixedly at Martha.

Anson has worried, but Martha doesn't even seem to notice his siblings. She smiles up at him, he takes her in,

"This is a really great door knocker," Isidore enthuses. Lulu nods solemnly. "The best," she agrees. River mutters something about it not being polite to talk about her knockers, but Martha doesn't notice. She stands back. Anson, who has apparently forgotten that anyone besides himself and Snuggles the dryer girl exist here on earth, follows her in. The door shuts behind him. Isidore considers leaving him there. But Lulu opens the door and reluctantly, Isidore enters.

Anson and Martha the pastor's daughter are chastely embracing in the middle of a grand living area. The house looks quaint on the outside but inside it is so expensive, Isidore couldn't even afford the magazine with the pictures of it. Huge pine logs run across the ceiling, which is vaulted skyward like good Lutheran ideals. On the far end is a stone fireplace, surrounded by couches of warm brown leather, floating in a sea of endless varnished pine. It looks exactly the type of place other women like Martha would gather in pajamas to talk about Bibles. Here and there the skins of dead animals are on display, but it's not as macabre as Isidore would have thought. There are antlers, too, whitened and dry, but like Martha they manage to appear robust and Hemingwayesque and don't reek of death like they should. The kitchen beyond gleams like an enchanted forest, like someone sang a hymn and it was born. Lulu leans in toward Isidore, almost loses her balance, and mutters, "I think I just had an orgasm." They have disturbed Anson and Martha's modestly-clad bliss. Isidore expects a bitch look, a forced kindness, but no. Martha can't even give her this. She smiles enthusiastically. "Anson. You've brought your family!"

"Anson has," says Lulu. "He's like that." Martha takes Lulu's hand first, awkwardly, and then says, "Oh!" sounding for all the world like she's going to follow it with "fiddlesticks" and switches to a hug. "I'm Martha," she says. "I can't tell you how happy I am to meet you all."

Next to Martha, Lulu is wan and ridiculous, an albino insect. She nods her head repeatedly, doesn't remove the sunglasses. Isidore feels awkward and shamefully pagan. Anson introduces them one by one. Martha hugs them and doesn't wrinkle her nose at the smell or pointedly avoid commenting on the t-shirts. She doesn't even seem to notice the t-shirts. "I know you've been travelling," she says. "Come on into the

kitchen, I've got some iced tea and Mom made chicken salad."
Isidore blinks. Iced tea and chicken salad is just the thing. How
did Martha know that? Isidore begins to weigh the likelihood
of Martha being an undercover hostile. "Mom," Martha calls.
"Daddy. Anson's here and he's brought his family."

Anson follows Martha into the kitchen. It's like he has
forgotten Isidore completely. His hand is on Martha's lower
back. He doesn't flinch at the mention of the mom and dad
and does not, certainly does not, glance back at his siblings.
Isidore fights the urge to kick him, remind him of her presence. She looks at Lulu, expecting to share a glance of sisterly
disdain, but alas. Lulu is admiring the copper cookware and
River is smiling at Martha like she is a rare and delicate prairie
flower. They settle in around the whale-sized island. Lulu runs
her hand across the flecked top, shiny like a novelty rock from
a tourist shop.

"This cost twenty-thousand," Lulu whispers. "At
least."

"That's not so bad," Isidore whispers, her eyes roam-
ing the rafters and the skylights. "It is pretty big."

"Not the house, Isidore. The fucking counter."

"Isidore?" Martha says. "Tea?"

"No thanks. I mean yes. Please." Isidore doesn't drink
tea but she fears offending Martha. The anger of a righteous
woman might be a signal beacon to angels.

"Everyone?" says Martha. "Tea? Or—" she glances at
Anson, who only smiles at her with unchecked admiration. "I
don't know what mood you're in, but we have stuff for mimo-
sas."

"Jesus," Lulu says. "I think I'm in love. With Jesus,"
she corrects when Martha looks at her alarmed. "I'm so in love
with Jesus."

"Me too!" River chimes in loudly, happy to have a line.

Martha's bright smile falters. "I'm sorry. I could swear
Annie said you guys drink. It's not like we're getting drunk all
the time. But we're all German, you know. All us Lutherans."
She is apologetic without attempting to excuse her own habits.

Isidore is starting to get it. Martha is solid. Grounded like a tree that knows how to iron a collar.

"They drink," Anson said. "Lulu's just, uh. She can't have any alcohol now. She's on medication."

Isidore looks up and realizes Anson is bug-eyed, looking to her for backup. "She's pregnant!" Isidore improvises. Martha's eyes flutter wide in pleasant surprise.

"Oh my god, Lulu, congratulations!" River says too loudly.

"No," says Lulu. "I just hope to be." She smiles smugly and touches her belly for effect. She's greatly pleased with this quick cover up. "Soon." A glow in River's eyes extinguishes. He seems genuinely disappointed.

"Oh!" Martha says. She glances at Lulu's hand, where there is no ring. Isidore expects a comment but Martha only says, "That's wonderful!" and she seems, strangely, to mean it. Then she clears her throat. Isidore realizes the subject of babies is probably not a comfortable one for this twenty-six year old virgin who is hoping to pin down Anson.

"Should we, um. Let's have the tea." Isidore's mind races back to her four years at Lutheran High School, her only experience with these people. They used to pray before dinner, she remembers, but not before lunch. She doesn't remember the rules for tea. Is this breakfast? Is dinner the only meal one prays over, or is lunch the only meal one doesn't? She looks at Anson for help. For heaven's sake, this is his girlfriend here. They're all here for him, the least he could do is make a little friendly conversation. "Anson has so much to tell you," Isidore says.

Martha glances up. She's set out five glasses filled with ice and is in the process of pouring tea. Lulu snatches a glass and knocks two cubes into her mouth, spits one back out, and starts crunching. Martha waits politely for her to finish, then pours Lulu's tea. "Oh," she says. "Does he?"

"Yes," Isidore says, nervous now. "So many, uh, Bibles he's been slaying. Selling. So many, you know. Brown people, who have the wrong religions and everything." She knows she's gone wrong somehow and takes a long gulp of tea to shut herself up. "Jesus," she says. "This is the sweetest tea I've ever had. What do you put in here, southern cheerleaders?"

"Well look here!" a deep voice bellows and Isidore jumps. Coming into the kitchen is a large man, a blonde with scrubbed pink skin and a massive belly. Isidore is profoundly confused; he is not wearing a white collar, but he is wearing a cowboy hat. He's got his arms outspread like he's going to hug them all at once, or maybe eat them. Lulu panics and shoves back her seat, rising as she thinks etiquette requires. He chuckles. He is benevolent and jolly like Santa Claus. To cover her faux pas, Lulu goes to embrace him. She goes in two-armed, a Hollywood embrace, kiss-ready, but the pastor somehow maneuvers it so that he only gets a side hug, one armed, and they look for a moment like they're posing for a picture or about to do the can-can, which is awkward. Not only because Lulu has been made excessively aware of her own breasts, but also because the idea of her doing the cancan with this fat bonhomous man is absurd to the point of agonized amusement. Isidore giggles and chokes.

"Pastor Svenson," Anson says. "That's my sister Lulu."

"Pastor," says Lulu. "What church?"

"Christ Almighty," proclaims Pastor Svenson.

Lulu jumps. "What? What is it?" She glances around, expecting maybe a snake or a hairy spider, and then, failing to see one, pats her hair self-consciously, as if it's her appearance that has made a pastor take the Lord's name in vain.

"I'm sorry. Christ Almighty Lutheran Church is where I'm a pastor. And you must be the missionaries." He releases Lulu and moves away. Shakes River's hand. Isidore is farthest from him and hangs back uncomfortably, hiding herself behind Anson because she cannot fathom the physical protocol.

"Yeah," River says. "Spreading out the word. Or however you want to say it."

"Definitely involves spreading," says Lulu.

"The point is, we're preaching God. And Jesus too. And that third thing."

"Oh," Lulu agrees passionately. "Definitely the third thing."

"It's difficult work, I remember from my days in Haiti," says Pastor Svenson.

"So worth it, though," Lulu says. "Casting out the heathens."

"You've been working mainly—" Pastor Svenson begins.

"Miracles," Lulu interrupts confidently. She is drawing on four years of Bible class in which she mostly painted her nails and flipped through Bust magazine, the young male teachers clean-shaven and flustered around her. She hadn't understood it was because of her insouciant sexuality until it was too late to use it for ill. "Lots of miracle working, lots of, uh. Fruits. You know. Totally into those. And the apostles, sometimes. Sometimes." She nods sagely.

"Lulu—" Isidore says.

"No, Isidore, don't be modest," says Lulu. "You know you've done the apostles, too."

"We've been taking up our crosses," River says.

"Oh yeah!" says Lulu. "And laying them on our hearts. Definitely that."

Pastor Svenson's smile has shadows at the edges. "I was only asking where you've been working," he says. "Where you've been."

"Oh," says Lulu. "Hollywood."

"Hollywood!" Pastor Svenson is impressed. "Excellent. Tough crowd down there, isn't it?'

"Not particularly, no," Lulu says sharply. Isidore looks at Anson. She doesn't know why he won't stop this. He's not even looking at Lulu. He is lost in the eyes of his girlfriend. Isidore has spent her life in hot pursuit of entirely physical pleasures, chasing down every barroom, bedroom, and back alley fight glittering across the interstates. And here is Anson, driven to this gingerbread house on the edge of the prairie in search of rewards that are emotional and perhaps even spiritual, though she doubts Anson would admit this to himself.

"We just like to talk to God, you know, man?" River says, shaking his head. "We just wanna talk to him. You know? We just wanna ask him why. Don't you ever just want to know why, Pastor?"

"Well yes," Pastor Svenson says. "I think we all ask that question. That's part of developing our faith."

"You look like a cowboy," River says.

Pastor Svenson chuckles. "Matthew four nineteen," he says. It's clear this cipher has meaning to him.

"Copy that," says Lulu.

"Wranglers of men!" Pastor Svenson explodes the punch line, laughing great booms at his own joke. He waits for the Campers to join, but they don't get it. Lulu's laugh is too late and painfully forced.

"Sorry," Anson says. "We're all just a little tired." Anson actually likes Pastor Svenson. He's never given Anson a hard time or tried to get him to come to church. This is because he has Anson pegged as a member of the flock, doesn't know Anson is in need of saving. But Anson appreciates it nonetheless.

"It's good to see you," Pastor Svenson says, clapping Anson on the back. "It's always good to have you in this neck of the woods. Patsy and I were just wondering if we'd get to see you for the holiday. Patsy said she sure hoped so. You know you're always welcome here."

Isidore is confused by this speech, which seems to be laced with double meaning. Surely the bit about the holiday was a jab at what they have recognized for Anson's paganism. Surely Patsy's hope to see Anson is not truly guileless. This must be about the ring that Anson should have provided by now, the home and the babies that Martha deserves and Anson withholds. She looks to Lulu for help, and it's then that she realizes a woman has entered the room. She is standing behind them all, beaming like a benevolent house elf. She's short but not slight, a panda in a denim jumper.

"Oh my god!" Lulu squeals. She reaches out and pats the woman on the head. "And who is this?"

A moment's pause. "That's my wife. Mrs. Svenson," Pastor Svenson says at last. Something is obviously wrong with Lulu. They've been made.

Pastor Svenson smiles at Isidore. Before he has the chance to violently scorn her, a thunderous noise arises, possibly from the depths of the earth. Like boots or many hooves on the wood floor, a stampede of beasts, perhaps, or catamites. Doors are slamming and a general cry is going up. Isidore had no idea pastors wielded this much power, to conjure avengers down from the heavens. She smiles bravely at River. He leers at her, wet-eyed.

But it's not the Armageddon. It's only Lutherans. Isidore turns and there appear to be hundreds of them, though of course this isn't possible. Wind-chapped blondes, all of them, tall and thick boned, blue eyed, their pigmentational discordance with the life they lead evident in their painfully pink skin, the spots of cherry lemonade scalps in places of thinning hair. Anson goes to them. They open like the Norwegian sea and swallow him whole. Slapping him congenially on the back, repeating his name and insisting how good it is to see him. Swedes are supposed to be stoic, Isidore knows. These ones must be drunk on Carlsberg, the lot of them.

Lulu is at Isidore's side. "It's a fucking ambush," she mutters into Isidore's ear. "Save yourself." Isidore calculates the difficulties of getting both Lulu and River to Pacey, but before she can form a solid plan, Martha is at her side and is introducing her to these people, whatever they are.

"Isidore," she says, and then intones a litany of names, like they used to do during chapel with the prayer requests. Pesky Jack, Little Tim, Big Tim, Aunt Sarah, Aunt Jane, Aunt Erika, Aunt Rachel, Uncle Mark, Uncle Carl, baby Grace—baby Grace is unnatural in her beauty, an enormously brown-eyed abomination with wispy white curls—her sister Rosie—unfortunate for Rosie, thinks Isidore, who has the tiny eyes of her Nordic ancestors—several more who press in, smiling or shaking her hand before moving on to the others.

"Who are all these people?" Isidore asks.

"Oh, family," Martha says. "I mean, they all feel like family, one way or another. Some started out as hands but they've been around so long," she shrugs. "It's nice, having everyone so close all the time. All my nieces and nephews running around." Obviously another barbed reference to Anson's failure to marry and impregnate her. "People ask if it drives me crazy, but I couldn't imagine it any other way. But that must be how you feel. All of you together all the time."

"You bet your ass!" cries Lulu, swinging against Isidore's arm. Isidore is ready to apologize but Martha begins to laugh.

At last Anson emerges from the tide bearing four bottles of beer. He hands them around. Isidore is on edge, certain that one of them will commit a faux pas and get Anson booted from the congregation. But Anson seems unworried, like this is a place where acceptance is taken for granted. River approaches, lurching like Frankenstein doing the electric slide. "Where's my beer, man?" he drawls.

"Oh," Martha says. "You're bleeding."

They all look. River is indeed bleeding through his bandages and his shirt. Before a lie is formed on anyone's tongue, River pokes the wound, then raises his hands in the air, waving them clownishly.

"Oh my god!" he cries in a falsely high-pitched voice. "I'm bleeding!"

There is a beat and then Martha waves her own hands and cries, "Oh my gosh! It's the Poodle flu!"

"Oh my god," Lulu goes next. "The world is ending!"

"Oh my god," goes Isidore, overly enthusiastic. "My mom's a drag queen!"

Martha's mouth makes a little 'o', but it's all right. They clink their bottles together and drink.

SVENSON'S LUTHERAN RANCH
OKLAHOMA
4TH OF JULY

WHEN ANSON WAKES, he thinks he has made a
serious mistake and had a one-night stand with a teenager. He
is sleeping under a pink quilt, surrounded on all sides by minia-
ture half-naked cherubs and figurines of children with worri-
some teardrop eyes. On the dresser, and this can't be good, is
an angel with fiber optic wings, the tips shifting purple to red
to green and back again, an acid trip for the devout. He sits up
and checks for Isidore. She isn't there. This is the first time in
twenty-five years Anson has woken and not known exactly
where she is, and he remembers. He is in the Svenson's guest
bedroom. To reassure himself, Anson gets out of bed and goes
to the window, which overlooks the front drive. The Airstream
is there, gleaming in the sun.

In the antiseptic bathroom there is a puffy pink toilet.
It brings on a kind of crisis. What sort of people have lives in
which it is possible to attend so carefully to every manner of
comfort? What choices lead a person to a life that offers time
to procure extra comfortable toilet seats, ceramic effigies of
angels? Anson won't touch the toilet seat. He pees in the

216

shower, washing his hair with Pert Plus, while in his heart spreads an uncomfortable and alarming softness. He urgently wants to provide his siblings with every luxury they've ever been deprived of, and he can't do that staying here. Isidore's search across the country for every carnal pleasure America can offer suddenly makes perfect sense. It makes a religious sort of sense: a quest a person might rightfully model their life after, and die, if not happy, at least sated. He remembers that Lulu's audition is today and texts River, telling him to buy her a ticket back to L.A. He has to do what he can for his siblings, while they are here on earth, and that means no more forced family gatherings and certainly no more sweaty shrimp cocktail. He will do his best, Anson swears to himself, to help the bastards find their father and while they're at it, he will stop at every restaurant the food channel has ever featured and let them fill themselves before driving off into the sunset. This determination in mind, Anson dresses and makes his way downstairs. He has a primal need to see that Isidore has made it through the night. He hopes to be able to slip out the front door undetected, as the prospect of breakfast in an unfamiliar kitchen produces a gnawing sense of panic in his gut.

There is no luck. Martha is with her parents in the sunlit kitchen, sitting at the counter and drinking coffee while Mrs. Svenson rolls out dough and the pastor, in a red apron, beats eggs. Her smile sends dead leaves skittering nervously across the paths in his heart. He goes to her because it is required, allows himself to be kissed chastely on the lips. She offers him coffee and it feels like a marriage proposal. "No," Anson says. "I mean, yes please. Coffee. Look, I gotta—we can't stay."

Pastor Svenson looks up from his eggs. Martha frowns with a cute wrinkle between her eyebrows.

He can't tell them that he needs to leave because their time on earth is limited. "We have to go because of—get the—we're looking for my Dad," Anson says before he can chicken out. "And I promised my brother and sisters that we'd find him."

He figures he deserves any frantic questioning that might come. But Pastor Svenson only nods. He doesn't even look sorry for Anson.

"And you think he might be in Tulsa?" Pastor Svenson says.

"He might be anywhere," Anson says honestly, beguiled by the calm with which both Martha and her father have absorbed this revelation. He wonders if the ranch is somewhere everyone comes looking for the things they've lost.

"What's his name?"

"Randy Camper."

Martha winces and then politely clears her throat. After a moment a smile breaks on Anson's face.

"Wow. I never realized until now how that sounds."

"Randy Camper?" Pastor Svenson repeats.

"It's bad, isn't it?" Anson says.

"No—well—I suppose it's—no, Anson, what I mean is, I know a Randy Camper."

He supposes he should be stunned, but it takes a lot to surprise a Camper. "It can't be the same one," Anson says. "Can it?"

"Luckily we don't know many Randy Campers," Martha blurts. Anson doesn't think it's all that funny but Martha explodes into laughter. Pastor Svenson looks like someone is strangling him and he feels secretly mirthful about it. This is how Lulu and Isidore find them. They enter the room quietly with their pleasant faces on, looking surprisingly presentable, and a deep tension seeps out of Anson just to see them here, alive another day. They're not in the Minxy shirts. Isidore wears a clean white tee and jeans, and Lulu's in a yellow sundress. It astounds and pleases him that his sisters have snuck out in the middle of the night and done laundry in order to make a good impression. He doesn't care that it's all a charade. Their entire lives are a charade and he has grown accustomed to duplicity.

"Hello?" Lulu calls. She smiles uncertainly, entering a stranger's home and finding them all conspiring at the table.

"Can we—"

"Oh, come on in," Martha says. "Please."

Not only is Lulu not dressed like a whore, she is proffering a wicker basket with a blue and white checkered napkin peeking out of it. She looks, Anson thinks, like Dorothy Goddamn Gale. Sweet and out of place but willing to make a plucky go of it.

"Good morning, everyone," Lulu says, her smile revealing two straight rows of perfect white teeth. She holds up the basket. "Hope we're not disturbing anything. Just wanted to bring over these peaches, and some cherries. Picked them up at the Farmer's market this morning. Thought they'd make a nice complement to whatever delicious thing Mrs. Pastor has baking in the oven."

She is perfect. Anson doesn't know how she's managed it, but she has. And Isidore. Isidore looks weird, but nice. She moves awkwardly into the room, coming very close to human for someone who really isn't.

Even Lulu calling Martha's mother Mrs. Pastor seems to charm the Svensons, who smile broadly, making Danish apples out of their rounded cheeks. Mrs. Svenson accepts the basket, overflowing with fresh, fragrant fruit, from Lulu's arms and takes it to the sink for washing.

"A farmers market, eh? On the Fourth of July?" says Pastor.

"The Fourth of July?" says Lulu. "Today is the Fourth of July?"

She sends a significant glance at Anson. Isidore licks her lips and moves her fingers up to her mouth, to bite. Lulu pushes her arm back down. They all get skittish on the Fourth of July. The constant pops and bangs sound to them like holy warfare.

"Yes, yes," says Pastor Svenson. "You girls must be early risers, to have been to the market and back again."

"Well," says Lulu, sliding onto a stool at the island. "We were just in a hurry to get over here, I suppose. We had some questions, Pastor Svenson, that we were hoping you could answer. Isidore," she says sweetly. Isidore shakes herself out of her panic and sits next to Lulu. Anson winks at her.

"You do?" Pastor Svenson pops a cherry in his mouth and yanks the stem.

"Yes. You see, we were wondering about the Old Testament. When God is killing everybody? We're curious—"

"We were just discussing your father," Martha interrupts. Lulu and Isidore's smiles freeze on their faces.

"God the father," Lulu nods voraciously. "Yes. God the son. Absolutely."

"Yes," says Martha. Anson can tell she's annoyed, something he's never before seen on her. "Of course that. But what I mean is, we were discussing your real father. "

"Now Martha—" Pastor Svenson begins.

"Your earthly one," Martha says, with what Anson senses is a barely contained eye-roll. He doesn't know why she's interrupted the pastor. He wonders if she's heard her share of discourse on infant baptism already. "My father knows a Randy Camper," Martha says with a giggle. There is only a brief second for Anson to worry because Isidore gets it right away.

"He won't need any help pitching his tent," Isidore says, lifting one finger. Martha's laugh begins as a raspberry between her lips. She covers her mouth self-consciously and looks at Anson. Her delight at this stupid joke seems extreme, but no one knows to be worried yet.

Patsy pulls a coffee cake from the oven and Anson gapes. Moments ago she had dough on the counter. The coffee cake has appeared by magic or witchery, surely. She sets it before them on a trivet, the scent of cinnamon and nuts filling the room.

Isidore picks at bread with her fingers. Anson is embarrassed, until Martha does it too. If Isidore is feral, Anson supposes he is somewhat to blame. "So you know our Dad?" Lulu says, managing to sound breezy or maybe she really doesn't give a shit. The Svensons must be curious about the story with their father, but they don't show it.

"I know a man named—Randy Camper," Pastor Svenson says, but by now the joke has worn off. "Let's see. Met him about five years ago." He glances at Martha, bothered at being pulled off his infant baptism soapbox.

"At an art show, or something?" Isidore says. Mrs. Svenson begins cutting thick pieces of cake and sliding them onto plates, handing out forks, so that Isidore can stop acting like a cannibal and Martha can stop pretending to be one to cover her.

"An art—no, not an art show," Pastor Svenson says. "It was a barbecue competition, actually."

"He was painting the sausages?" Isidore says.

"He wasn't doing anything to the sausages," Pastor Svenson says. Martha makes a helpless sound in her throat but hangs on to herself. "He was smoking a pork butt, actually."

"But actually what?" Lulu says.

"What? No, I mean, uh," Pastor Svenson chuckles. "It's a cut of meat. A pork butt."

Licking her fingers, Isidore says, "Still. Dad shouldn't be smoking."

"Oh my god. Gosh," Anson says. River is right, it must be an act. She can't actually be this stupid. "He means he was barbecuing, Isidore. Like Bobby Flay."

"Then why didn't he say that?" Isidore frowns.

"No way that's our Randy Camper," Lulu says. "Dad doesn't barbecue. He went to college."

"I suppose the odds aren't good that the man I know would be your father," Pastor Svenson says. "Still, it's worth looking into, wouldn't you say? You never know. A man might take up barbecuing unexpectedly, later in life. There is no telling what a man might do. In this world or the next."

"What verse is that?" Lulu says. Anson forgets any feelings of goodwill he may have had for her this morning and the urge to kill her returns. But to his amazement, Pastor Svenson is charmed. He smiles at her indulgently, the way Anson has seen him smile at Martha. Lulu smiles back, like she made the joke on purpose. It's a fine line, between companionable

221

teasing and outright mockery. Lulu is treading it like a pro. Anson wonders what her life is like out there in L.A. Does she go out evenings, make herself a hit among producers and friends? He decides to make a point to see one of her movies. Has she done a movie?

"Do you have his number?" Anson says. He can't believe Pastor Svenson would know his father, that it could be this easy. But he doubts there are bounties of men out there unfortunate enough to be named Randy Camper.

"I'm sorry to say I don't. We spoke briefly about his rub—his, uh, you know it's the mixture of spices that go onto the meat before you cook it? It was the best smoked pork I've ever had. I wanted to know how he did it, and we got to talking. He said his children were grown, his wife had left him and he'd come to Tulsa on the competitive barbecuing circuit and decided not to leave."

"There's a competitive barbecue circuit?" Lulu says. "That's depressing." She catches herself. "If only we could get men as excited about baptism as they are about meat."

"Amen to that," Pastor Svenson nods approvingly. "I invited him to church. He seemed a little lonely. He came to Christ Almighty a few times—"

Pastor Svenson is interrupted by Isidore, who has choked on her pastry. "I'm sorry," she says, pounding her chest. "You mean he—he came to Christ?"

"It's the name of the church," says Martha. "Christ Almighty."

Isidore takes affront. "I'm sorry," she says, neck bobbing slightly backward. "I didn't know."

"No. It's the name of the church, goddammit," Lulu says. Her performance might have its strong points, but it's also spotty as a fake Irish accent. Pastor Svenson flinches visibly. "Christ Almighty."

"Jesus, Lulu," Isidore gasps. "Show a little respect—"

"Here," Martha says. She has somehow produced—Anson suspects Patsy—a pamphlet or tract sheet, and the name is printed on green paper beneath a scrolling of flowers.

222

"Christ Almighty Lutheran Church," It says. There's an address and then Pastor Svenson's name, a graphic of a funny-looking 3-D cross.

"Oh," Isidore says. She opens her mouth and then shoots her eyes to Anson. "That's a lovely name." Martha accepts the compliment with a raised eyebrow.

"Only saw him a couple three times," Pastor Svenson says. "Then I went to an interfaith meeting at the Prayer Tower and heard he'd been over 'round Holy Hill Baptist."

"Oh no," Lulu says. "Oh God no. He can't be a Baptist."

Pastor Svenson chuckles. "Don't worry. They'd lost him too, were trying to track him down. It's a shame. I think he vanished from the church circles after that. And with the Holy Hillers after him, I can't blame him."

"Imagine that," Anson says wryly. "Holy rollers after Dad."

"We could Google him," Martha says.

"We have," Lulu sighs. Anson looks back toward Martha and startles. Patsy Svenson is bearing down upon Isidore with a phone book raised over her head. Panic overcomes him. Oh God, oh God, Mrs. Pastor is an agent of the Lord, she is going to murder his sister, and Anson must decide who to save. He stands, feeling for his knife and uncertain what exactly he will do with it—save Isidore, or save Mrs. Svenson. Mrs. Svenson slams the book down onto the counter with a resounding bang. "Well of course," says Martha. "The phone book. I swear, I never think to use a phone book anymore."

Anson catches his breath while Martha flips quickly through the white pages. Isidore watches him as if she knows what the result of his Sophie's Choice would have been and does not approve.

"No," Martha says. "No Campers at all. These things really are worthless." She shoves the phonebook away like it has insulted her. This worries Anson, though he can't say why. "Well. There's only one thing to do then."

This takes the Campers by surprise. Their life has never been so boiled down. When is there ever only one thing to be done? How does one know what the one thing is? None of the Camper's can manage this trick. Instead they look to Anson until he barks out a flustered order. Now Martha has put the world into neat form. They lean forward to hear it.

"We'll go down to the cook-off," she says. "Today, at a park near downtown. They're having a barbecue competition, and you never know. Maybe your Dad'll be there."

"Oh my gosh," says Lulu. "That was beautiful, Martha."

Martha nods. "Just seems the thing to do."

TULSA
OKLAHOMA

THE CAMPERS CONVENE in the Airstream. It's a relief to Isidore, who is anxious for things to get back to normal. On any other visit to Tulsa, this is the point at which they'd leave town, and she is ready for the road. She wants Anson to be happy, but wishes he had picked some obsession less treacherous than Martha. Like cock fighting or whores.

Anson runs his hands through his hair in an uncharacteristically agitated manner. "What if we get heat?" he says.

"Boy are you two episodes behind," says Lulu. "Now you start to worry about heat? Shouldn't you have thought of that before all the times you came to Tulsa to visit Goldilocks in the first place?"

"We don't get heat in Tulsa," Isidore says quietly. She's slumped, surrendered, in the sofa, her hands folded across her pooch.

"Oh, that's rich," says Lulu. "Nice set of rules you've made for yourselves here, guys. Real convenient."

"They're not our rules, Lulu," Anson says.

"I'm only going to say this one more time. And then I'm going to stop, because it hasn't made any difference before and I'd be nuts to try and keep explaining it to you." She takes a deep breath and folds her hands across the dinette. They would both look away but she gave a hell of a performance this morning, and they feel grudgingly indebted. "Anson. Isidore. The angels aren't real. They don't exist, they never existed. You made all this up in your heads." Anson and Isidore nod solemnly, offering no contradiction, until Lulu visibly relaxes.

"We should go now. We have to leave Martha," Anson says as soon as the moment has passed. "I have to get you guys out of here. This was a mistake." Lulu nods, filled with the calm this ritual of denial provides her. Anson's personal bag is still upstairs but contains nothing that can't be left behind. He didn't bring any guns into the house, didn't want to risk them around all those kids. He glances around the cabin. The bedroom door is open, but it doesn't look like anyone is in there. "Where's River?"

"Oh yeah. He's gone," Lulu says.

"Where'd he go?" Anson says, thinking maybe the grocery store, or Starbucks.

Lulu shrugs.

"Isidore," Anson says. "What the hell?"

"We meant to tell you earlier," Isidore says, sighing heavily. "We put him in the bed last night. Lulu got the sofa and I got the floor, which wasn't very comfortable by the way. When we woke up he was gone."

Anson can't be hearing them right. His sisters are certified basket cases, both of them, but he thought even they were better than this. Surely they would not allow their former-addict brother, who is having his first encounter with drugs since cleaning up nine years ago, to disappear into a strange city and wait hours to do anything about it. Get dressed, fix their hair, fuss over their clothes—it's too much, Anson begins to breathe heavily—do the goddamn laundry—he wants to speak, he opens his mouth but can only gasp, he thinks he might be having a heart attack—shop for peaches—oh God, his chest hurts—sit in a kitchen and—

"Coffee cake!" he explodes, throwing one finger in the air at the sheer triumph of speech. "You sat there eating coffee cake!"

Isidore raises her palms. "Are we not allowed to have coffee cake, now, Anson?"

"You know, I have to sleep on the galley floor all the time, Isidore. All the fucking time."

"You never complained," Isidore says, like it's his own damn fault.

"And River—eating cake while River is—is—shit," he says.

"Relax," says Lulu. "He'll be fine."

"He probably just went out to get laid," says Isidore. "It's about time."

"Ok," Anson says to himself, formulating a plan. "Ok. We find River. We find him first," he repeats loudly, anticipating his sisters' protests. "I don't give a damn about Minxy and Dad, I never did. Dad left us and that's his problem, if Minxy dies without him. River's our brother, he's been in this with us all along and he comes first. Now. Where would River go?"

Lulu is utterly stumped by the question. "Uh . . ." she says.

"He would—um—" Isidore chews her lower lip. "He'd . . . " She squints into the distance.

"Come on," says Anson. "This is our own brother here. Somebody has to know what River likes? What he's into? Pool, or . . . " Anson is at a loss. He tries to picture River doing something he enjoys and can only conjure up an image of his brother with one hand around the Xbox controller and the other down his pants. "Darts, or something?"

"He likes the cooking channel," Isidore says weakly. "Maybe he'd go to . . . a restaurant supply store?"

The answer is embarrassing. They are sitting in a terrible silence when a series of rapid pops and the distinct whir of a fiery sword comes from outside. This is what Anson has always been afraid of and now it's happening. Isidore realizes she didn't hear the heat meter, and then she remembers that River's gone and he must have taken it with him. She slides the Smith and Wesson at Anson and then they are on their feet, pistols raised because the door has banged open.

"Oh my God," Martha says.

"Get down!" commands Anson. Martha hits the floor like she is accustomed to being told to drop and give twenty. Stepping over her, Anson looks out the front window.

"I don't see anything," he shouts. "Lulu?"

Lulu has made herself useful and hustled to the back windows. "Nothing here," she says, affecting her signature ennui.

Isidore looks out the passenger side window and sees nothing. She glances at Martha, motionlessly awaiting orders like a good soldier, and crosses to the driver's side window. "Nothing."

"Where is it? Where is it, then?" says Anson.

Isidore looks. There's prairie, the cement driveway, and a gaggle of Martha's nieces and nephews, ranging in ages from about five to fifteen. They stand in a cluster, all but one, who is bent over something in the driveway.

"Dammit," Isidore says. "It's just the fucking fireworks. Those lotus blossom things."

"Fucking fireworks," Lulu and Anson say.

"Can I get up?" says Martha.

Anson glances out the window again. "Yeah."

Martha's eyes are sharp and miss nothing. The Camper siblings armed for battle. A colorful assortment of guns and knives on the table like sweets at a candy shop. Anson has played this scene out in his mind hundreds, maybe thousands, of times. Now that it's here, he is calmer than he always imagined he would be. There is a sense of relief.

"Ok," says Martha. "What is this?" Anson has always pictured her accusatory, tearful, but she is neither.

"We're arms dealers," Lulu says, spinning out a quick lie. "We couldn't tell you because the Muslims are trying to kill us."

Martha looks like she might faint. Anson shakes his head. He appreciates Lulu's effort, but this has gone on too long. "Martha," he says, bracing himself to be slapped or dumped. Isidore feels sorry for him. And squeamish. She doesn't want to witness this. But she also does. Her eyes fix on the spectacle and refuse to liberate themselves from basic nosiness. "I'm not a Bible salesmen," says Anson. Lulu cranes to see past Isidore. If Anson's going to get slapped, she darn well wants to see it.

Martha's eyes are wide and pretty. "You're not?"

"No, honey," he says. Anson watches her struggling to reconcile what she has just witnessed with the person she needs him to be. An impossible task.

"You've lied to me," she says.

"He could shoot an apple off your noggin from a hundred paces," says Isidore. "Doesn't that count for anything?"

"Not now, Isidore," Anson says. He is worried that Martha might shatter like glass. He can tell this is the first time life has ever surprised her. Watching it fills him with a sick horror. He has made a terrible mess and there is no clean way to end this.

"So you're . . . " Martha is looking at the guns. Each Camper is holding a big one. Lulu has a knife in her second hand. "You're like, the Lutheran CIA?"

"How would you feel about that?" says Lulu. Anson holds up a hand.

"We're not the CIA," he says. "We're—"

"But you're still Lutheran, right?" Martha says. Her eyes are wide as offering plates. All three of the Campers can see that Martha desperately needs this to be true. There is a pause. Martha shines her eyes at Anson, begging him not to let her down. After a moment, Anson flashes his winning smile at her.

"It's not that I'm not—"

"I need to sit down," Martha says. She goes boneless. Anson braces her as she falls limp into the captain's chair. Isidore and Lulu rush to her. They push Anson out of the way.

"Give her some air," says Lulu.

"You're Wisconsin Synod, is what you mean," Martha says. She winces. "Or even—ELCA? I could work with that.

Oh God." She braces her palms on her knees, sucks in air.

"Here," says Isidore, holding out a bottle of water. She has no idea what Martha is saying about Wisconsin sinners. Clearly Martha has snapped. She doesn't take the water, just frowns at Isidore suspiciously. Isidore presses it to her lips. Bottle smashing her flesh to her teeth, Martha submits and drinks. Lulu begins to fan her with her hands. "Anson, roll the windows down for heaven's sake. Give her some air." Anson does as he's told.

Martha is starting to breathe too quickly. "Slow down," says Isidore. "Come on. Close your mouth and breathe through your nose, you don't want to hyperventilate. Imagine—there are Lutherans all around you. You are safe in your Lutheran world. There you go. Now what is it? You can tell us."

Martha has locked her eyes on Isidore like Isidore is a map of home. She nods. Takes a few measured breaths. "It's just been so hard," she says. Isidore nods.

"Of course it has. Tell us why."

Martha hesitates.

"Don't worry about hurting our feelings," says Lulu. "You can tell us. Is it Anson? It's Anson, isn't it?"

"Jesus, Lulu—" Anson says.

"Shut up Anson. Give us some room."

"Anson's wonderful," Martha says.

"Isn't he?" Isidore glows.

"But all my friends are married—"

"I know, honey," Isidore says soothingly.

"All my friends are married," repeats Martha. "And I'm not, and that's fine. I thought that was fine. I just kept praying that God would work in Anson's heart," Lulu flinches at that, the idea of asking God to manipulate her brother, but Martha doesn't notice. "And I trusted that He would. But He hasn't. And now I'm twenty-six and Anson isn't Lutheran!" She's panting again. Isidore shushes her, stroking her hand, but Martha is too flustered to be calmed. "Now I either have to convert him, or start all over with some other guy! And I'm

230

old! And I've never had sex!"

"Come on now," Isidore says. "I mean, is that really true?"

Lulu raises an eyebrow at Anson. "Shut up, Lulu!" Anson says. He is watching this unfold in red-faced horror, the way men witness grief or babies being born. Completely useless.

"I'm just starting to feel," Martha says, and her eyes water and spill over. "I'm just starting to feel like God is punishing me!"

With those words, a vast world of possibilities opens to Isidore. She can hardly speak, she is so stunned. "Martha. He hunts you too?"

"Oh God," Lulu says. "That's not what she means, Is."

"Of course it is. God is punishing her? He's trying to kill her. What else would that mean?"

Martha has stopped crying and is staring at Isidore the way people start to, when they've been around her long enough. "Hunts? What are you talking about?"

"You said God is out to get you," Isidore says. "Since you were born, or did you mess something up along the way?" Isidore figures that if someone like Martha can deserve to die, maybe her own fumbling attempts at life aren't so iniquitous by comparison. She probably never even had a chance.

"No," Martha shakes her head. "I'm talking about the fact that all my friends are married, and I'm not. And Anson's not Lutheran. And we don't even have an Ikea in Tulsa. I mean, come on!" She sniffs. "Why did I have to be born in a city without an Ikea?"

Anson catches Isidore's hand before she can bring it down hard across Martha's tan cheek as she obviously intends. "Let me go, Annie," Isidore says. "No fucking—no fucking Ikea—Anson I swear to God—"

If it was up to Lulu, Martha would get the smack in the kisser but since it's not, she merely says: "God isn't out to get you, Martha. God is out to get us."

Martha rolls her eyes. "Yeah right. God obviously loves you guys the most. You've got this sweet Airstream, you don't have jobs. And you all have really awesome bone structure. Mostly." She casts a quick glance at Isidore.

The Camper siblings all stare at Martha Svenson, shocked into silence. They are aware their lives have been more difficult than most. They don't spend a lot of time asking why, they are in general too busy trying to stay alive. Who, after all, does get explanation for the events of their lives? While the Campers don't dwell on feeling sorry for themselves, it is still a shock to hear this from Martha: that they, heaven's most wanted, should in fact feel grateful. That they are the lucky ones.

"He is a sweet Airstream," Isidore says finally. "My Pacey. I'll give her that."

"My bone structure is pretty nice," Lulu muses, running a fingertip along her ski jump nose. "Thanks for reminding me."

"Yeah but—" Anson says. It feels imperative not to overindulge in happiness. To let the guard down is to let the angels in. "God is still out to get us. I think."

"But at least we have each other," Lulu says. On her last word, a loud stream of pops erupts from the driveway. Isidore and Lulu hit the floor, pulling Martha with them. They land on top of her. Anson raises his gun out the windshield. "Where are you bastards?"

"Fireworks," Martha says. Her voice comes out small, Lulu and Isidore's weight pressing her against the floor. "Just fireworks."

"I think you need to count your blessings," Martha says. She stands and adjusts her blouse back into perfection. "You guys have a lot to be thankful for."

Anson is chagrined. "You're right," he says. "I know. It's just—it can be so distracting. Always worrying about getting our heads cut off, or castrated. Those Bible guys were really into castration, you know."

Lulu makes a sympathetic noise. "Annie," she says.

She rubs his back. "I didn't know you worried about being castrated."

"I do," Anson confesses.

"It's me," Isidore tells Martha. "The angels want to kill me. They're on orders from God. We think. I mean, we pretty much know, but it's not like they've ever said that. God forbid he should ever be direct." Isidore speaks to the sky, rolling her eyes like God is a husband she's been married to for too long.

"They're not your kind of angels," Lulu says, attempting tact with Martha's beliefs. "They're the real conservative type, you know. They hate women's bodies, and . . . dairy."

"Dairy?" repeats Martha.

"River panicked and chucked a Frappuccino at one, once. It scattered. We're pretty sure it was the dairy. They're allergic or something," says Isidore.

"Are you guys making this up?" says Martha.

"Yes," says Lulu. "Thank you."

"Yes," Isidore says to placate Lulu, but she shakes her head at Martha and mouths "No."

"Ok," says Martha. Her eyes roam Anson up and down, full of a purposeful intent they all ignore. "First things first," she says, and they all know what she means: later, she will be reading to him from the catechism and taking him out to coffee, which will not be merely coffee but attempts to sway his spirituality. But all that must come later. "First I'm going to go tell the cousins to stop setting off the fireworks."

"Praise Jesus," says Lulu. It is hard, sometimes, to shake a role.

"And then we're going to get you to the cook-off. First we'll see to the earthly father. Then the heavenly one." Lulu and Isidore wince. They look to Anson, wondering if he's going to dump Martha now that the jig is up. But he's clearly distracted.

"Shit," he says. "What are we going to do about River?"

"What's wrong with River?" asks Martha.

"He could be anywhere," says Anson.

"Vanished in the night," says Isidore. "Such a tragedy. He was so gentle."

"And he didn't answer his phone?" Martha says.

Isidore blinks and looks at Lulu.

"Lulu?" Anson says. "Is? Did he answer the phone?"

"I guess we could—try again," Lulu falters.

"Wouldn't—wouldn't hurt."

"Jesus Christ," says Anson. "You're telling me you didn't even call him?" Anson takes out his phone and dials River. It rings once, and then a voice which Anson does not recognize as his brother's croaks, "Hello?"

"Who is this?" Anson demands.

"Annie?"

The voice is parched, bone dry, and if it wasn't for the nickname, Anson wouldn't have believed it was River. "River? That you?"

"Who else would it be?" River says, more than a touch smug. "Where are you, man?"

"I'm at Martha's house. In Pacey," says Anson. "Where are you?"

"What?" River says. "You can't be in Pacey. I'm in Pacey."

Because Anson does not put it past his sisters to look in the bedroom and simply miss River's body on the bed, he moves down the galley to the bedroom and throws open the door. No River. He walks around to the other side of the bed to see if he's wedged between it and the wall. He toes a tremendous heap of dirty laundry to be sure. No River.

"No you're not," Anson says. "Listen to me man. I'm standing in Pacey with Martha and our bitch-whore sisters right now, and you're not here."

"Oh my god," says River. "Do you think I'm in an alternate dimension—"

"Look around you," Anson barks. He does not have time for this. River is obviously on drugs again, something stronger than the Vicodin, Anson suspects, because he hasn't heard River sound this narcotized in years. In nine years, to be

234

exact. Since before River was busted for possession and sent to prison for eighteen months. Goddamn Lulu for shooting him. Anson doesn't have the energy to talk him down from another high and into another attempt at sobriety. He's tired. He might be converting to Lutheranism. "You're not in the Airstream. Look around and tell me what you see."

"Okay, except only I am," River says in a singsong voice. God help him. Then River starts laughing. "I see the flat screen, and the overhead, and the galley, man. I see the bathroom door and the dinette. Shit. I think I ate all Lulu's lemons. Shit, she's gonna kill me, man."

"Quit screwing around and tell me what you see," Anson says.

"That's what I'm doing. I see the sofa—I'm lying on the sofa. And the—holy shit. Oh God. Hey man. What's up?"

"What?" Anson says. There is the sense that River is speaking to someone there with him, wherever he is, and not into the phone.

"Who are you? Dude, were you with my sister? Gross," River says.

"Oh my god," says Anson.

"What?" says Lulu.

"He's in an Airstream," Anson says. "He's just not in our Airstream."

"How the hell did he find another Airstream?"

"The barbecue competition," says Martha. "They all have trailers."

"It's cool man, you can chill with us," River is saying. "Play a little Xbox, whatever." And then—"Oh shit. Anson. Annie, help me! Oh God, help me!"

"What's happening?" Anson says.

"He's got a frying pan, man. He's chasing me with the—shit." Anson hears a tinny bang and then a gravelly skidding noise. He thinks the phone has been dropped. He waits. "River?" he says after a moment. He pictures some old RV lifer coming out of his commode to find River stoned on his couch. He imagines the man thumping River over the head and killing him. "River?"

"Oh my god," River breaths into the phone. "That dude almost killed me. He almost killed me, man."

"Is he coming after you?"

"Of course not," River says, deeply offended. "I'm me. I got away. And I got my gun."

"Do not pull your gun on any tourists," Anson commands. "River, listen to me. Are you at the barbecue competition?"

"I don't know! How would I know that?"

"There'd be a bunch of dudes with grills," Anson says sharply. He is losing his patience.

"Oh. Okay, yeah. I guess I am. There's all these big guys in aprons and they've got meat."

"Stay where you are, River. You hear me? Stop right where you are and don't move."

TULSA
OKLAHOMA
4ᵀᴴ OF JULY

ANSON DRIVES WITHOUT allowing himself to dwell on the situation. Martha insisted on coming and is next to him in the navigator's seat. Lulu and Isidore are in the back. They seem to be silent, but Anson senses they're whispering about him, or sharing glances at least. He's jittery, wondering what it might be like to see his dad. He wonders if the opportunity to shoot something might present itself. He'd like the man to see how much his aim has improved.

As they approach the park, the streets grow more crowded. There are people everywhere, all in red, white and blue. At a stop sign a family passes in front of the Airstream. A slender young mother in a blue sundress, a dad in khakis, three black haired children, the baby with her hair in two shiny pompoms tied with explosions of patriotic ribbons. All five of them check out the Airstream as they pass. The little boys point and jump. Martha waves. Anson is unaware of his own grip flexing and clenching on the steering wheel. There's something he doesn't like about this. There is a sense that one of these things is not like the other, and he doesn't want to consider who doesn't belong.

"The Fourth of July is my favorite secular holiday," Martha says.

"It's gonna be a bitch to park," says Anson.

"This looks like a propaganda film," says Lulu. "I mean, yay America, but isn't this a little obscene?"

"It's just patriotic. The competition's that way," Martha points. "In the square. There's a pie-eating contest, Annie, maybe we could eat some pies." She smiles like a firecracker.

"Yeah," Anson says through his teeth. "Maybe." He wishes she would stop calling him Annie.

They circle blocks. The crowds and all the closed off streets render the task Herculean. Finally they find a lot with enough empty spaces to fit the Airstream, a short distance from the festival. Anson parks in the shade of a high-rise. He stands and puts the Glock 26 in his pocket holster. It's too hot to wear a jacket to conceal the shoulder holster and he's not expecting any problems from the angels. Big crowds, Baptist families, this just isn't their gig. Lulu slips a Colt into her hip holster where it hides beneath her gauzy sundress. Isidore brings only her knife, tucked into the ridiculous red boots that Lulu has made her wear.

"Ready for Mission River Rescue?" Martha chirps, alighting from the trailer. She has recovered from her breakdown and has clearly set forth with a new determination to save them all. Anson is too embarrassed to look at his sisters. "This way." She takes Anson's hand and starts off down the sidewalk, speedy in her sensible shoes.

Behind them, Lulu is forced to link her arm through Isidore's like they used to in high school, because Isidore is tottering on her one-inch boot heels. "Seriously, Isidore?"

"Seriously Isidore? Seriously Lulu," Isidore snaps. "You're the one who owns these ridiculous things."

"They're vintage," Lulu says. "I just thought you'd want to look cute. Because you're a whore."

"Yeah," Isidore agrees. "When should we tell Martha?"

"That her boyfriend's sister is the Whore of Babylon?

Probably after the wedding."

"Or during it."

"Now you're talking."

They join the throng of happy families and young couples making their way toward the park where the competition is set up. Somewhere a band is playing patriotic tunes, drums and tubas that make Isidore imagine a gazebo, men in red-and-white striped pants. The scent of roasted meat is pervasive and mouthwatering. It smells like the world's last supper. The barbecue competition must be underway.

"Can we get some brisket?" Isidore calls to Anson. She had brisket once at a roadside stop in rural Missouri and has never forgotten it. The way the meat melted like chocolate on her tongue.

"River first," says Anson. Martha looks over her shoulder and rolls her eyes at Anson for the benefit of the girls. Lulu and Isidore both flinch.

"I can't do this," Isidore says when Martha turns back and laughs. There had been a moment there, in the trailer, when she'd believed it was all going to be okay. That they'd found another and, between the five of them, would form a tribe. God's Hated Few. Then Martha had said the thing about Ikea and Isidore had known she wasn't their tribe, and never would be. She doesn't mind if Anson wants to keep sleeping with Martha, she just hopes she won't have to cede the navigator chair again. It is her chair. She doesn't bring her conquests home and can't understand why Anson must.

"Maybe there's beer," Lulu says. A mother pushes a stroller past them, her child's cluster of balloons bombarding Lulu's face. Lulu bats them away. "There's gotta be beer somewhere. Goddammit." She punches the balloons again. The mother's look is withering. Lulu flashes a grin and then gives the bird behind the woman's back.

The scent of smoked meat grows heavier the closer they get to the square. Isidore's mouth waters. Lulu groans lustily that they must get some of the meat, and even Anson admits that he's starving. "Let's just find River. Then we'll get something to eat."

"Call him," Isidore says. They have reached the competition arena. It's on a paved area next to a sprawled out green, under the baking sun. There are dozens of white tents sheltering men in aprons and the loveliest barbecues Isidore has ever seen. Some of them are black and silver and barrel shaped, chipper little pipes sticking up from the sides, puffing savory smoke. Others are like the gas grills they have to stop for River to lust over every time they pass a Home Depot, only four or five times the size. They pass a tent as a man in a white apron with a smiling pink pig on the front pops one open to reveal four rows of plumpy chickens. He's got a jug of sauce, and he uses a brush to paint it on to the happy little chicken breasts, which are beginning to char ever so slightly at the sides. The sauce is scented peppery and sweet; Isidore catches a sun-soaked tomatoey aroma and the pleasant burn of bourbon.

Lulu makes climaxing sounds. It might upset Isidore to realize how similarly lecherous they are—she has a corner on lust—but she is distracted by a rack of beef turning on a spit. It's dripping fat into a grated fire beneath it, each drip hissing and sending out an intoxicating scent. She moves toward it, pulled against her will by the fleshy siren song.

Anson grips the back of her shirt and stops her. He knows from experience that losing Isidore in a crowd is a mistake and eventually someone will call the police. He's got his phone raised to his ear. "Where are you?" he's saying. "Tell me what you see." He squints in the glare, perspiration forming at his hairline. Martha in her crisp blouse looks snowy by comparison. Anson turns, searching, and then he stops. His face goes strangely blank, which puzzles Isidore. "Stay there," he says.

He snaps his phone shut. Takes a breath. He turns to look at Isidore and Lulu, his lips parted like he's going to say something. But he doesn't. He looks at Martha and then he rolls his shoulders back. Isidore recognizes his battle-ready body language, but there are no angels and, as a quick glance

240

around proves, no Grandma Ruth either. She follows him deeper into the heart of the cook-off.

They walk only a short distance, avoiding the aromatic lure of the smoking meat around them with considerable effort, and then Isidore sees him. River is in the space behind two tents, leaning against a tree in its shade. Anson reaches him first and embraces him with a hug, which Isidore finds unnecessary and overly dramatic.

"You guys have gotta try this barbecue," River says. "Oh man, it's out of this world."

"We were waiting for you, you bastard," Lulu says. "Anson made us wait."

Anson's harsh tone evicts River's smile from his face. "What are you on, man? Don't try and fuck with me."

River is wounded. "What? I was on Vicodin this morning but I think it's worn off. I'm kind of hurting here." He nods at his shoulder. "Did you bring it? I think it's been eight hours."

Isidore thinks Anson is going to make some thumping male display and maybe shove River, which bothers her only proportionately to the amount of time she figures it will delay her getting a taste of the barbecue, but Anson doesn't. "I said don't fuck with me," Anson says low. "What are you on? Heroin? Meth?"

"No. I've only had the Vicodin Lulu gave me—"

"Which you've already burned through, and now you're asking her for Xanax, or Valium, or whatever the Mormon movie stars are taking—"

"Oh God no," Martha whispers. "Not Mormons."

"No," says River. "I gave the bottle to Lulu, actually. So that I couldn't do that. I don't want to go on drugs again." Most of the time Isidore's feelings for River vacillate from fond indifference to mild disgust, but River's innocent dismay tugs at her and she feels an upsetting desire to make him a sandwich.

"Right," Anson says. "How am I supposed to trust you—"

"Because," River interrupts. He looks at Isidore. "You really never told him?"

Isidore shakes her head. At another time his doubt might offend her, but to her left a husband-and-wife team is luxuriously coating a huge piece of meat in a grainy red paste, a process that looks erotic to Isidore. The husband is good looking, and behind them another cut is smoking so that now Isidore is not only ferociously hungry, but also a little aroused.

"I'd never go on drugs again because of what happened last time."

"Prison?"

"No. I mean, that was bad too, but," River sighs. "Isidore kicked my ass."

Anson frowns. Martha giggles, presumably at the idea of Isidore kicking ass. Isidore inches toward the barbecue.

"She what? Don't move, Isidore," Anson says, stopping Isidore in her tracks. Truly he is a proxy parent, to catch her like this with his gaze turned away.

"She came in when I was using. With my dealer, man. It was me and a few other guys, couple hot chicks in some dude's basement, and Isidore came in, and she kicked my ass, man. She was seventeen. She was all Hulk, but they didn't know that. You ever had your ass kicked publicly by your kid sister? You'd do just about anything to avoid that again."

"And I would," says Isidore to the pork. "Do it again."

"I know you would," says River. "I know she would. I'm not using. I don't ever wanna go through that again."

Anson searches River's eyes and decides he believes him. He looks embarrassed enough, recounting the story here in front of only family and Martha. "Well," says Anson. "Good. You're bleeding again."

"Yeah, I know," says River. "My high's all gone, too."

Anson considers his brother and decides he is contrite enough to be given pain relief. He tells Lulu to administer a Vicodin, only to see panic enliven Lulu's eyes before she pastes on a bright smile and tosses her mane like a haughty pony. From this Anson knows that Lulu has swallowed whatever

242

remained of River's medication. He thinks back to her perky mood this morning, her dress, her basket of fruit. He should have known it was not come by naturally. Natural good cheer is not something the Camper's are capable of. Not the human ones, anyway.

Isidore begins to whine. She's hungry, she's going to go Hulk if she doesn't eat something, does Anson agree the man is rubbing his roast that way purposefully to taunt her. Martha has taken a few steps back and is now glancing around and smiling at strangers, in what looks to Anson like the actions of a crazy person but may be some sort of attempt to produce a positive front. For once, Anson has no regrets about turning his back on all of them. He leans in to River.

"Where is he?"

River jerks his chin. "There."

TULSA
OKLAHOMA
4TH OF JULY

IN A STALL across the path from where the Camper siblings are gathered, their father is violating a chicken. Dressed in an apron a shade of turquoise uncannily similar to the Minxy's Last Stand tee shirt that River is still sporting, Randy Camper is caressing tender white flesh that lays dimpled and motionless beneath his ministrations. The awkwardness of catching their father in this private, carnal moment is only compounded by the cartoon chicken on the apron, bulging out of a smallish yellow camper, waving one white wing. Inexplicably printed underneath the grinning chicken are the words RANDY CAMPER'S BEANS AND WEENIE. The Camper siblings wince upon reading the words. Anson feels nauseated.

The beans and weenie man is shifty, shuffling his eyes back and forth between the siblings and the chicken carcass with which he is becoming intimately acquainted. Anson doesn't know how River and Isidore watch the cooking channel all day, if this is what it's like. He feels he should put a stop to it. Defend the honor of the fowl.

"Annie," Isidore says. "That's not him, is it?"

Since she was ten, Isidore has seen only pictures of their father. Pictures from fifteen years ago or more; pictures that are not of the man making the truest sense of food porn here before them. The man before them is fifty-six. His blonde hair has gone white. It's still thick on top, and he's let it grow out just a touch long, to show it off, probably. He looks older than he is the way Nordic people who go in the sun tend to, his face tanned and wrinkled, sunspots on his arms. He has the same broad shoulders, but he's gone a little fat-bellied, a state of sloth he never would have allowed himself when they were young. When he was still at their side, fighting angels.

"That's him," Lulu says. Anson envies her certainty. He remembers the times he most wished for his dad. When the Airstream broke down in the center lane of the 405 during rush hour. When he'd been driving through the roughest parts of town looking for River, who had gone to see his dealer three days before and hadn't returned. When Aunt Jackie had married a serial killer. He'd been a twenty-one, or twenty-six, or thirty-two year old man. He'd felt that he should have known what to do. But he hadn't. He hadn't had a father since he was eighteen and despite that, he'd all that time tried to be a father. To Isidore, mainly, but to Lulu too, before she'd run off, and even to River, who hadn't let him but who, he'd suspected, had wanted to.

"Doesn't he see us?" Isidore says. Lulu puts her arm around her shoulders.

"He can't even look at us?" says River.

Anson doesn't plan what happens next. Like getting pregnant, or sick after quesadillas, some things are simply functions of the body and occur without intent. Martha flutters around him like a tiny dog. Anson pushes her away. The next thing he feels is his Glock 26, cold and familiar in his hand. It feels separate from him, bionic maybe. Beyond his control. Then Anson does something he was drilled, in his youth, never to do. He advances with a drawn weapon on his father.

People around them scream and curse their time-and-placing, but Lulu claps and cries giddily, like she's just won a spot on a game show, and this juxtaposition surprises the crowd and prevents a full panic. The other people in the booth behind their father, basting his Camper chickens and squeezing his Camper sausages, spill back like ants at a picnic, pouring out of the tent and falling over themselves and each other in the process. They are not willing to take their chances.

Randy Camper stands his ground.

"Whoa there, boy. I know it smells good but you'll have to wait like everyone else." There is laughter. A kid pulls out his cell phone to take a video. Quickly Anson calculates that he cannot shoot the phone without killing the kid.

"Quit screwing around," Anson says. And then he spits the word like a weapon. "Dad."

His father's eyes drench Anson in moist sympathy. Clearly he pities him and his pathetic gun, these misguided men-and-women-children in strange, stupid clothing. River rangy, unwashed and bleeding; the women with alien-orb eyes and scrawny Area 51 limbs. "I'm afraid I don't know what you mean, buddy."

Isidore's eyes are blue Danubes of dismay. "Dad—it's me. It's us."

Randy Camper squints at Isidore, leaning in like she is a melon to sniff. "Did we—did we compete together? Back in Arkansas, or?"

"No," says Isidore. "You're our dad." It is unclear to Anson whether she is pissed, or pitying, or both.

"Mmmmmm," their dad says, as if he's searching way back in his memory, really trying here. "No, dear. I'm afraid not."

Anson can feel them all eyeing him. His siblings for direction, the crowd for the show, and his father almost a challenge, daring him to engage. He doesn't know what to do. He isn't sure if, had he been better fathered, he would have been confident in this and other situations, or if everyone uncertain of their course, even those who hadn't been abandoned. He holds steady. "This is what you're going to do? You're going to pretend you're not our father?"

"Your—your father?" Their father laughs. "I can't blame you for wishing, what with the smell coming off these beauties." He says it to his audience, an aside. "But I'm afraid you're mistaken. I don't have children. I've never seen you before in my life."

River looks like he could cry, and he's not a man who could pull it off. Anson won't shoot the civilians. River actually might.

"You're pathetic, you know that—"

"Who are you people? Is this a prank? Mitch sent you, didn't he? That Mitch, he's always up to something. Where are you, Mitch?" Randy Camper is grinning. Anson thinks he should have been an actor, or a preacher. He is a true charlatan. "Mitch Morrell, come on out, buddy!"

"Is?" Anson says quietly, checking in. Ever since River told him, over the phone, that he could see their father, he has been thinking of Isidore. He has been remembering the way Isidore, at age three, would sit near their father, craving his presence, but never on him. Never with him. Because she knew, even then, that she frightened him.

Isidore answers Anson with a shrug. She's thought about this moment often, on the road in New Mexico or West Texas. Even when they'd been slamming back tequila and dancing to cowboy songs, it had hovered in the back of her mind. She had imagined a grand reunion, sweeping emotions, but here, under the Oklahoma sun, she feels mostly dull and hungry. She wonders if this is why God wants her dead. She has little memory of her father's voice, the sound of his laugh. All the pictures she has seen have not captured this man before her. They've captured a younger version, one with kids hanging off his neck as he rolled around in the backyard. A man in red swim trunks with a trim belly, next to three scrawny kids and one chubby baby in goggles and floaties. She doesn't know this man, who panders to the crowd and pretends not to know his children, and she's relieved to find she doesn't want to.

"We need to get out of this heat," Martha says, no-nonsense. "We need to sit down in the shade, with a cool drink, and discuss this."

Their father's gift is for working every moment to his greatest benefit. He does it now. "That your girlfriend, there?" He points not to Martha, but to Isidore. "She's a real looker, isn't she? What are you, honey, a C cup?"

"Shut up, Dad," Anson says wearily.

"You're an asshole," River says. The anger in his voice is clean, not ugly or bitter. He looks at Anson. "Was he always an asshole?"

Anson remembers his father pretending to sleep in the backseat while his wife and children fought off the angels. "Yeah. I guess he was."

Anson waits for his words to hit home, but his father is distracted. "Oh my god!" he says. His eyebrows shoot up the way they used to when River would bring home a toad, or fire a potato gun at Anson. Like never had he imagined his life would contain such uncontainable mess, such base domestic chaos.

"Gosh," corrects Martha. Randy Camper waves his hand at her dismissively. Isidore can't decide if the fact that he hasn't acknowledged Martha is a mark for or against him. Peering at River's shirt like it holds the secrets of the universe, their father displays emotions usually reserved for a child's first step or start of college.

"Is that—is that Minxy? Is something wrong with Minxy? Is she okay?"

"God, Dad," says Lulu. Although her disgust is aimed solely at their father, all three siblings and probably some of the crowd recoil at its vigor. Anson doesn't care if it's true emotion or affected for the moment; either way, he thinks, his sister can act. "What the hell are you trying to pull? I told them. How we've kept in touch. Just with me. How the hell do you think that makes them feel? I mean, I know I'm the only one of us who's accomplished anything worth mentioning. That can't be easy on you, I get that. But to pretend you don't even know them? You're a douche, Daddy. A real chubby douche." The crowd applauds. A few of them cheer. Lulu has swayed the audience.

Randy Camper is wily. He knows when he is trapped. He slaps his palm to his heart like a true patriot. "Lulu, is that—well hallelujah, folks, oh praise Jesus!" he cries, turning open-armed to the crowd. "It's my prodigal daughter! My Lulu! And Anson! Isidore! Is that really you?"

"Shut up," says Lulu. "He knows who you are. Mom sent him pictures, I know she did. He said Isidore had nice legs and River turned out to scrawny. Well that's what he said," she snaps defensively.

"Fine," their father says. Glaring at Lulu like she is responsible for this mess, and Anson's gun comes back to half-mast. "Fine, you assholes. You win. You're my kids, okay? Feel better now?" He glares the father-wrath at them and they all withdraw under it, never mind they are grown-ups now and can check their own oil. Anson, at least. "Would you just tell me what's going on with Minxy? She's all right, isn't she? If she's not, I swear to God your mother. She wouldn't let me have Minxy, did you know that? My own dog, and that bitch-"

"She's dying, you dick," River says. "And you're seeing your kids for the first time in fifteen years. Do you think you could stop staring at the picture of the damn dog and look at us?"

"Yeah!" someone calls. "They're your kids, man!"

"I'm sorry," their dad says. It's not clear whether he is addressing his children or the audience. "Sorry guys, it's just. This is all a little much to take." His voice is thick. None of the Camper siblings flatter themselves by imagining it's over then.

"Mom sent us to come find you," Isidore says. "As soon as she found out Minxy was dying."

"She wants you to come home and take Minxy for a walk for the last time. Before she goes," says Lulu.

"Minxy's Last Stand," their father reads off the shirt with a misty smile. He wipes at his eyes. Drags his gaze off cock-eared Minxy and truly looks at Anson for the first time. Anson waits for reaction. Approval or disdain, something. What he gets is shallow interest, like Anson is a work of modern art, not one that particularly grips him. Then Randy Camper moves on to River. Here he winces, it is unclear why. It could be the blood seeping from the shoulder wound, or the hair, which has grown a little long. The crowd waits in rapt anticipation. He turns to Isidore. Assesses her. Not as a daughter, but as a threat. Backs away, like he's placed her at orange. It makes Anson furious. "Stop it," he growls.

"Look, guys," he says. "I know I've got some explaining to do. I have a lot of regrets, and a lot to account for. I know that. But first, I really have to get these birds in the cooker. I have a real shot at winning this thing, this time. That goddamn Mike Mills—" his voice rises. The crowd gasps in horror. "You leave Mike Mills out of this!" someone cries. Their father takes a deep breath, like he's practicing something he learned in anger management class, and reaches down for his pan of chicken.

"Put the chicken down, Dad," Anson says. "Or I swear to god, I'll kill you here."

"You wouldn't. This place is swarming with cops. You'd have a particularly hard time in prison, Anson. Being so pretty."

Anson has forgotten this, how his dad calls him pretty to keep him small. "You think Isidore can't get us past a few cops?" he says proudly. "Yeah. She does that now."

"I've developed," Isidore chimes in.

"You're upset," their dad begins. "I get that—"

"Upset?" Anson says. His hand goes to his gun again, pure habit, and his father edges away. "Do you have any idea what this has been like for us? For Isidore and Lulu, growing up without a dad? Isidore's a complete mess, and Lulu? Lulu's a fucking actress. And River—did you know we almost lost him? You think he had an easy time in prison? And Mom—"

"A complete mess?" Isidore says at the same time their dad says, "Lost River? What do you mean, you almost lost him? Weren't you using the heat meter?"

"What's a heat meter?" asks a child, who is shushed by his mother. "I think we're going to find out," she stage whispers.

Anson blinks at his father, dumbfounded. "Not to the angels. To the drugs."

"River was on drugs?" his expression reduces River to a misbehaved child. River shuffles closer to Anson.

"Yeah," Anson says. "Mom never told you that?"

"I don't talk to your mother," their father huffs. "Gross." The crowd titters nervously.

Lulu's disdain might as well be sparking in red flares out her sea-green eyes, but Randy Camper doesn't even have the good grace to notice. "Look, kids," he sighs. "Did that woman even try to explain to you why?"

"That woman?" Anson says. His mom is a pain in the ass, but she never faked her own death.

"Why I had to leave? Did she tell you the whole story? Because there's a lot to it. The decision wasn't easy. It was a very painful time for me—for all of us. For all of us, Anson."

"This is a little much for me," says Martha. "I think we should call a pastor. I think we should pray. I don't think I can do this, Anson." She looks to the crowd for help, but they are not participants. They are only the audience, incapable of providing aid.

His siblings are looking at him, waiting for orders. Anson is aware of the audience, their expectations to be entertained. "All right," he barks bracingly, perhaps with more testosterone than he would use were they alone. "Let's hear it." He hopes to be proven wrong. Maybe Dad left to keep them safe. Maybe, Anson's brain spins out quickly, he realized he was the one drawing the angels, and he didn't want to leave them but he had to, to spare his children's lives, and now the angels haunt Isidore to track their dad and he's been watching all this time from the wings, like Indiana Jones in the hangar, waiting for the right moment to swoop in and—

"It was really hard for me to focus on my art," he says.

The crowd hisses.

"Oh my god," says River.

"Yeah. Fuck this," says Lulu, and now she has drawn

her weapon. She holds it casually at her side, which is some-how more menacing than when Anson trained it directly on him. Anson expects screams, but the audience is silent like at a horror flick. They are transfixed.

"Y'all wonder why God is after you," mutters Martha.

Anson nearly turns to her, but checks himself. He can deal with Martha later. Take her out to Chili's and tell her he's become a Mormon. Right now, he needs to see this through. "You were having a hard time with your art," he says. "And then?"

Anson wants more, but he can read it in his father's eyes. There is no more. Randy Camper goes jumpy-throated. He senses himself irretrievably in the maw of the lions. He takes one step backward, slowly, his eyes on Isidore. He is ter-rified of Isidore.

"And then—and then, I wasn't able to finish a paint-ing, you know. With the distractions. Was I supposed to just—what, muddle through? Raise you kids and try to make a liv-ing?"

"Yeah," says Anson. "That was exactly what you were supposed to do."

Their father blows air out his cheeks, like this is the single most ridiculous thing he's ever heard. "Don't be absurd," he says. "I know this is hard for you guys, but parents have needs. You think we want to spend our lives making forts and sitting through your interminable tea parties? You think Candy Land is fun? Let me ask you this: have you actually tried to sit through a game of Candy Land since your IQ hit seven? You talk about hell, Isidore, that's hell. Having to pour someone's goddammed white grape juice into the right Rainbow Brite sippy cup at six in the morning before you've had your coffee, that's the real hell. I don't care where we go when we die, it can't be as bad as that."

"As bad as tea parties?" Isidore says.

"And you, telling me the entire time what to say. As if sitting in a chair the size of a muffin and drinking Kool-Aid out of a plastic cup isn't bad enough, you've got to do it with a three-year-old Stalin. A tiny tyrant who scripts your every word and raises the seven hounds of hell if you don't do it exactly right. Can you imagine, Isidore? Me? Me, with the talent of Jackson Pollock meets Weird Al Yankovic—oh, have I said that before?" he pauses to ask, when all four of his children speak the quote with him. It was the one review written of their dad, after his sole art show, staged in an abandoned coffee house he'd paid for himself, and he took it as a compliment and worked it into conversation at least three times a day. "Forced to sit there asking Miss Polly if she's been a good girl and would she like to pass Mr. Bear Face the crackers now? Jesus Christ, Isidore. I mean, Jesus Christ."

Anson tries to meet Lulu's eye to signal her to do it. Take the shot. Shut him up. He supposes he should be the one, but what his dad has said isn't completely untrue and deep inside Anson is a bit of sympathy. He knows the burden of a family, is like Randy Camper in this way, and he doesn't think he can muster the nuts. To kill his father. Okay maybe not kill, but wound. Bust a kneecap. Plus, Lulu would get off easy, being famous. But Isidore speaks.

"So you mean—what you're saying is, it wasn't the angels?"

Their dad frowns, like he doesn't want to be tricked into giving her too much ground. "Well, it was partially the angels—"

"But not the angels alone, right? That's what you're saying, isn't it? The angels made it worse, yeah, but really you were already fed up just from being a parent. From tea parties, and—"

"And catch," their father rolls his eyes. "And monster, and bush-man, and tickle-daddy—"

"Ok," Isidore interrupts tersely. "Ok, yeah. So it was all of that." She looks at Anson. "Do you hear that?"

"Yeah, Is," Anson says. He gives her what she's looking for. She deserves it. "I hear it." Isidore has been carrying a stain. Unworthy by all standards, even by God's, who might have loved hookers and tax-hiking Democrats, but could find no place in all creation for Isidore. And now, for the first time—Anson feels terrible, but it is the first time—someone's telling her it isn't true. That it isn't her fault. All her life, she's wondered what she's done wrong to deserve this. And now, she hears the answer.

Nothing.

"I hear it too, Is," River says. He puts his arm around her waist companionably. Anson thinks maybe he's still feeling the Vicodin after all, but it doesn't matter. He ignores the sniffling crowd, the whirs of camera phones snapping.

They look at Lulu.

"No way," Lulu says. "I'm not going there with you. Dad didn't leave because of me, I never made him sit through any goddamn tea parties."

"So you didn't leave because of Isidore," Anson says, reaching an arm around and pulling Lulu's earlobe. Squeezing hard. "You left because you were a shitty parent."

"Ow, you fucker!" says Lulu. She swings back at him with her gun arm.

"Anson, don't hurt your sister," their father says.

"She's hitting me with her gun!" says Anson.

"I've got the safety on," Lulu snaps.

Their father goes shoulder-slumped, a defeated soldier. Sweat dripping off his brow, he stares numbly at his sad, naked chicken. "Yes. I suppose that's true. It wasn't because of the angels, not only."

"Is this a Christian play?" a man says nervously from the crowd.

"And then you didn't even succeed at that," River points out. "You left us to do your art and now you're standing here in the sun, surrounded by rednecks and religious guys, elbow deep in chicken offal."

"River was an addict because of you," says Isidore. Anson nods approvingly.

"River was a sissy boy. They always take the drugs, his type. Not strong enough to deal with life. Say, how's your mother? She didn't lose a bunch of weight and get all hot, did she?"

In the back of Anson's mind there is a sound, a nagging feeling that there's something he needs to be aware of, but he's caught up in this moment, senses numbed by the injustice of it all.

"Mom took a Latin lover," Anson says and, for the first and only time, takes pleasure in it. "She lives down in San Miguel de Allende. With a bunch of artists."

"No!" says their father. Anson hears Martha humming. He wishes she'd shut the hell up, she's distracting his rotund enjoyment of the scene. "She got out?"

"She's out," Anson says. Relishes it. "She lives a peaceful life drinking coffee and eating pan dulce, and she hasn't seen an angel in years."

Their father exhales what could very well be a death moan. His hand clutches at his chest and he pitches forward, bracing himself on the table. "He's having a heart-attack!" a little boy cries. "Life is cruel," says their father. "Oh, son, but life is cruel!"

Lulu is delighted. "It's been what—seven years, for her?"

"Oh God no," Randy Camper gasps, grape-faced. "No, no, no."

And Martha is humming still. Damn her. This is going to have to end. Martha is behind him, and she is humming, oh when the saints. Go marching in. Oh when the saints go marching—

"Son of a bitch. Lulu!"

But it's too late. Reeling around, Anson sees the light coming off the Gabriel. Martha's face glows beatific, like a saint receiving enlightenment, an Oklahoma Moses. It's only an instant. She steps into the light, her arms raised to them as if ready for embrace, and says, earnestly, "Welcome Lord—"

The lead Gabriel, the one heading the charge of about fifty others behind him, flicks his sword and lops her head clean off.

In that same second Lulu's bullet finds the Gabriel between the eyes and its head explodes. But it's too late. Too late for Martha and too late for everyone else. No amount of Lulu's charm could calm the audience now. A huge swarm of Gabriels hovers in the air above the barbecue competition. The Campers are used to them, but Anson supposes to these Oklahomans they must look rather alarming. Fifty long-locked men in diapers bearing swords and floating on the air, their feet clapped in beatnik sandals. The panic is profound and complete. It is, or may as well be, the end of the world. Some scream, some run, others faint dead away. They trample each other. Men beat back women, women beat back children and old ladies, any sense of honor forgotten in the need to preserve their own lives. The enticing scent of barbecue in the air is quickly replaced by the scent of humans fouling themselves in panic, control over one's bowels merely a fad for better times. Across the way, a retreating competitor overturns a large vat of homemade barbecue sauce. It covers him from the neck down and he screams and runs, arms outspread like he's been covered in tar and lit on fire.

"It's only barbecue sauce," Lulu screams at him. "It's not even hot! Shit," she says, looking at Anson. "What are we going to do?"

"It's spicy in my eyes!" the sauced man retorts.

"Show them your boobs, you idiot!" River screams. There might be tears streaming down his brother's face, Anson doesn't let it register.

"Oh! Right!" Lulu says. Turning her back on them, Lulu gives it her Spring Break all. She raises her shirt, taking her bra with it. Anson absolutely does not allow himself to think about why his sisters are such pros at this. "Hey!" she screams. "Hey! Looky here!" She jumps up and down.

"Stop!" one man in the crowd cries. "You're defrauding me!"

"That's the word!" Lulu is a jubilant pixie.

"That's such a stupid word," says River.

Anson isn't listening. He is watching the angels. They turn away from Lulu, but that's it. This time, her breasts fail to produce the desired fleeing in scandalized terror.

"It's not working," Lulu says, giving her chest one last shimmy. "It's not working, Annie. Shit."

There are too many Gabriels. They don't have the Airstream. Isidore prepares to throw herself into the fray. Like an athlete visualizes winning, she has visualized this moment in preparation for the day it would be necessary. She has always known it would come, that when it does there won't be time for goodbyes, that the lives of her siblings might balance on a second's hesitation. Her muscles quiver in preparation.

"Hold!" Anson shouts at Isidore. "Hold!" She throws him a pleading look, but freezes. In the street, Martha looks like a headless mannequin knocked down for fun, painted gore around the neck. Anson drags his eyes off her corpse, chest down in the street, her head having already been kicked away like a pretty blonde soccer ball, and takes stock of the situation. He is not a monster. Martha's corpse is disturbing, but he has no time to take the vapors over it now. He's got three siblings to keep alive. In the air are fifty hovering Gabriels. There are four of them, no way his father counts. They were so certain they wouldn't get heat, here in the Bible Belt—the Bible Belt, God, Anson thinks, or prays—and have packed one weapon each. He doesn't know if River's armed. He glances at his brother, is relieved to see he's drawn a Glock. River feels his gaze and shakes his head. "I've only got one shot left," he says. And then:

"I'm sorry, Annie."

Anson refuses to allow his heart to recognize the desperation they are in. They are looking to him for direction and he shakes his head.

"Run," he shouts.

"Anson—let me—" Isidore says. But Anson isn't ready. He shouts it again.

"Run for the Airstream. Go!"

The desire to go on living wins. They run. They leap, all four of them, over their father's table, and their father scrambles out of the way. They dart out the back of the tent, between the other booths, leaving their dad to fend for himself. He can stay behind or follow them, nobody cares. Weaving between men who are soiling their pants and women fallen to their knees in prayer—as if that won't just bring more of them—they manage to stay together. Anson runs past a smoker. Smoke floods his eyes, burning them until they water. His Lutheran school lessons return to him and leave him stunned. "It's the barbecue!" he shouts over the chaos. "They think it's a burnt offering!" They've walked, not into a trap, but into something akin to angel happy hour, and here's Isidore all trussed up for them. They have to get the hell out of here. The scent will continue to draw more.

"Son of a bitch!" Lulu screams, her feet pounding the pavement. She turns and fires a shot. Anson feels blood spatter his neck and knows her aim was true; she was always good on the run like this. He is so deeply grateful for Lulu, her comic book pluck. "It's not a sacrifice, you fuckers! It's a meal!" she shouts. Isidore could cry. No one can make like as bearable or unbearable as her sister, why has she not realized this until now? She prepares to split off from them. She just has to wait for the right moment. It needs to be quick.

They dart behind a tent off the main square and crouch in the flimsy shelter of white canvas. At least, Anson thinks, they are in the shade.

"I can take three or four down if you guys can hold off the rest," says Isidore. She feels stupid and ridiculous for not bringing her gun, but maybe it's better this way. It will be over faster.

"I've got four left," Lulu says.

Isidore lets Anson make his plan and avoids his eye, afraid to give her own away. "Ok," he nods. "I've got ten. So that makes nineteen. Hey, that's half of 'em. We can take out about half—shit."

A Gabriel has soared over their tent and hovers between them and the sun. Anson takes quick aim and fires. The angel goes down hard.

"Shot was a little off," says a voice from behind him.

Their father.

"Shut up," says Anson, merely surprised, and nothing close to relieved, that he's there. Anson will get them through this. It's going to be a bad one, but one they'll remember later over beers and guacamole. His father is of no consequence. "Look at me, guys. Look at me. We're getting out of this one, okay? We've got Isidore. We'll take out the few we can, and then we'll leave it to Is. Isidore's got it. Right?"

"I've got the bastards," Isidore says, and Anson doesn't know if she's faking it or not, but it doesn't matter. This time, there isn't another option.

"Watch each other's backs," he says. "And head for Pacey—"

He is cut off by a sextet of Gabriels who soar over the tent, swords flashing. There is no time to call out orders, no time to do anything but run. Anson and River dive one way, Lulu and Isidore the other. Anson hears someone firing and is furious to see that it's River. He's spent his one shot—taken out an angel, but still, that shot was all he had.

"Goddammit," says Anson. There are more angels. They are spilling over the pork-butt tent, a white tide. "Here," he says. He draws his knife and thrusts the gun at River. Isidore and Lulu are on their feet and running, the opposite direction, away from him. River shakes his head. The gun is survival. Whoever holds the gun holds the chance of getting out of this. He won't take it. But Anson roars, "Take it goddammit!"

River takes the gun.

TULSA
4ᵀᴴ OF JULY

"SHIT," LULU IS SAYING. "Shit shit shit shit shit—"

"That's enough," Isidore snaps. She's mad at Lulu for following her. The angels have swarmed mostly after Isidore, only a few remaining behind to menace Anson and River, keep them separated. Lulu should have saved herself and stayed with them.

"What do we do now?" Lulu says.

"You run for Pacey," Isidore says, taking shelter behind another white tent. She knows it won't last but hopes it will buy them a few moments, here in the sea of identical white tents. "I'll cover you."

Lulu's eyes go so venomous that Isidore is reminded of Grandma Ruth. "Don't give me that bullshit, Isidore. I'm not leaving you here."

"Why?" Isidore says. "Seriously Lulu, why?"

"Because you're my sister," Lulu is gathering steam. "You're my fucking sister and I didn't come all the way to this prairie hellscape to let you die!"

The few people with enough sense to run are surging

past them from either side of the tent, looking back over their shoulders in terror. Isidore sticks her head out and sees the angels are advancing. "Follow me," she says.

They leap out from behind the tent, guns raised. Moving backwards, they take aim and fire, again and again, into the swarm of Gabriels. It's worse than Isidore imagined. The angels are metastasizing like an aggressive cancer. She can't take on this many. She doesn't know what she is, but she is not limitless. It settles upon her gently, like a quiet snow draping itself across the barren desert. There is exactly one way out of this. It is up to Isidore alone, yet she has no dominion over it. She summons her apocalyptic power, the explosive ability that is, perhaps, the reason God wants her dead, or they're all going to die here.

They take refuge inside the next white tent, under a table. Crouching on the hot pavement Lulu pants, dripping sweat. The asphalt hurts her knees. "That was all I had," Lulu says.

Everything drops away and Isidore sees only the eyes of her sister. Lulu holds her gaze and Isidore thinks there is emotion there, that Lulu's eyes are brimming with all the love and tenderness she has never been able to express. She wonders if this is the time for a hug. Lulu's hand reaches up and the she snatches a chunk of shredded pork between her fingers. She drops it like communion on her tongue. Her eyes roll heavenward. "Glory hallelujah, Isidore, you have to—"

But Isidore is already savoring the meat melting on her tongue. She echoes Lulu's moans and tells her they can die happy now. Lulu laughs and the entire tent rips away like a trailer home in tornado alley. But it's not a tornado. It's three Gabriels. Isidore shouts for Lulu to move, but they are both already running.

"Isidore," Lulu shouts over her shoulder. "Think you could do your thing now?"

"I'm trying!" Isidore screams desperately. "It's like a sneeze. I can't just make it—"

She senses the trajectory of a sword headed directly

for her neck and she spins. There is no choice but to engage the angel in hand to hand; it's either that or end up like sweet Martha. Lulu screams for Isidore not too, but it's too late. Isidore matches the angel blow for blow. There is a swell of joy. This is what she was born to do. She tries to ignore the fifteen others gathering behind it.

Isidore grabs an angel around the neck and breaks the bones of its wings. She tells herself she isn't going to die. She is going to survive this, like she always has. Seconds later, she realizes she's wrong. First two more are on her, but then four, and then a fifth. Any wrong move will be her last. Isidore whirls and kicks, wrenching a sword away from one and running him through, but then there are three more. There are dozens and dozens gathering behind her and out of Isidore's mouth comes a desperate laugh that pitches downward into a sob. She doesn't want to die.

She's going to die.

The sword is knocked from her hand. Isidore moves to kick an angel in the chest and he seizes her leg and tugs, like Isidore is a roasted chicken and he's hungry for the drumstick. Hands are all over her, on her legs and thighs and neck. Isidore wishes they would reclaim their squeamishness over the female form. She is enveloped. In the sun above her is the flash of at least twenty swords. She moves her lips in something like a prayer, for it to be fast, for it not to hurt, for something to save her even though she knows she will end up in hell. Hands are closing around her throat. Isidore looks for Anson in the crowd.

Isidore smells smoke and coughs. Is it the approaching fires of hell? The hands clawing into her loosen. She looks up, prepared to see a thin blade of metal plummeting to cleave her brain in two, and instead sees twenty angels hovering sloppily in the sky above her. They look woozy and begin to faint away. Smoke swirls thick and finally the last one releases her and crashes to the ground, stumbling like River after half a glass of wine.

Isidore lands on her feet and hears Lulu screaming her

name. She searches for her sister in the smoke, gasping for breath. She is almost certain she has not peed her pants. She has spent more time than most worrying that, when the end comes, she will soil herself.

She finds Lulu. Her big sister is crouched behind a giant fan, manning it like it's the mini-gun. Isidore gets her sea legs back and runs to Lulu, trying to survey the perimeter as Anson taught her. It's not her natural instinct, which makes her wonder how truly necessary it is for survival. In front of Lulu's fan is a blazing barbecue.

"Help me," Lulu says. For a moment Isidore thinks her sister is grilling angels. Lulu releases the wheel and grabs handfuls of hamburger buns. She throws them into the fire. Catching on, Isidore takes the fan and aims, blowing smoke at a cluster of angels. They wobble like drunken debutantes and faint dead away.

"It's the wheat!" Lulu screams. She jumps up and down. "Isidore, it's their wheat allergy!"

For a moment Isidore thinks Lulu has chosen a particularly bad time to have her requisite mental breakdown. Then she remembers: wheat and dairy. She sees the bag Lulu is pulling the buns from; they're the hippie whole-wheat buns. Isidore bursts into tears, or maybe she's laughing. She can't tell. She grabs two handfuls of whole-wheat bread and, yelping giddily, tosses them into the fire.

TULSA
4TH OF JULY

ANSON IS LYING on his back and thinking of surrender. The majority of angels have gone after his sister, but they have left behind too many to be defeated. Heaven is here. In God's favorite country, on what must be God's favorite holiday. Anson has only seen this many angels one other time, in the canyon, before Isidore exploded some force out of her like an atom bomb. River holds them off for a moment with the three rounds left in Anson's gun, but then they swarm, swords whirring like the wings of ancient beetles. One of them catches River and River's blood sprays across the blueberry sky like strawberry syrup with the wrong kind of smell. He sinks lifeless to the asphalt.

Anson doesn't know if he cries out; there are too many voices around him to pick out his own and he's disoriented, floating in and out of consciousness. He thinks he has taken a blow to the head. He senses that he could make the effort and revive himself, but doing so would ultimately prove futile. There is no way Isidore is going to survive this, and once she's gone, Anson simply isn't necessary. He never was very necessary, with Isidore being a supernatural assassin and Anson just a man with an overdeveloped sense of responsibility and a sniper's aim. But once Isidore dies—if she hasn't died already—Anson is obsolete. Hamburger helper without the hamburger is just a packet of salt.

Sweating and nauseated in the sun, Anson tells himself it's okay to die. This trek across the ass of Texas with his contentious, spoiled siblings has been his own hero's quest, and he's through with it. There are times when Lulu rants, River whines, and Anson is sure that death would be a mercy. Even if he's destined to be tortured by pitchforks in the afterlife, he won't have River to look after while they're doing it.

He believes he is alone now, here in the grips of heaven, but then he hears his father. His father is sobbing. Anson takes small comfort. If one has to die, it's a relief to be noisily mourned.

Then Anson makes out the words. "Minxy!" his father sobs. Outrage injects Anson with enough energy to turn his head. The man is holding his face and rocking. "Oh, Minxy! Minks-saay! One last walk! Please, God, let us have one last walk together—"

"Fucking hell," Anson mutters. The pain overwhelms. His vision swarms black and he fights the darkness. He doesn't know how long he can hold out, but it won't be long. He raises his head and almost faints. Squeezes his eyes shut, and raises his head again.

River is alive. Anson gasps in relief. River is crawling toward him, hand over hand, across the asphalt. He is bleeding profusely from a wound across his forehead. If he doesn't die today, he'll have a geeky scar. Like he tried to make a headband out of barbed wire.

"Annie," he says. Anson forces himself to a sitting position. He goes dizzy, his torso circling, and then steadies himself. River grabs Anson's shirt with two fists and shakes him. He forces Anson to look him in the eyes. Anson expects a thorough scolding, for what River must read there, but all River says is:

"Not yet, man. Not yet."

Somehow Anson understands. He nods and touches River's shoulder. Their father is sobbing behind them. Anson would knock him out, if he had the strength.

"We gotta get to Is," Anson says, avoiding what they both know is true. They have to get to Isidore because they don't want her to die alone. If he can help it, Anson will not allow that. He will hold Isidore's hand through her final moments and hope with everything in him that there has been some kind of mistake, that Lulu was right all along, that there's no such place as hell.

If there is, he figures at least he'll meet her there.

"Can you walk?" says Anson.

"I think. Can you?" River sounds doubtful. Anson forces River away from him, putting his weight on his own tremulous legs. About ten tents away, he can see them hovering in the sky. A cozy coven of angels, like a Biblical plague. He knows that's where Isidore will be. He isn't sure, but he'd bet Lulu has stuck with her. He resolves to tell Lulu he's always loved her, after all.

"What do we have?"

River shakes his head.

"Come on," Anson says. "Come on." There has to be a way. They always find a way. "We've got to have something."

"You idiot children are all going to die," their father says. Anson sees only one option.

"We gotta get to Pacey," he says. He plans to drive the Airstream into the angels, come out guns blazing. He doesn't think beyond that. They run down the emptied streets and toward the camper. The damage isn't too bad. Many tents have been overturned and the pavement looks like barbecue chicken rained down from heaven, but the angels have only one target and the streets aren't littered with corpses. Anson hears emergency vehicles screaming nearby. He wonders what they'll make of this. He reaches the camper and gets in, starts the engine. It roars up over the whine of the heat meter.

"Get in," he says to River.

"Look," River says.

266

Anson can't believe it. "Get in or I'm going without you--"

"They cut the tires. Anson, look. They're all flat."

Anson can't breath. He climbs down from the captain's chair and sees that River is right. The tires are still wheezing, leaking out their lasts breaths of life. River starts to cry.

Anson kicks the deflating tires, their rubber cleaved apart by ancient swords.

TULSA

ISIDORE LOOKS FOR ANSON. They have gone through all the wheat buns. Lulu tried using white in a desperate last attempt, but it was no good. The angels are regaining their senses. It's like watching frat boys wake up on a Sunday morning. They're lumbering now, unsteady and graceless, but you know in a few minutes they'll be back to their chest-thumping, raising their swords.

They are surrounded on all sides, pressed back to back. The world is a sea of angel flesh and white garments that flutter in the wind and stretch as far as Isidore can see.

"Isidore?" says Lulu. "What do you think we should do?"

"I'm trying," Isidore says. To do the thing she did in the canyon that saved all their lives. She can feel the beginnings of it, a vibration low in her body like a long-forgotten instinct. Or at least, she thinks she can feel it. It might be simply the urge to fight, to fling herself into battle. She tells herself it's more. It's the thing that will save them.

"That's what I'm going to have to do," she says.

"What?" says Lulu. Isidore can feel her sister's skinny shoulders pressing in to her back. Their asses align, it reminds

268

Isidore of sleeping in the same bed, back to back. After Dad died, they shared a lot of motel beds and rooms in tiny houses. They press in close to one another for comfort. Isidore can hear Lulu crying, trying to hide it from her.

Isidore knows what she's going to do. "Listen."

"No," Lulu sobs. "No, Isidore."

"Lulu. Listen. I'm going to get you out of here. I'm going to throw myself into them—"

"Anson will come. He'll come, goddammit—"

"Anson's not coming," Isidore says. She can't think about it now, but she knows Anson is probably dead. If he weren't dead, he would be here. "This is it, Lulu. Okay? This is it, and I'm going to throw myself into the Gabriels, and Lulu," her voice catches. "You are going to run. And you're not going to look back—"

"No," Lulu says.

"And I'm going to die knowing I saved you. That's all I want." It's true, what Isidore says. Not an attempt at bravado. If she can't save them all, she can at least try to save Lulu.

"I'm sorry about the circus peanuts," Lulu says tearfully. "I know I was the one that always picked them. I was just trying to piss you off."

The Gabriels are reviving their warrior shine and beginning to work their swords. "It's okay," Isidore says. "It's enough that you've said it now."

"Oh god, Is. Can't you just do your thing?"

Isidore can feel the hum. It's growing to a glow. But anything might scare it off. Lulu doesn't deserve to die waiting on Isidore's parlor trick.

"I don't think so," Is says quietly. Lulu sniffs.

"Lu," says Isidore. "I'm going to count to five—"

Lulu screams. Isidore understands that this is a big moment for Lulu, but this is Isidore's death scene, dammit, and she wishes Lu could tone it down a notch and let her have her fifteen minutes. It takes her a moment to realize why Lulu is screaming. She cranes her neck and sees that, on Lulu's side, a gap has opened in the angels. A few of them fall to the sides, beheaded and bloodied. Lulu is shouting for Isidore to look.

Isidore can't turn her back. "Rotate!" she orders. She and Lulu spin in tandem. The angels part like the red sea, falling to bullets and the slice of a Gurkha knife, and through them burst her brothers. Anson is in the lead. He wields the knife like a sword, takes out two more Gabriels. He's covered in blood, Isidore doesn't know how much of it is his. In his eyes is an oily sheen that frightens her. He grins like a mad man. Then he tosses her a gun. She catches it and shoots the left eye of a Gabriel whose sword is bearing down toward Anson's head. He wipes blood from his face.

"I told you," Lulu is screaming. "We're gonna get out of this, Is. I told you he'd come."

Isidore doesn't argue. She doesn't tell Lulu what she can see in her brother's eyes: that Anson hasn't come here save them. There are too many. They are beyond the help of anyone but Isidore and God himself.

He's come here to go down together.

"You're so stupid, Anson," Isidore says. She starts to cry. "You're so stupid. You should have stayed away."

River is behind him. He looks like a chocolate fountain, one coursing blood for a wedding in hell. He winks at Isidore. Together the brothers enter into Lulu and Isidore's ring, and the angels seal the gap behind them.

"Yeah," Anson says. "I guess I am."

They have trained for this together over the years and hours, since they were children. The Camper siblings, if given the chance, might emotionally miscomprehend and agitate each other into loss of sanity, but they possess a physical familiarity with one another that, in these tight circumstances, will pass for a language of love. Anson pulls another gun from his belt and slaps it into Isidore's waiting hand. River arms Lulu. The four of them easily form a square, backs in, shoulders out, facing the onslaught.

The Gabriels rise in levels and form a coliseum around them, a sword-wielding wedding cake. The Campers are a stubborn human form in the middle, surrounded by enemies so great in number that they blot out the sun. Around them the world is an abandoned hush. Either the beating feathered wings block out all sound, or the humans are all gone and the Campers stand alone in a world of death and angels.

Racing for Pacey and then for his sisters, Anson hasn't considered what he might say. Isidore is at his right shoulder. Lulu is at his left. He can still smell the barbecue. He wishes he had let Isidore eat instead of insisting they find River first.

"Hey, Is," Anson says.

"I'm trying," Isidore screams. Her voice is ragged. "Just give me a goddamn minute."

Anson hadn't intended to ask her to turn herself into a bomb. But in her voice is the answer he would have received. She isn't going to do it.

The realization settles gently and silences the world. His brain travels far away, across years and miles, to a soft place far inside him. His eyes are unfocused. He doesn't hear the gunshots, doesn't see his family around him. He sees a room he once knew well. Red evening light. The dusty floral scent of baby powder. Skin warm and ripe like cherries.

Then he swallows hard. Pulls himself back. "Calm down," he says easily. "That's not what I was going to say." A Gabriel presses in. Anson shoots it.

"What were you going to say?"

"Anson," Lulu says. It's a plea. She's sobbing. "Annie, I'm sorry. I'm so sorry—"

"Hey," Anson says. His voice is low and calm. "Lu. It's all right."

"It's all right," Isidore says. She wants to tell Lulu how sorry she is, but that won't bring her any comfort.

The angels press in, closing the diameter of the corral. For a moment, the Camper siblings fire into the multitudes. The angels are unbothered as their brothers fall at their sides. The dead are not spared a glance.

"Isidore," Anson says. He's almost out of rounds in his first gun. "Remember that time we didn't make it to the Grand Canyon?"

"Jesus," Isidore says. "You're going to bring that up now? Look, I'm really sorry—"

"Remember what we did, after?" Anson interrupts her.

Lulu and River are listening. Shooting angels and listening to Anson's memory. What else is there to do?

"No," Isidore says. "I told you. I don't remember any of that trip."

The angels press close enough that Anson could touch one, were he to stretch out his arm and lean. The Campers fire wild. In the end, it will be quick. There are too many for any of them to last more than a few seconds in hand-to-hand, even Isidore. In a moment, Anson knows, the angels will be upon them.

And that will be the end.

He keeps shooting. He raises his voice. Shouts over the report of gunshots so they can hear him. So his voice reaches Is. Lulu and River too, but he's about to die and there's no longer time to pretend he loves any of them as much as he loves Isidore.

"We drove up to the river," he roars. "Just you and me. And you know what? Lulu was right. I was sixteen, and you were eight. Lu and River were off somewhere alone and I was giving you whiskey."

Isidore has spent her life missing any and all subtleties. She takes things as they are, exactly, and misses all the layers that Lulu and Anson and any normal human gets instinctively.

But Isidore doesn't miss this. She knows what Anson is telling her. Something escapes her that is mostly a laugh. He is able to lean in close to her ear. His words are for her only. "If we go one way," Anson says. "Is. The angels will follow us."

Isidore shakes her head. Her face is covered in soot, grime, and blood. Her tears cleave two clean paths down her cheeks. Her body keeps insisting no, but she mouths, almost soundlessly, "Okay."

In a moment Anson is going to grab Isidore and pull her hard left. Cleave the two of them from Lulu and River, who might then live. He is going to throw himself on top of Isidore and they will have to tear him off her. He hopes it's quick for Is. He hopes he goes first. He doesn't want to watch her die.

"You could get drunk, back then," Anson says. "You got drunk and went Hulk and split my eye wrestling me for more."

Isidore wipes away a tear. "I bet you wouldn't make that mistake again."

Anson pulls the trigger and it clicks. He pulls it and it clicks three times fast.

It's empty.

Anson turns his back to the angels. He spins on one heel and grabs Isidore by the shoulders. Her eyes are terrifying, alight with hellfire, but to him it doesn't matter.

"No," he shakes his head." Isidore. I'd do it all again."

Isidore meets his eyes and nods. She holds up her gun.

"I'm out, too."

Anson grins. "How's the pit, Isidore?"

Isidore searches for something to say but Anson pulls her head into his shoulder. Her fingers clutch his shirt. He smells like Anson. Something hits them, Isidore feels only impact. He makes a strange sound from his throat and Isidore says, "Annie?" and tries to raise her head. But Anson holds her tight. There is a flash of heat and then a sensation like falling. A sense of the stars.

From Anson's view, the world goes white.

He shuts his eyes.

THE BEGINNING

TAOS
NEW MEXICO

HE GOT HER TO SLEEP only an hour ago. She went down sucking her thumb and squeezing her purple armadillo. It's after two in the morning. He has to look at the phone book to find out where he is. Time feels slippery and unfixed. Like a labyrinth, and if he knew the right turns he could find a way to go back. After everything—after everything—mom threw them into the car and handed Anson the keys. He drove for hours and they ended up here after taking the long way through Mesa Verde. He'd worried about the girls, expecting tears he wouldn't know how to stop. But they hadn't cried. Lulu had taken Isidore's hand and she'd stared, pale, out the window, watching the trees for hours, her expression making it clear she was seeing nothing.

They've taken out two rooms in this motel. In the parking lot, beside the fake Kiva and the incongruous totem poles, River had lifted the cooler from the trunk and then raised it above his head and slammed it to the ground.

The cooler had always been their dad's job.

To keep the girls from his brother's rage, Anson had ushered them into one room, leaving his mom to deal with

274

River in the other. Lulu had lain back on the pillows, clutching at the peach and teal comforter, and promptly fallen asleep. Isidore had sat cross-legged on the bed and stared at the wall. Anson asked her if she wanted the TV. She hadn't answered. He asked again and she dragged her eyes to him, heavy with effort. She didn't speak. Finally, Anson had looked away.

Before he turns off the light, Anson stands over her. He wants to tell her it's not her fault but of course, that would be a lie. She has strange ways. Sometimes she moans in the night, a rhythmic tonal noise that might be a chant. Now she is still in her sleep. Her winter-white hair rests across her face.

He remembers when she was a baby. Because they were afraid, Isidore was often left to cry alone. A whimper she could be coaxed out of but when she screamed, the family feared what she might do and abandoned her to herself. Anson was forbidden to enter the room. But he'd creep to her anyway, in the buttery nursery light. Above her spun a trinket sea of whales and narwhals and sharks. Anson wanted to know the baby. He'd seen the blood, the monsters in the delivery room, the same as everyone else, but he couldn't assign her blame. A tiny thing with knowing eyes, see-through skin.

Anson would lift her from her crib. Isidore would coo in her sleep but wouldn't wake. Her cheeks were flushed with cherried heat. She smelled of milk and tears. His mother cried and carried a sour smell, clearly not the woman she was before Isidore's birth. He didn't know who Isidore had other than him. She was alone in this world, Anson realized, but that night he promised her she wasn't anymore.

His family asleep, unknowing around him. Anson would rock the baby Isidore and sing.

ABOUT THE AUTHOR

Brittany Tuttle is a graduate of Colorado State University's creative writing program and the author of the novella "Stone and Spring". She grew up in Colorado and took many childhood roadtrips across the western states. She now lives in North Carolina with her family. She is a sharpshooter and is probably wanted in at least seven states.